THORNHILL

Road

a love me tender novel

ISBN: 9798349210136 (Paperback)

Library of Congress Control Number: 1-14435306301

First printing edition 2024.

Untapped Publications, LLC

CONTENTS

THORNHILL Road

CHAPTER *One*

Tess

I PULLED INTO THE driveway on Ramshorn Avenue and checked the time.

A sigh of relief passed between my lips when I saw I was ten minutes early.

"Hey, Siri—set timer, ten minutes."

My phone talked back to me, alerting me to my ten-minute timer, then I leaned my head against the seat and closed my eyes. I was four hours away from the end of my double shift. That meant two more stops. Two more patients.

Ten minutes.

Ten minutes of sleep was going to carry me through.

It was all I needed.

Just ten minutes.

A knock sounded at my window.

I pulled in a deep breath and opened my eyes.

Seven minutes. I'd gotten seven minutes.

It would have to do.

Glancing out the driver's side window, I saw Mitchell Jones offer me an apologetic smile and a timid wave. I smiled back at him. Not timid. Not apologetic.

Real.

Genuine.

Tired, but genuine.

He was a major reason why I was there. His mother was dying. Stage four lung cancer. Inoperable. Never smoked a day in her fifty-nine years.

Her life expectancy when I met her had been three months. Now she had weeks left. Six, maybe less. She wanted to spend what time she had remaining on this earth in the comfort of her own home, surrounded by family, and it was my job to make sure she got her dying wish.

I also considered it my responsibility to make sure both of her sons were well supported and looked after during such a difficult time.

I canceled my timer, grabbed my purse and my bottle of water—water I wished was coffee, even though I'd already had my fill—then moved to get out of my car.

"Hi, Mitch. How you doin'?"

"I'm so sorry to wake you. I'm sure you're burning it at both ends. I saw you pull up, and I wanted a chance to talk before you came inside."

Mitchell was average height with dark blond hair I was sure he got cut every four weeks, like clockwork. He had brown eyes, a strong, masculine jaw, and a subtle cleft chin that wasn't unattractive.

"No need to apologize," I said.

I meant it. Mitchell was the eldest of the two brothers. He was always so kind and gracious. It was obvious he loved his mother and felt quite helpless. He couldn't fix her, but wherever he could step in or show up, he would. He was a good son. A good man. The kind of man I thought I should consider for myself.

Not *him* of course. Aside from the fact that he was already married—and I made it a point not to date married men—he was related to one of my dying patients. Family members were strictly out of bounds. For ethical reasons, first and foremost, but also because I had unwavering boundaries when it came to mixing my work and my emotions.

It was critical in the field of hospice care.

All that aside, someone *like* Mitchell was who I thought I should keep an eye out for. Someone stable with a good head on his shoulders. A man with a corporate job. Maybe even a job that required him to wear a tie.

As boring as it sounded, it also seemed quite safe.

My dating history was littered with men who were far from safe. Mitchell wasn't exactly my type—but for the last couple months, I'd thought it was time for me to reconsider my options.

However, at present, my pathetic dating life was not a priority.

I was at the house on Ramshorn Avenue, which meant I was there for Sharon.

"What's on your mind?" I asked Mitchell as we slowly made our way toward the front door.

We chatted for a few minutes on Sharon's porch. Mitchell's youngest daughter, Emilia, had come down with a cold. She'd been in the house the day before, and he was worried. I reminded him that sick toddlers were inevitable, he couldn't possibly blame himself, and I'd monitor Sharon carefully for any sign of a cold; then we both headed inside.

I could barely remember a time when I didn't want to be a nurse. Since I was twelve years old, it had been my plan. I had no alternate routes for my future. Hospice care, in particular, was my end goal. For the last six years, that's exactly what I had the privilege of doing.

And it truly was a privilege.

It was exhausting in every way—mentally, emotionally, physically. It was hard work. The schedule was shit, and I didn't know the meaning of *work-life-balance,* but it was worth it. Not once had I regretted my career choice, because it was more than a career.

It was a vocation.

It was my calling.

It was medicine, sure. I was a registered nurse. But a hospice nurse was so much more than that. I addressed my patients' spiritual and emotional needs, too, as they journeyed toward death. I was there to make dying dignified, peaceful, and comfortable—or as comfortable as possible. It's what made the job such a challenge. It was also what made the job so rewarding.

Hard as it was, I loved it.

I went through my usual routine with Sharon, checking her from top to toe. Once I was done with her physical exam, we discussed how she was feeling, and I got an assessment of how alert and oriented she was. Then, like I did with most of my patients, I sat with her for a few minutes and visited while I charted.

I was wrapping up, checking to see if she needed any of her prescriptions filled, when the sounds of an argument drifted into the room. I looked toward the doorway and frowned.

Lance had arrived.

"My boys...they're having a rough go of it lately," murmured Sharon.

It had become clear to me where Mitchell had gotten his personality. She was busy dying, and Sharon hardly spent any time worrying about herself, too concerned with the family she would leave behind. It was why I liked to spend a few extra moments with her each visit, so we could focus on *her* for a little while.

I offered her a small smile, then reached for her hand and gave it a gentle squeeze. "I'll talk to them. You get some rest, okay? Call me if you need anything."

I stowed my tablet in my purse, then double checked to make sure I had all my supplies. I bid Sharon farewell and ventured out toward the living room.

I didn't need Sharon to tell me her sons were having a *rough go of it* lately. This wasn't the first argument to draw me away from my patient. They were two men who were losing their mother. Rather than bond over it, they were hurtling their grief at each other like grenades.

"Guys—guys," I interjected as I went to stand between them. "We agreed. No arguments without a mediator. As I understand it, Renee is home with a sick toddler, which leaves me. So—are we good here, or do I need to get a chair?"

"No. Sorry, you're right," said Mitchell.

"Yeah. All good here," agreed Lance.

Lance, though younger, was the taller of the two brothers. His hair was lighter. His nose was sharper. His jawline squarer. One might have said he was the more attractive brother—until he opened his mouth.

I hadn't met their father. He and Sharon were divorced. When I considered Lance, I wondered if his personality was his own, or if the apple hadn't fallen far from the tree. He was certainly the more selfish of Sharon's offspring. Most of the arguments were instigated by him; and most of the time it was about money, or whose turn it was to help with laundry or house chores.

In the two months I'd been coming around, I hadn't seen Lance even so much as fold a single tea towel.

There was also something slimy about him that made me feel uncomfortable.

Nevertheless, people experienced pain in a variety of different ways, so I did my very best to offer him as much patience and grace as I could muster.

"I'm going to go check on mom," Mitchell told us before he left.

I blew out a breath and looked up at Lance. "You sure you two are okay?"

"We'll be fine. Thanks for stepping in." He reached for my shoulder and gave it a squeeze. "I don't know what we'd do without you."

As he began to let me go, he trailed his fingertips a short way down my back before dropping his hand to his side.

I gave no response to his touch but did a mental shiver.

He made me feel so *ick.* Like he was incapable of platonic affection.

"I should get going. I've got another patient to see."

"Of course. It was good to see you, Tess."

I nodded, waved, and said, "I'll be back in a couple days."

Once on the other side of Sharon's front door, I closed my eyes, stretched my neck, then rolled my shoulders back.

One more patient. Two more hours.

I was on the home stretch.

On my way to my car, I pulled up Edmond Thomas' address. He was my newest patient. This was going to be my first trip to his house on Thornhill Road. My GPS told me I'd be there in about twenty minutes, and I didn't waste any time before I began the short trek north.

When I pulled into his driveway, the first thing I noticed was the unkempt yard. It was the middle of June, and we hadn't had snow in several weeks, which meant it was lawn mowing season. Only, Edmond Thomas had a yard full of weeds, not grass.

The house looked old and almost as neglected as the lawn, and I wondered what I'd find on the inside. Since it was my first visit, I took some extra time to go over his chart before I got out of my car. He was dying from pancreatic cancer. According to his list of medications, he also had cirrhosis of the liver and a few other long-standing conditions he'd been dealing with, as well. Aware I wouldn't know the full extent of what I'd be dealing with until I met him, I grabbed my things and was at his front door in under thirty seconds. After a quick knock, I waited for someone to answer.

Edmond filled the doorway a minute later.

He was a tall man with hunched shoulders. One look at him, and it was obvious he'd once been formidable. Now, at only sixty-one years old, he was on the verge of appearing frail. His clothes hung on him like they belonged to someone else, and his eyes—while a pretty hazel-blue—were sad.

"Mr. Thomas?"

He jerked his head in a nod. "You my nurse?"

"Yes. Theresa McBride," I said, extending my hand as I offered the name the care center would have provided. "But, please, call me Tess."

He accepted my hand with a stronger grip than I anticipated, and this made me smile.

"Call me Ed. Come on in," he muttered.

He turned and left the door open as he made his slow return trip deeper into the house. I followed after him, closing us inside. We didn't go far. It was a split-level home, but he'd obviously dispensed with dealing with the stairs. In what I assumed was once a living room, there was an unmade bed, a well used recliner, a television that sat on top of a wooden dresser, and a bunch of clutter on every flat surface there was. On the opposite side of his living area, partitioned by a wall, was the kitchen. I assumed the bathroom wasn't far, either.

Ed made his way to the edge of his bed and took a seat.

"So, how does this work?"

I set my purse at my feet, took out my tablet, and proceeded to explain what a typical visit would look like. I then asked him a list of questions and proceeded with my exam. When I was finished, I grabbed a chair from his kitchen table so I could take a seat next to him while I charted.

"Ed, other than me, who is going to be helping with your care?"

"Got someone who drops by to take care of the laundry and cleaning 'bout once a week."

I nodded, hugged my tablet to my chest, and clarified, "What about any family or loved ones?"

He shook his head. "My wife died a lifetime ago, and I haven't seen my son in years."

When he said *son*, I saw the slight nod he gave to the frame that sat beside him on his nightstand. It was the only picture frame I'd seen on the main level of the house.

"May I?"

He nodded and I laid my tablet in my lap in order to pick up the frame. I was surprised to find not a picture but a clipping out of the *Gillette News Record*, our local paper. There was no date, so I wasn't sure how old the clipping was, but I recognized the establishment in the photo and knew it couldn't have been more than a few years old.

The article was about Steel Mustang, a popular biker bar located on the edge of town on the Wild Stallions Motorcycle Club compound. Even though bikers were the typical patrons, the bar wasn't exclusively for those in the club, and it drew quite the crowd. They were known for their live music and the great bands they hosted.

I didn't know this via hearsay.

I'd been a couple of times.

I could attest, it was awesome.

However, I didn't recognize the man in the photograph.

Not that it was a great quality photo. It was black and white. He was leaning against his motorcycle with his arms folded across his chest and a pair of sunglasses covering his eyes. I knew enough to be sure the leather vest he wore was a *kutte,* and I was certain the patch on the back matched the tattoo he was sure to angle toward the camera on his right bicep. It was difficult to see the details in the clipping, but everyone in town recognized the Wild Stallions logo. It was a skeletal stallion head, only it was designed to appear made out of metal. And the mane wasn't hair, but fire.

It was badass.

I'd never officially met anyone who rode with the Wild Stallions—but the members who made up the *heartbreaker club,* known informally as my *exes,* were men who could have been cut from the same cloth.

Or, if not the same cloth, they'd at least have been found in the same fabric section at the store.

All that to say, I didn't need to actually read the article to know what it was about—but I did glance at the caption beneath the photo.

Sullivan Thomas, long time member of the Wild Stallions MC and majority owner of Steel Mustang, poses in front of the up-and-coming biker bar.

"Sullivan, that's your son?"

"Sully," Ed corrected. "Turned out alright, no thanks to me."

I studied the dying man in front of me for a second, curious about the details behind the sad look in those hazel-blue eyes. He was all alone, and I didn't like it.

"Says here he's the owner of this bar. That means he's local," I pressed gently.

"We don't talk, Tess. He doesn't even know I'm sick. It's just me. Move slow on account of the pain, but I can still manage to get around most of the time. If you're gonna be comin' by for night visits, I got a spare key I can give you."

"Okay, Ed," I murmured, setting aside the photo frame. "Let's try that for a while and see how we get on."

I stayed for a few more minutes, then collected my things and the spare key to the house on Thornhill Road. I bid Ed farewell, assuring him I'd be back in a couple of days and insisting he call me should he need me before then. It was a few minutes after four when I got behind the wheel of my car. I was done for the day. I was free to go home and sleep, which was exactly what I wanted to do.

Except, I couldn't.

Ed Thomas was all alone in the house I'd just left, and that didn't sit right with me.

I understood families were complicated. People had falling outs and relationships were torn apart. But I also knew what it was like to lose a parent to an illness they couldn't beat. Sully didn't even know his dad was sick. I didn't understand what that was all about, but death had a way of changing people's perspectives. Maybe whatever was broken between father and son could be reconciled with the threat of losing their chance on the horizon.

I figured it was worth a shot.

I didn't know Ed, but I knew it was my job to make sure he died in peace and comfort.

It was obvious he was lonely, and it felt like my duty to reach out to Sully, just in case all they needed was a little intervention.

So, I didn't go home.

I put my car in reverse, I backed out of the driveway, and I pointed my car toward that bar.

CHAPTER *Two*

Mustang

T RIX WAS LATE. FORTY-FIVE minutes late.

Mustang looked at the clock and felt his blood start to simmer.

It wasn't just that he needed to be at the bar half an hour ago.

If work was the pressing matter, he could have called Winnie. Bull's ol' lady was always more than happy to help out where she could when it came to MK. She understood what it was to be a parent. She and Bull had three boys, the youngest of which was only a year older than his MK.

This worked out for his little girl, as Otto had become her best friend.

Mustang was alright with that and foresaw he would be until Otto hit puberty; at which point, should he get any ideas about changing the nature of his relationship with Mustang's princess, he didn't care if Otto was his president's youngest son or not—they'd have words.

It was two forty-five.

His custody agreement with Trix stated Mustang had MK Sunday morning until Wednesday afternoon. His schedule revolved around his little girl, so long as he had a say in the matter. He closed the bar Mondays and Tuesdays not simply because their Friday and Saturday night draw alone was enough to get them through the entire week, but also because he wanted to be home with his girl.

It pissed him off knowing if Trix was more than forty-five minutes late, it was because she was prioritizing something else over their daughter.

If she didn't show in the next fifteen minutes, he knew he could tag in Winnie. He'd take MK with him to the clubhouse, which was routinely kid-friendly during business hours, and have Winnie meet them there. Possible as it was, this wasn't his preference. It was a gorgeous day outside, and he wanted to be on his hog. MK still had a couple inches to grow before she'd be able to ride, which meant he'd be in his truck if Trix didn't show.

He looked from where he stood, leaning against the kitchen island, into his living room. MK was on her knees playing with a couple of her stuffed animals. Her dark, curly locks were wild and loose—the way he loved them best—and she swept a few strands out of her eyes as she continued the scene she'd been enacting on the coffee table in front of her. She was completely oblivious of her mother's lateness.

It still pissed him off.

He heard it when a car pulled into his driveway five minutes later, and he looked in the direction of the front door.

"Princess, time to put your toys up."

"Oh, but daddy, do I have to?" she whined as she got to her feet. "Can't I take Mr. Snuggles and Mr. Twinkles with me this time?"

He pushed himself upright and started for the door. "No, baby. You know the drill. They'll be here when you get back."

"Okay," she said on a sigh, her shoulders slumped as she made her way to her room.

Mustang waited until she was out of sight, then opened the storm door and stepped out onto his front porch. He then proceeded to meet Trix halfway.

Four years he'd had his house. Not once had she so much as peeked inside.

His home was his sanctuary. It was MK's safe haven. He'd bought it for her, and the only other woman who'd ever stepped foot inside was Winnie. Trix might have been the mother of his child, but she sure as hell was not welcome into his home.

As she approached, he took in her appearance.

Her long, curly hair was piled on top of her head in a messy knot, and she wore a pair of jeans that sat low at her hips. Her cropped Guns-N-Roses tank top revealed her narrow waist and flat stomach. She had on her usual amount of caked on makeup, barely concealing the dark circles under her eyes. She looked like she hadn't slept in days and could put on a few pounds.

Every time he saw her, he wondered how on earth he'd ever found her appealing—let alone desirable for the three months he'd fucked her on the regular. Like most of the sheep who hung around the clubhouse, she'd been easy pussy. She was never more than that, and he'd never claimed her, but she certainly wanted him to—as evidenced by the four-year-old daughter they shared.

She'd poked a hole in his condom thinking she could trap him into making her his ol' lady.

She'd thought wrong.

That was back in the day, before the club was clean. Back when the code of the Stallion brotherhood was being compromised from the top down.

The Wild Stallions were always going to straddle the line when it came to the letter of the law—clean or not—but Stallion code was something else. The code of the brotherhood was sacred, or so it should have been. The number one rule of the house was no drugs. It was their job to *move* the drugs, not consume them. Addicts were sloppy.

Stallions were outlaws.

They knew how to party.

But they weren't supposed to mix business with pleasure.

Back then, Trix was a hang around who hung around too much. She was into that shit, but Mustang wasn't. When he found out she was pregnant, he warned her that if she didn't get clean, she was on her own with the kid. She sobered herself up, hopeful he'd change his mind about them.

What she failed to understand was, clean or not, he would not be manipulated.

She was pissed when MK was born and he still refused to claim her as his woman, but she'd needed the help, so she didn't cut him out of their daughter's life. Unfortunately, it wasn't long before Mustang realized Trix was incapable of staying on the straight and narrow. She wasn't into the hard stuff, not anymore, but she was a fan of the high, and he couldn't trust her.

She'd never totally fucked up, but he was always on his guard. The only reason he hadn't sued for full custody was because he knew MK loved her and because she used to be a hang around who hung around too much.

She knew things. Things she shouldn't know.

She threatened him with that shit all the time.

"You're late," he muttered as she came to a stop in front of him. "You work from home. What the fuck, Trix?"

"Whatever. I'm here. I'm sure you're both fine."

He clenched his jaw and reached for her chin, angling her head up so he could look her right in the eyes.

She tried to jerk out of his hold, but his grip was too tight, and he wasn't going to let go until he was sure. She'd given MK her dark, curly hair—but their daughter had gotten his eyes. Trix's were russet brown, and currently clear.

She wasn't high.

Good.

"You bastard," she grumbled, swatting at his arm.

He let her go.

"Stay," he told her before he returned into his house. "MK, come on, baby. Time to roll."

He loaded MK into the backseat of Trix's car and pressed a kiss into her hair before he said goodbye. He watched them leave, then went inside to grab his keys and his kutte. Not sixty seconds later, he was on his blue Harley Davidson Road King, headed for the compound.

The compound was where the Stallions spent most of their time. If they weren't at the clubhouse, they were working; and if they weren't working, they were at the clubhouse or home. For some, the clubhouse *was* home. It had been for Mustang when he first joined, until he'd saved up enough money to get his first apartment.

Work came in a variety of forms for those in the MC—and not all of it was club business. Since MK was born, for Mustang, it rarely was. After the hostile takeover that ended with Bull as the president over all the Wild Stallions, things had been different. A lot of their business was legit.

The garage had been around as long as the club. They did good work which meant they had a faithful customer base, allowing them to earn their keep. Fixing up bikes was their specialty, but their guys could handle anything with a motor.

The auto-parts store was a late addition. Mustang had been a Stallion for a good five years before someone suggested they expand. The club was growing, and business—on and off the books—was good. They had the capital, so they made it happen. Turned out to be not just a good idea, but a profitable one.

For a while, things were steady.

And then they weren't.

When business got messy, it was Bull who started recruiting guys to side with him in an effort to clean up the club. Their off-the-record work was getting more dangerous, brothers were getting caught, a couple had gotten themselves killed. Mustang knew he wanted to be around, not in the ground, and he was quick to pick a side.

It had been his idea to go one step further than righting the ship.

He thought they could change the game entirely.

That's when he tossed out the idea of building a biker bar.

It was something he'd been thinking about for a while. He'd even stashed a good bit of his earnings to make it happen. The timing seemed right, if the club could put up the funds to get him the rest of the way there.

Bull had been surprised that Mustang, of all his brothers, wanted to open a bar. As far as Mustang was concerned, it was a sure way to rake in cash that could supplement what they would lose if they got out of the drug trafficking business.

But it was more than that, too.

It was also his chance to have a place where good bands could come play. He'd cross state lines to find and enjoy a killer show, but he liked the idea of bringing great talent to the northeast corner of Wyoming.

Shit went down. Civil war ensued. The good guys won. Then Steel Mustang was born.

He pulled onto their lot in under four minutes and took a sharp right turn, headed straight for the bar. There were already a couple bikes parked out front, and he was quick to make his way inside. The overhead sound system was playing, a couple of his brothers were shooting pool in the corner, and Rodeo was behind the bar while Wrangler sat with a beer on the other side of it.

"Hey. You good?" asked Rodeo with a jerk of his chin.

He was one of the first brothers to join the club under new leadership, voted in just two years ago. He was a good kid, and Mustang liked him, which meant he worked behind the bar most nights.

"Trix," was all Mustang said in response.

"Fuck. 'Nough said," muttered Wrangler.

Wrangler was the club's enforcer. He'd been around for more than a decade and was elevated into his role when Bull became president. It had been the right call, and not one of them disapproved of the appointment.

"Phoenix?" Mustang inquired, speaking of his bar manager.

Unlike the majority of his crew, she was not part of the club—she just kicked ass. From the moment she showed up for her interview, he knew he'd be a fool to turn down a woman who could hold her own in a bar full of bikers the way she could. Phoenix always had a fire in her belly and a knife on her hip. Their regulars knew not to mess with her.

"She's—"

"Right here," she interrupted as she shoved her shoulder into the swinging door that opened up behind the bar. Her arms were full of five bottles of unopened liquor. "Little help," she said, looking to Rodeo.

He was quick to unload her arms. With her hands free, she sighed, planted her palms against the edge of the bar, brought her eyes to meet Mustang's and teased, "Nice of you to join us."

It may have been a stereotype to assume all redheads were feisty, but this one certainly was.

"Trix," he repeated.

Phoenix scrunched her nose. "Oh." She then shrugged and added, "Well, we're good here. And we've still got a couple hours before the band shows and business starts to pick up. If you need to get anything done in the back, have at it."

Mustang nodded in a silent show of appreciation, then headed for his office.

CHAPTER *Three*

Tess

A FTER I'D ARRIVED IN the parking lot of Steel Mustang, I freed my hair from the clip I'd worn all day and shook out my wavy locks until they brushed to tops of my shoulders. Then I looked at my reflection via my rearview mirror and frowned.

What am I doing?

This was exactly the wrong place to be for someone who was on a *bad boy* hiatus.

I'd moved to Gillette right after college. Since then, I'd been in a series of failed relationships. None of them lasted very long. My most recent attempt had gone on three months before it ended in disaster.

He was a bull rider.

A real cowboy.

A total heartbreaker.

Admittedly, that was exactly my type.

I was a sucker for a bad boy.

I liked them rough around the edges and slightly dangerous. I found the devil-may-care attitude sexy. It was a total turn on when a guy said *screw it* to the rules of society and did what he wanted to do.

Not to say I wanted a felon in my bed. I seriously didn't. But a rebel who pushed the limits just to see how far he could go? That was my kind of dare devil.

When a man like that wanted me, it made me feel like more of a woman.

It was hard to explain why, but I'd fallen for that guy and chased that feeling time and time again. And, without fail, I'd ended up with a broken heart—a heart I'd recklessly given away too easily.

Difficult as it was to admit, after a decade of failures, I realized I was the problem. It wasn't like there was anything wrong with the guys. They were who they were—unapologetically; and who they were, were men who didn't know how to handle my tender heart. I couldn't be mad at them when their devil-may-care attitude extended to how they treated me.

In a way, I'd asked for it.

Now it was time I tried something different.

I needed to look for a guy who was more gentle than rough.

Safe.

Reliable.

Maybe a guy who knew how to tie a Windsor knot.

I gathered my hair and put it back up in a clip.

Man, I needed sleep.

I wasn't there to impress anyone. I was there for Ed.

It wasn't unheard of when patients died alone. Except, usually those patients were in a hospice care facility, not at home. The whole point of choosing to spend one's last days at home was to have the freedom to enjoy their loved ones in a place filled with warmth and memories.

Ed's house was not full of memories. It was full of clutter.

I knew I couldn't get emotionally wrapped up in his situation. I needed to remain objective, and I promised myself I would—*after* I spoke with Sully. I didn't want Ed to die alone. Also, I didn't want his son to live with regret having not gotten to say things he might have needed to say but didn't know he was running out of time to say.

I wanted to help.

I wanted to *try*.

Glancing around the parking lot, I noticed it wasn't too busy yet. The couple nights I'd been in the past, the place was so packed I wondered how many fire-safety laws had been violated.

I'd wondered, but I hadn't worried.

I was too busy having a good time.

The reputation the bar had was actually pretty impressive. I couldn't remember exactly when it opened, but it wasn't older than five years, and they were known not just in Gillette, but in the surrounding towns, as well. I would have gone more often, but it was the kind of place one went to party all night—and I didn't have that luxury most of the time.

I got out of my car, adjusted my purse on my shoulder, and tried to ignore the thrill that shot through me at the sight of a dozen Harleys parked out front.

Like the bar, the garage, and the auto-parts store, the Wild Stallions had a reputation of their own. They were as respected as they were feared. I didn't know any of the specifics behind why they were feared other than they were a bunch of badass bikers. It wasn't like they were in the news for stirring up trouble—even though it seemed unlikely they weren't the kind that stirred the pot every now and again. Of course, there were rumors and conjecture, but one could never tell fact from fiction.

As I approached the front entrance, I drew in a deep breath and let it out on a heavy sigh.

I was on a bad boy hiatus—that meant no badass bikers, no matter what I found inside.

I was there for Ed.

I pulled open the door and stepped through it, allowing my eyes a moment to adjust to the lack of bright sunlight. When I looked around, I found the place just as I remembered.

To my left, toward the back, were a couple of pool tables. That half of the bar had a number of high-top tables with barstools. On my right were the low-top tables and chairs. The seating was strategic, as the stage for the bands was along the far right side of the building.

The walls were covered in neon lit signs, framed photos of old motorcycles and famous musicians, posters, flags, and metal wall art that made it clear their bias was for Harley Davidson.

The bar, opposite the high-top tables and tucked in the corner, was L-shaped. The front was decked out in old motorcycle license plates from all over the country. There was a custom neon *Steel Mustang* sign that hung in the back corner, and the walls were full of shelves stocked with booze. There were no televisions, like one might have found at a typical bar. No one came there to watch sports. They came for the drinks and the music.

My favorite part was the ceiling.

It was plastered with vinyl record sleeves.

"You lost, sweetheart?"

I looked toward the bar, where the voice had come from, and noticed two men were staring at me. I remembered I was wearing pink scrubs, and I couldn't fault him for his question.

"No," I said, making my way toward them.

The guy behind the bar appeared to be younger. Maybe twenty-five. He had a baby face, his hair trimmed on the sides, but longer and messy on top. He wore a kutte, as did the guy sitting on the opposite side of the bar. I couldn't help but notice him, too. He did *not* have a baby face. He had a biker mustache that totally worked for him, and his hair was thick—with just the right amount of lazy curl—and hung down to his shoulders.

I reminded myself I was on a bad boy hiatus.

I was also in the middle of a biker bar wearing pink scrubs.

I got straight to the point.

"I'm looking for Sullivan Thomas."

The guy behind the bar frowned. "Who?"

"Sullivan? Maybe Sully?"

The man with the mustache chuckled while Baby Face said, "I have no idea who you're talkin' about."

"She's lookin' for Mustang," Mustache drawled.

I gave him my attention just in time to see his eyes trail slowly up and down my body. He did not appear put off by my scrubs. I tried to ignore that.

"Mustang?" I asked, attempting to stay on track.

"You're in his bar, darlin'. Best call him by his rightful name."

"Mustang's name is *Sully?*" asked Baby Face incredulously.

Just then, the door behind the bar swung open, and the man who walked through it stated, "Sure as fuck ain't to you."

Baby face laughed.

I did not laugh.

I could hardly breathe.

That was because those hazel-blue eyes hit me, and I could barely think.

The same eyes on his father were sad. But on Sully, they were vibrant and *alive.*

The black and white photo I saw earlier didn't do him justice.

He was a chestnut-brunette, his straight hair overgrown, but not enough to be considered long. His beard was full, and maybe a little unkempt—like he'd get around to trimming it when he felt like it, and he hadn't felt like it in a few days. He was tall, like Ed—maybe six-foot-two—but unlike his father, he was far from frail. He didn't look like a body builder, but he certainly looked sturdy.

The black and white photo also failed to capture the decent sized tattoo he had on his left bicep.

It was an old school, American traditional style *mom* tattoo. It was in full color. Even though it was clearly not new, it still looked good, the artist obviously no novice. The heart was red. The bird holding the ribbon with *MOM* in the center was blue, and the flowers that completed the piece were purple and pink. If done wrong, it would definitely have been a cheesy disaster of a tattoo—but it most certainly was *not* done wrong. It was so clearly in memorial of a woman he loved.

It was badass and sweet in equal measure.

He gave me a half-smile, and a zing shot straight through my belly.

"You, on the other hand—you can call me whatever you'd like."

Oh, god.

I wanted to call him a lot of things.

Like *mine.*

But I was on a bad boy hiatus.

More importantly, he was a family member to one of my dying patients.

I needed to focus.

"Are you Sullivan Thomas?" I managed to ask.

His smile disappeared. "Except that."

"Okay—but you're Mustang?" I stammered. "As in *Steel* Mustang?"

"Yup."

He folded his arms across his chest, and I couldn't help but notice the tattoos he had scrawled in massive, intricate cursive lettering across the back of both forearms. One read: *ride wild*. The other: *roam free*.

Oh, god.

Why did he have to be so hot?

"Um, okay. Could I have a word? In private?"

"About?"

"Your father."

I watched as those hazel-blue eyes went cold—*instantly*.

"I don't have one of those."

Alright. So, things between father and son were bad. Worse than bad.

I pressed on anyway.

"Ed is dying."

Sully—*Mustang*—didn't even flinch.

Our evolving exchange made it easier for me to ignore how attractive I found him. I hoped there was a small chance I could get through to him, somehow.

I took a step closer to the bar and explained, "My name is Tess. I'm Ed's hospice nurse. I just came from his house and..." I lost my words for a second, intimidated by the icebergs his eyes had become. "Look, it's very obvious your relationship is broken, but I thought you should know. You should at least know that he's dying."

"Now I know."

It was all he said.

Stubbornly, I asked, "Do you think, maybe—?"

"No," he interrupted, clearly not interested in anything I had to say in relation to his father.

I thought about the sad look in Ed's eyes as I stared into his son's cold ones—cold at the thought of his father, but vibrant when he first looked at me. I wondered what caused the giant chasm between them, but it wasn't my place to pry. I wanted to try to help them, but I knew some things couldn't be fixed.

Still, I gave it one last shot.

"My next visit is scheduled for Friday night around ten. I understand it's been a long time. If you change your mind and you want to stop by, I'll be there. You won't have to do it alone."

"Like I said—I don't have a father."

"Right," I murmured with a nod. "Okay. Okay..."

I turned on my heel and started for the door.

I knew I shouldn't have been, but I couldn't help it.

I was disappointed that hadn't gone as I'd hoped.

Mustang

His dick got hard just looking at her face.

Fuck, she was beautiful—with those golden-brown eyes and plump, sweetheart lips.

Her hair was pulled back, save for a strand she hadn't captured by her ear, but he could tell it was dirty blonde—more dirty than blonde. He wondered what she looked like with it down, and what she looked like out of her uniform.

Though, she worked those fucking cotton-candy pink scrubs just fine.

She'd tucked her short sleeve top into the thick, elastic waistband of her pants. This meant he knew she had a subtle hourglass figure with breasts that appeared just large enough to fill the palms of his hands. The pants weren't baggy, like the nurses he'd seen on TV, but fit her legs down to the elastic bands wrapped around her delicate ankles. Never would he have imagined he could be turned on watching a woman walk away from him in a pair of white, New Balance sneakers, but there he was.

He didn't like the reason she'd walked into his bar.

He didn't like she was leaving so soon.

But he sure didn't mind the view of her nice ass as she left.

She was at the door, pushing her way out into the late afternoon sun, when he thought about what she'd told him. He didn't give a damn his old man was dying, and he sure as hell had no intention of dropping in to say his last goodbye. He hadn't said goodbye twenty years ago and didn't see the need to do so now. He thought that bastard deserved to die alone.

Mustang *did* wonder what sob story Ed had fed Tess to get her to walk into his bar.

Wrangler whistled, pulling Mustang from his thoughts.

"Shit—I sure wouldn't mind a checkup if it meant I got a piece of that."

Rodeo chuckled, but Mustang shifted his gaze back toward the door.

No way in hell he'd let Wrangler get anywhere near her.

She'd come in looking for him.

Tess was his.

Tess

MY EYES FLUTTERED OPEN Friday morning, and he was the first thing on my mind.

Mustang.

His friends didn't know him as Sully.

Having met him, I had a few guesses as to why.

Sully was the name of a schoolboy, or that guy who worked behind the counter at the post office, or that pilot who landed that plane that one time on the Hudson—and Mustang wasn't any of those *Sullys*.

He was a badass biker who owned a badass biker bar.

He was a Wild Stallion who rode wild and roamed free.

It had been two days since I met him, and I hadn't forgotten.

I barely had the chance do anything other than work and sleep in that time. The fact that he was there in my head, first thing in the morning, was like a taunting reminder of my horrible idea to try and mastermind a reconciliation between two men I didn't even know.

It hadn't been a horrible idea because it hadn't worked.

I did what I thought was right, so my conscious was clear.

It had been a horrible idea because when I started my Wednesday,

I didn't know an incredibly hot badass biker with vibrant hazel-blue eyes and a *mom* tattoo I just knew he wore with love and not a drop of irony. Now I did, and it was Friday, and I couldn't forget it—forget *him*—even though I knew he was out of bounds *and* the embodiment of everything I was trying to keep out of my bed and certainly away from my heart.

I freed a pathetic whine, clapping my hands over my face, but didn't move to get up.

I should have. I needed to. It might have even helped to distract myself with the responsibilities of the day—but I was dragging.

I'd gone to sleep the night before only to be roused two hours later by a call from the husband of one of my patients. She had been struggling with insurmountable pain. I was out the door ten minutes later. I didn't walk back through it for another three hours. I'd turned off my alarm after crawling into bed in the wee hours, but my body was gracious enough to make sure I didn't sleep away the entire morning.

So, I was awake…thinking about Mustang.

My cell phone rang, and I was quick to roll over to reach for it.

I didn't care if it was a patient or the pope, I needed the distraction.

I smiled when I saw it was *Jenna* calling.

"Hey," I spoke in greeting, putting her on speaker.

"Hi! I didn't wake you, did I?"

"Nope. Your timing is perfect."

Jenna and I had met shortly after I moved back to Wyoming. My first job out of school was as an oncology nurse at the hospital. Jenna was an ER nurse who'd been on the job about a year longer than me. I thought she was crazy for staying in the ER for the last decade, and she thought I was nuts for leaving the hospital to tend to patients who never survived—but we remained each other's best support system all the same.

"I just finished an all-nighter and wanted to call to confirm our plans for Sunday before I crashed. Please say we're still on, because my feet are *dying* for some tender love and care."

I looked down at my own feet, even though they were tucked under my covers. I didn't need to see them to be reminded they were in need of a fresh coat of paint.

"Fingers crossed neither of us gets called in, because I am so totally there."

Pedicures once a month was our ritual, but it was more than just a chance for a little self-care. It was basically a mandatory check in. She and I kept each other sane. Our jobs were hard and emotionally draining. It would have been so easy to burnout, but we had each other to lean on in order to make sure that didn't happen.

Like me, Jenna was single and had no one to pick up the slack at home. Her dating history was quite different than mine. Her exes weren't the heartbreakers so much as the heartbroken. It wasn't that she was a tyrant when it came to dating relationships, she was just picky. She never gave her heart away too soon, as she was incredibly overprotective of it. If she saw even a hint of something she didn't like, she was out.

I wasn't entirely sure if it was the healthiest way to go about dating—but she felt the same way about how I did it, too. In so many ways, we were each other's opposite, but I supported her in her pursuit of happiness all the same. She was a gorgeous, lovely human who deserved to find the right man for her—whatever that looked like.

"Okay, good. We'll keep each other posted. But, while I have you, quick check in. How you holdin' up?"

We chatted for the duration of her drive home, then we said our goodbyes so I could start my day while she wound down from hers.

I didn't tell her about Mustang, and I wasn't sure why.

Maybe I'd fill her in on Sunday.

With him on my mind again, I wondered if he'd show at the house on Thornhill Road that night. He said he wouldn't, and I knew better than to hope—but I still wondered.

I was genuinely getting ready to finally get out of bed when my phone rang again.

This time I sat up in excitement when I saw *Andy* was calling.

"Hi!" I answered without delay.

"Hey, sis." I could hear the smile in his voice, and that feeling I associated with *home* washed over me.

"It's good to hear your voice. How are you?"

Andy was older than me by five years. We hadn't been incredibly close when I was really little, but our bond certainly grew after mom got sick. When she died, it grew even stronger. It sucked, but our losses were what kept us so tight, no matter what distance separated us. We were all each other had left in the world.

Andy was a pilot in the Air Force. He flew C-17s and loved it. I was incredibly proud of him, even if I wasn't crazy about the places his work took him. He was currently stationed down in Texas, which felt like a world away sometimes; but he checked in on a regular basis, which always meant a lot to me.

We spoke a few minutes about the mundane.

Given what each of us did for a living, I was generally good with the mundane.

"So, how are things going with Gwen?" I asked, digging for the juicy stuff.

"They're good."

I shook my head, not at all satisfied with his answer, and probed, "Are things getting serious yet or...?"

"It's still early to tell."

I rolled my eyes. They'd been seeing each other for three months, and he still refused to call her his girlfriend. I didn't know how the poor woman put up with him. It wasn't that I thought he should be out ring shopping or anything, but the man wasn't getting any younger. I wasn't sure where his commitment issues came from, but they were large and in charge. He was the only one of his buddies who'd never been married.

Then again, he'd never been divorced, which wasn't a bad thing.

"Listen, I've got a job coming up overseas," he told me, changing the subject. "Not sure this time how long I'll be gone. Could be a few days, could be a few weeks."

"Oh, the uncertainty of it all," I teased.

He laughed softly, saying so much without speaking a single word.

"We leave tomorrow. I'll call you when I'm back."

"You be careful."

"Always am, Tess."

"Well, I love you. Thanks for calling."

He returned my sentiments, and we said *talk to you later* before disconnecting.

My next call came from my bladder, which meant I finally got out of bed.

Two days a week, I worked the night shift. The best part of my Friday night schedule was that it wasn't immediately followed by a day shift. This always put me in a particularly good mood when I left my place at eight. That night, my first stop was the house on Ramshorn Avenue.

When I pulled into Sharon's driveway and saw Mitchell's car and no sign of Lance, my mood got even brighter. It was Renee who opened the door when I knocked. The first thing she told me was Mitchell was at home with Emilia that night, while Bristol—their six-year-old—had come to visit with her grandma. They were fifteen minutes from the end of a movie, and that was reason enough for me to spend a little extra time chatting with Renee.

I loved families like the Jones'. It was so heartwarming to see the way they took advantage of every lucid moment they could find. It meant a lot to Sharon, I knew—but I was even more aware of how much it would mean to Bristol when she got older and all she had left of her grandmother were memories.

My visit at Sharon's took a little longer than I anticipated, and it was a few minutes after ten when I was headed to my car. I was late for my visit to Thornhill Road, which could have potentially been the beginning of a long domino effect. As I started my journey north, I was so focused on trying to figure out how I could find ways to make up the time in my schedule throughout my shift, I wasn't thinking about whether or not I'd see Mustang that night.

So, when I was three houses down from my destination and I saw a man and his motorcycle parked on the far side of Ed's driveway, I almost forgot how to breathe.

He came?

He actually came.

I couldn't believe it.

Even when I pulled into the spot right next to him, turned off my car, then stared at him through my driver's side window, I couldn't believe it.

He stared back at me, waiting, lit by the floodlight mounted above Ed's garage door.

He was wearing a sleeveless graphic tee underneath his leather kutte, his arms folded casually across his chest. His black-jean clad legs were spread wide, his booted feet firmly on the ground as he leaned against the seat of his blue Harley. His hair, wind-blown from his ride, hung disheveled on either side of his forehead.

I wanted to run my fingers through it.

What is wrong with me?

Him.

He was what was wrong with me.

He was a sight to behold behind the bar, but the vision of Mustang with his bike right next to me sent a zing straight to my belly—a zing that hit and ricocheted like crazy.

When he ducked his chin to catch a better look at me, I understood that meant he was getting tired of waiting. It wasn't safe outside of my car. I knew this because my willpower had reached dangerously low levels the moment I saw him in the driveway. Nevertheless, I had to get out. I'd never make it inside the house if I didn't first get out of my car—and I had a patient I needed to see.

I anxiously licked my lips, grabbed my purse, then finally stepped out of my car.

"Hi," I said, shutting the door behind me.

There was a good four feet between Mustang and me, and I made sure to keep it that way.

"I—I didn't think you'd come."

"Not here for him," he stated plainly.

I ignored the thrill his words sent racing up my spine, as well as what he may have been insinuating.

He was out of bounds. So far out of bounds it wasn't even funny.

"What? What do you mean?"

"Go out with me."

Oh, shit.

It had been a horrible idea to go looking for Sully Thomas.

Before Wednesday afternoon, I didn't know an incredibly hot badass biker with vibrant hazel-blue eyes and a *mom* tattoo I just knew he wore with love and not a drop of irony. Now I did, and even though I knew he was out of bounds *and* the embodiment of everything I was trying to keep out of my bed and certainly away from my heart—there he was.

Right in front of me.

Asking me out.

He wasn't insinuating anything. He'd made it plain.

Why did I have to love it when a man was so bold?

Reaching up with both hands, I grabbed hold of the straps of my purse, looped over my shoulder. I'd brought this on myself, and now I had to face the consequences.

"I'm afraid that's not going to be possible."

It almost pained me to say it.

"Why not?"

This one was a bit easier to spit out.

"I don't get involved with the family members of my patients."

He was quick with a rebuttal.

"Told you, that man in there is nothin' to me."

I couldn't accept this. Not because I didn't think he meant what he said, but because I needed this boundary like I need *air.*

"Yes, you have made that abundantly clear. But I'm stubborn enough—or maybe stupid enough—to think maybe, just maybe, I could change your mind about going inside of that house." I nodded toward the aforementioned house and continued, "In the event that I do, I can't go out with you, as that would be unethical on my part."

"Tess, I'm not goin' into that house. How about we just skip to the good part and forget the old man?"

My name on his lips made my heart skip a beat.

My god, I should have never gone looking for Sully Thomas.

I squeezed my hands around the straps of my purse even tighter, unable to find my words.

"Come on. Go out with me. Bet we'd have a good time."

A laugh forced its way out of my throat, and I was quick to press my lips together, cutting it short. I then hummed in embarrassment and forced a smile.

I needed to get away from him.

I was losing my grip.

"I really should be getting inside. If you don't want to join me, I'll have to say goodnight."

I paused a beat, not ready to leave but certain I should.

When he didn't say a word to stop me, I nodded and started for the house.

I took two whole steps before he said, "Maybe I'll think about going inside if you let me take you out."

I stopped and looked his way. "You'll go inside if I go out with you?"

This was an interesting if not cunning proposal. If I wasn't so freaking attracted to him, I wouldn't have considered it for even a second—but I'd gone into that bar with one objective, and Mustang had shot me down before I could even get the ask out of my mouth. Now that he was turning the tables on me, it felt silly not to explore the option.

"Said I'll *think* about it, which is a hell of a lot more than I'm doin' now," he clarified.

My shoulders slumped a little in disappointment.

"That's not exactly a guarantee, Mustang."

No sooner had the words come out of my mouth than he was up

off his bike. He got close. Real close. So close I knew he smelled like leather and fresh air. So close I could touch him. So close he could touch me—and I'd be a liar if I said I didn't want him to.

I held my breath as I looked up at him, willing myself to remember he was out of bounds. Very, very, very *far* out of bounds.

But then he spoke, and my willpower was suddenly on empty.

"I don't know what you think you know, but that son-of-a-bitch deserves nothin' from me. Not even a stray thought about me visiting him on his deathbed. And what you should take from that is you took one step into my bar in those pink scrubs, I took one look at you, and what I saw was worth a second look—so fuckin' worth it, I dragged my ass out here, down a street I haven't been on in years, just to get that look. And now that I've had it, I know I want a third, so much I'm willing to spare a thought to that bastard who led you to believe he still had a son all so I could guarantee that third look. Only next time, maybe we won't talk about that dying fucker. Hell, maybe next time we won't talk at all.

"So, what's it gonna be, Tess?"

It was an out-and-out miracle my knees still worked.

He'd said a lot.

There was a decent amount in there I didn't fully understand. It was like he'd thrown a bunch of puzzle pieces at our feet, and the only clues I had as to the picture they might make were locked in the depths of those hazel-blue eyes.

Eyes that wanted a third look.

A third look *at me.*

That feeling I chased every time a bad boy glanced my way with interest? It was there. It was there, and it was huge, and I hadn't even chased it. Mustang just gave it to me. Served it to me on a silver platter.

He wanted a third look.

It definitely wasn't a good idea.

But I'd already made a mess with one horrible idea—what was one more?

So long as I kept my clothes on, how much worse could it get?

Maybe I really could get Mustang to go inside.

At least, that's what I needed to tell myself before I told him, "Okay. A drink, then. But my schedule is—"

"How about tomorrow night? My bar. Nine o'clock."

Remarkably, I could make that work.

"Okay. Nine o'clock." Agreeing on a time reminded me I was late for Ed when I'd pulled into the driveway, which meant now I was even more so. "I really do need to get inside. Your fath—uh—Ed," I stammered, correcting myself, "he's only my second patient of the night, and I'm already behind."

"Tomorrow then."

He turned and went to get on his bike.

I wished I hadn't watched.

He mounted it like it was an extension of him, which was the reminder I didn't need that Mustang wasn't merely a bad boy—he was a badass biker. He was a Wild Stallion who rode wild and roamed free.

The light from above the garage highlighted the back of his kutte, and I took in its details. He had three patches. *Wild Stallions* was sewn in a slight arch across his shoulders. Along the bottom was his Wyoming location patch. Finally, in the middle was the metal skull stallion emblem. Unlike his black and gray tattoo, it was in color—the fire on the stallion's mane red and orange underneath the dinge and dirt he collected on the road.

I stood there, and I watched him, and I knew.

If I let him, he'd break my heart.

I just couldn't let him.

Before he started his engine, he glanced at me from over his shoulder and said, "Night, Tess."

All I could manage was a wave.

CHAPTER *Five*

I STARED AT MYSELF in the mirror and shook my head.

It was Saturday night, and I was dressed and ready to leave for Steel Mustang.

My outfit was a clear indicator a biker bar was *exactly* where I wanted to be that night.

But that didn't make any of this a good idea.

I wasn't a *frills* kind of gal. I never wore a ton of makeup, mostly because washing it all off was a chore in which I was not interested. Other than a pair of studs in my ears, I didn't really wear jewelry. I owned exactly *one* little black dress, and I wasn't sure when I'd last worn it, but I was sure I wouldn't be wearing it to meet Mustang.

I was keeping my clothes on that night, and that dress implied otherwise.

I'd opted for a pair of jeans.

Then again—I had a pretty kickass collection of jeans.

I wasn't a *frills* kind of gal, but that didn't mean I wasn't the kind of woman who would absolutely drop two-hundred dollars on a pair of jeans that fit just right. I couldn't go out in anything less than a great pair of jeans if I also wanted to wear a fabulous pair of shoes—and I had some pretty freaking fabulous shoes.

I was only twelve when my mom died. I wasn't old enough to absorb a lot of her wisdom, but there was one thing in particular she taught me that I would never forget. She told me life was short, and if I wanted red-sole Louboutins, I should buy them, wear them, and enjoy them.

I'd never been to Paris or Italy. I'd never seen Central Park or the Grand Canyon. I hadn't gone on a real vacation in years—but I did own three pairs of Christian Louboutins and four pairs of Jimmy Choo heels.

That night, I was going with Jimmy.

I did my makeup like I normally did—a little eyeliner, a bit of mascara, a touch of blush, and a glossy lip. I'd styled my hair down. Its natural wavy texture gave it body, so all I had to do was fluff it a little with my hands and it hung how I wanted, kissing the tops of my shoulders.

The shirt I had on was a black, sleeveless turtleneck. It clung to my body and was long enough that it tucked nicely into my favorite high-waisted skinny jeans. They were faded, dark-washed denim with a couple minor holes strategically placed on each thigh. Rather than a zipper, it had five buttons up the front.

I didn't have the perfect body by any means. I may have been thin-ish, but that was more on account of my odd schedule made my eating habits less than ideal, and I spent a lot of time on my feet. I wasn't toned or tight anywhere—but my kickass jeans made me look like I could have been.

The icing on the cake was, of course, my shoes.

I knew I was going to a biker bar. I knew some might find my choice strange.

But if wearing Jimmy Choos to Steel Mustang was wrong, I didn't want to be right.

I had on my ballet pink pumps.

They were made with both suede and patent.

They had a sharp pointed toe and a three-inch heel.

They also looked *awesome* with my outfit.

I'd have been a liar if I said I didn't select every item of clothing with Mustang in mind. It would have been smarter to show up in a pair of scrubs and sneakers.

Then again, I'd learned that was not as unappealing as I'd imagined.

In any case, I was dressed. I was ready. It was time for me to go.

I grabbed my purse and headed for the door.

Ten minutes later, I was reminded that Steel Mustang at nine o'clock on a Saturday night was a different experience than it was on a Wednesday afternoon at four-thirty. The parking lot was packed. Mine wasn't the only car there, but a good third of the lot was occupied by motorcycles.

A younger, dumber version of me would hardly have been able to contain her excitement at the prospect of a great time had by all beyond the doors of the popular biker bar. I could hear the music from inside the second I stepped out of my car. A live rock band, a good drink, and a bunch of badasses in a room teeming with testosterone was nothing less than a recipe for a wild night.

Admittedly, the older, wiser version of me still felt a thrill ripple through me as I made my way toward the front entrance. I knew, inside that bar, there were no rules. No boundaries. No sickness or sorrow. And while I couldn't let go entirely—first, because I was on-call, and second, because I needed to be sure things didn't get out of hand with Mustang—I didn't have to hold myself back in a place like this. All anyone who passed through those doors, or mounted a motorcycle, or even a wild bull—all *any* rebel really wanted was to feel *free*.

While I didn't consider myself a rebel, I was no different.

I made it to the door, reached for the handle, and pulled it open without a hint of hesitation.

I didn't know who was playing that night, but it was already standing room only. Even in my heels, I couldn't see from the door to the bar. I had no idea how I was going to find Mustang, but it seemed like my best bet to head in that direction.

I was squeezing and shimmying my way across the room when I felt a large hand wrap around my arm, just above my elbow. I stopped to look and see who had hold of me, but my cheek pressed against his before I could see his face—his lips grazing my ear as he spoke.

"Welcome back, darlin'," he drawled. "You still lookin' for Mustang, or are you here for a different Stallion? Cause I sure wouldn't mind your company."

Mustache.

I registered who the man was a second before another arm snaked around the back of my waist and pulled me firmly against his warm, solid chest. My nostrils filled with the scent of leather and fresh air—this time, with the welcome addition of *pine*—and I didn't even have to look up to see Mustang had me in his grip.

But I did anyway.

He wasn't even looking at me. His eyes were fixed on Mustache. I watched him wink at the man, but he did it with a straight face. When I felt the hand on my arm loosen, I understood that *wink* had been a warning.

I felt a familiar zing in my belly.

"Alright, brother," said Mustache, his tone laced in amusement.

Mustang didn't bother with a *hello*. Once he'd made his message clear, with his arm still around my waist, he escorted me toward the bar. It was significantly easier maneuvering through the crowd with him at my side. When we made it to the back, rather than signal one of the bartenders, he stood me in front of a very large man.

Even sitting, I knew he was taller than Mustang by at least a couple inches. He was older and broader, too. Not by much, but enough to notice. He had a thick beard he'd grown out down to his chest, most of it more salt than pepper, and he'd curled the ends of his mustache. His salt and pepper hair was cut short on the sides, the top combed back in a classic, clean look. Though, *classic* and *clean* didn't describe his vibe.

The front of his kutte was riddled with sewn on patches—but there were three on his upper-right chest that stood out the most. The top read *Bull*. The one underneath it, *President*. And the one underneath that, *Gillette*.

So, he wasn't just a big man. He was a big flipping deal.

He was also covered in tattoos. The V-neck of his tee revealed he had more than he cared to show that night, ink peeking out from the thin layer of chest hair exposed. The only skin I saw on him that *didn't* have a drop of ink was his face—but the wrinkles around his eyes told a story of their own.

And his eyes were piercingly beautiful.

They were the purest light blue I'd ever seen.

"Bull, you mind?" Mustang hollered over the band.

His blue eyes caught mine, and I swear I was struck in the middle of my chest by the depth of his character in a single glance.

His gaze didn't last long before he looked at Mustang and gave him a silent nod. He then got up and moved to squeeze into the space in front of the woman in the seat next to the one he'd vacated. She didn't seem to mind. She wrapped her arms around him, he leaned into her a little, and they both watched me settle onto the empty barstool—my back to the bar, like everyone else.

Mustang made room for himself at my side, and I ignored the pleasant sensation that came as a result of the heat radiating off his body and onto mine.

It came as little surprise to me that the woman who claimed the man *Bull* was gorgeous. Her platinum blonde hair was a few inches longer than mine and the texture slightly curlier. I couldn't tell if she got that color from a bottle or not—but it didn't matter. She rocked it.

She had a narrow face with angular features and a long, slender body to match. Her eyes were dark blue; and while her gaze didn't have the same effect as Bull's, I had no doubt she was a woman who could hold her own. She was also a woman no younger than forty who could pull off a cropped Sturgis tee, high-waisted black leather shorts, and fishnet stockings with killer boots.

Even in my Jimmy Choos, I was a little jealous of her swagger.

"Where're your manners?" called Bull. "Aren't you gonna introduce us?"

The blonde smiled, and it was contagious, which was how I found myself smiling up at Mustang as I waited for his reply.

"Tess—Bull and his ol' lady, Winona."

"Kickass shoes!" Winona freed up a hand and offered it to me. "And you can call me Winnie."

I loved her instantly.

Accepting her gesture, I said loudly, "Thank you! It's nice to meet you both."

I meant it more than either of them could know.

It was a relief to be sitting next to people who could help stave off whatever sexual tension Mustang had aroused the moment he touched me. Buffer people were good. Great, even—especially friendly female ones.

"Babe, what're you drinkin'?" asked a woman from behind the bar.

I was not the least bit surprised when I twisted and found a knockout redhead waiting to take my order. A place like this only let the pretty ones behind the bar. It was more surprising she had on a decent amount of clothing; and it was the fierceness in her dark green eyes I found most intriguing.

I cleared my throat and called out, "I'll take a ranch water, please."

She gave me the *okay* signal with her hand, then left to make my drink, not bothering to take Mustang's order.

Turning to look at him, I asked, "You're not having a drink?"

He shook his head once, then said, "Don't drink."

I frowned and tilted my head in confusion, "What?"

This got me a half-smile before he semi-repeated, "I don't drink."

I straightened, leaning away from him so as to get a better look at his face as I asked, "You're telling me you own a biker bar, you're a member of a biker club, and you don't drink? *Ever?*"

His half-smile stretched into a full one, and I felt another zing light up my belly.

"Nope," he answered simply.

I stared at him, stunned and intrigued.

There was a story there. There had to be a reason why this particular badass never drank. It made zero sense on its face. But I didn't want to pry, which meant I wasn't going to ask, no matter how badly I wanted to know.

The more I knew about him, the more I'd want to know about him.

It was a slippery slope—one I did not wish to traverse.

However, Mustang had no problem revealing the reasons behind his sobriety. As if he could tell I wanted to know even if I wasn't going to ask, he explained, "Lived with an alcoholic the first sixteen years of my life. Just in case that shit's hereditary, never touched the stuff. Can't ride drunk. I'd rather ride free than buzzed or high."

Just like that, one of the puzzle pieces he'd tossed at my feet the night before snapped into place.

Ed was an alcoholic.

Given the state of his liver, this was not startling news to me. He was sober now, though how long he'd managed to stay that way I wasn't sure. Nonetheless, for sixteen very crucial years, he'd succumbed to his vice, and I suspected that was a major reason why Ed and Mustang were no longer on speaking terms.

There were definitely more pieces yet to fit into place, but this one revealed a whole lot.

Mustang never drank. Ever. Because of Ed.

"You work today?" he asked, changing the subject.

It was my turn to shake my head. "No. But I am on-call Saturdays and Sundays, so I'm just going to have the one drink." I lifted a single shoulder in a shrug. "Hopefully no one needs me tonight."

He propped a hand on the edge of the bar, pressing in a little closer. "How long you been a nurse?"

"Ten years," I told him. I watched his eyes drop to my mouth as I went on to say, "I've been in hospice care for the last six."

His eyes found mine once more before he asked, "You from around here?"

"I grew up in Casper, then left to go to school down in Greeley. I made my way back home right after I graduated. Or, close to it, at least."

He jerked his chin in acknowledgement then I lost his eyes. The next thing I knew, he was lowering my drink in front of me. I took it, murmuring a thank-you I wasn't sure he heard as I noticed his knuckle tattoo for the first time. He moved too quickly for me to make out what it said, but I made a mental note to keep an eye out for it at my next opportunity.

As I sipped my drink, my eyes drifted over the patches on the front-right chest of his kutte. I hadn't noticed them the other day, too distracted by the rest of him. His patches were just like Bull's, only the top one read, *Mustang;* and the one underneath, *Sergeant-at-Arms.*

"What about you?" I asked him, lifting my gaze in search of his. "How long have you been a Stallion?"

He reached up and raked his fingers through his hair before dropping his hand and shoving his fingers into the front pocket of his jeans.

"Officially? Eighteen years. Unofficially?" He jerked his chin toward my opposite side and said, "Bull took me under his wing a couple years before that. Looked out for me until I was old enough to earn the patches on my kutte. All in—twenty years. Makes me more Stallion than anything else."

My eyebrows shot up in surprise.

Twenty years ago, I'd just lost my mom.

I was twelve. How old was he?

"How old are you?" I blurted.

"Thirty-six. How old are you?"

"Thirty-two," I told him distractedly, still trying to piece together the timeline of his life.

I noticed as those hazel-blue eyes dropped down to my mouth again, and suddenly I lost track of my thoughts. I took a sip of my drink, scrambling to think of another question.

"So—what did you do before the bar?"

"Same as the rest of us. Worked in the garage and the shop. Still do, when I feel like it."

I nodded and took another swallow of my ranch water.

I was out of questions.

Or, rather, I was out of *safe* questions. What else was there after work talk? Family was out. Hobbies were obsolete. I had no real hobbies, unless one considered power napping an interesting activity.

Deciding to leave the ball in his court, I turned my attention toward the band. Since I sat down, they'd played one or two covers, but there were some songs I'd never heard before. I wondered if they were originals. If they were, they were really good.

"Is this band local?" I inquired, barely taking my eyes off of them as I did.

"No, they're based in South Dakota," Mustang answered, his lips closer to my ear than they were before. "They're a crowd favorite, though. Found out about 'em a couple years ago, and I try to get them up here at least once every month or two."

I thought about what he said. Not so much about the band, but his role in getting them there. Then I put a couple pieces together myself, recognizing that while it made zero sense for a badass biker who owned a badass biker bar to never drink, it made a whole lot of sense that a badass biker who owned a badass biker bar but never drank could pour a whole lot of his focus into sourcing awesome bands to come play at his bar. A bar that was known for miles as the place to be on a Saturday night if you wanted to hear some kickass live music.

I didn't need another reason to like Mustang—but he'd given me one.

For the next forty-five minutes, I sipped slowly at my drink, enjoying the show. Mustang and I didn't ask each other anymore questions, but the silence between us wasn't weird. It didn't feel like we were ignoring one another. It wasn't just the two of us. We were in a crowded room, riding the vibe of the band. It was actually pretty great.

When I got to the bottom of my drink, I was a little disappointed I had to cut myself off.

Before I could twist to set my empty glass on the bar, Mustang's fingers brushed against mine as he took it and put it behind me. I'd just looked up to say thank you when the band wrapped up their set. The overhead music kicked on, decidedly less loud, as they started clearing the stage in order to make way for the next band.

That's when Mustang started grazing his knuckles up and down my side.

I stiffened at first contact, my eyes glued to the floor, but he wasn't deterred.

When he kept going, the excitement that sparked in my belly rippled through me, causing a wave of warmth to spread all the way into my chest.

Against my better judgement, I relaxed.

It felt good, and I liked that his manly, tattooed hand was capable of a touch so gentle.

Yeah—I didn't need another reason to like Mustang, but he'd scored one again.

I was in serious trouble.

As if she'd been waiting to take advantage of a quiet moment, Winnie turned toward me, mercifully pulling me from my thoughts as she asked, "How'd you two meet? I haven't seen you around before."

For a moment, Mustang's fingers stopped grazing.

Instead, he wrapped his hand around my side and squeezed.

Somehow, I knew exactly what he was communicating.

This was why I answered, "I came in the other day, when it wasn't busy, and he was behind the bar. I've been here a couple times, but on nights more like tonight."

I'd said the right thing. I knew this because Mustang let me go, then continued the steady up and down rhythm of his knuckles on my side. Rather than get lost in the feel of his touch, I tried desperately to focus on what Winnie was saying.

"It's nice to see a new friendly face. We get a lot of sheep, not all of them friendly, and certainly none with such impeccable taste in shoes."

"Sheep?"

This was a new term for me.

Winnie smiled knowingly, glanced over my head at Mustang, then fixed her gaze back on me. I wasn't sure what that look meant, but I was certain it meant something.

"Yeah, you know—hang-arounds. Club sheep. Always on the compound looking for a good time."

I nodded, catching her drift, while at the same time hoping my being there for a drink with Mustang didn't land me in the *sheep* category. I had a type, a *weakness*, really—but I wasn't desperate.

"Heard you're a nurse," she went on to say, rescuing me from my thoughts for the second time.

"Yeah. I am."

"Noble. *Brutal.*"

I laughed, as amused as I was impressed she could sum up my career in two simple words. "Yeah. That about sums it up. What about you? What do you do?"

"I'm part time over at the garage, handling all the admin work," she said, nodding in its direction. "And when I'm not there, I'm with our three hellions. We've got a seventeen-year-old, a fifteen-year-old, and a five-year-old. All boys."

I smiled at that. Knowing Winnie was a mom made me like her even more.

"I'm gettin' another," said Bull, turning to address his wife.

I'd spotted the rock on her finger and figured, in their case, *ol' lady* was synonymous with *wife.*

"You want one?" he asked her.

"Yeah, honey. I'll have another."

Bull then looked at me. "Tess?"

"I'm good, thanks."

He gave me a slight nod, then turned to order another round. As he did, the lead singer of the next band introduced them. The drummer marked the beat, and then the music drowned out everything else. Bull hooked his arm around Winnie's shoulders, and she nestled into his side as they settled.

Now, with no one to talk to, I was again hyperaware of Mustang and his hand at my side. I chanced a look at him and found his attention was on the band. He really was so handsome. I resisted the urge to reach up and run my fingers through his hair.

As if he sensed my gaze aimed at him, he looked down at me.

Another zing ricocheted in my belly.

His eyes searched mine for a long moment before he brought his mouth to my ear. I felt the whiskers of his beard, he was so close.

"You ever been on the back of a hog, baby?"

A thrill shot up my spine, and I had to fight the urge to shiver.

I'd been on the back of a motorcycle before.

But I'd never been on a Harley.

I shook my head in response.

"You feel like a ride?"

Oh, god.

I held my breath as I contemplated his offer.

It was a bad idea. The worst.

Me, on the back of Mustang's bike?

There'd be no turning back after that.

The second he took off, we'd be racing across every boundary I'd told myself I shouldn't cross.

But it was a perfect summer night.

I'd have been a liar if I said I didn't want to experience the power of his hog and the wind in my hair with me at his back—and I really didn't like to lie.

I ran out of oxygen.

I blew out my breath, inhaled another, and shifted so I could see into those hazel-blue eyes.

Then I nodded, waving a white flag of surrender.

In that moment, there was nothing I wanted more than to go for a ride.

The next thing I knew, he had hold of my hand, and I was sliding off my barstool. As he pulled me toward the door, I managed to glance back at Winnie.

She grinned and winked at me, then I lost sight of her altogether.

As soon as were outside, I had to move my feet double time to keep up with Mustang's long stride in my heels. His bike was parked near the end of the row closest to the building. When we reached it, excitement rippled through me knowing I was about to be on it.

"Purse?" he asked as he dropped my hand.

I gave it to him, and he flipped open the lid of his saddlebag and stowed it away. Once the top was latched closed, he mounted his ride, and it was just as hot then as it had been the last time I saw it.

After he was settled, he pointed at a foot peg and told me, "Use that to help you climb on." He then extended his hand to further assist me.

I hesitated for a moment. The bike was beautiful and slightly intimidating once faced with the prospect of straddling it in my Jimmy Choos; but I was going for a ride, and nothing was going to stop me.

I took his hand, held on tight, and found my way onto the seat behind Mustang. It might not have been entirely graceful, but with a Harley Davidson between my legs, I couldn't spare a thought to worry about it.

He pressed a few buttons, the engine roared to life, and I didn't fight my shiver.

Before we took off, he reached down, grabbed me behind my knees, and yanked me forward. My breath caught as I practically slammed into his back, every part of me now in contact with a part of him.

Leather. Fresh air. Pine.

He smelled divine.

"Hold onto me, Tess," he demanded.

I didn't have to be told twice.

My arms locked around his waist, and we were gone.

We rode casually off the compound's lot, Mustang pointing us I didn't know where. It wasn't long before I realized we were headed for I-90. He merged onto the highway, and we *flew.*

I was scared for all of thirty seconds—then I reminded myself Mustang and his bike were one. He was in control, and I was safe, no matter how fast we went.

When I began to relax and enjoy the ride, I tasted freedom like I'd never had it before. I emptied my mind completely, and it was *bliss.*

There was, however, one thing I couldn't ignore.

The vibration of the Harley coupled with the feel of Mustang between my legs turned me on.

There was no fighting it.

The wind was cool against my skin as it whipped through my hair, but Mustang was warm, keeping me that way, too. He steered us through the heart of Gillette and beyond, until there was nothing to see on either side of the road but the darkness of night. I pressed my cheek to the back of his shoulder as I closed my eyes, and I swear he rode even faster.

I didn't know if we were chasing a feeling or running from one—but I never wanted to stop.

We rode for a while. How long, I couldn't say. He eased us off the interstate at a rest stop, then turned us around, taking us back from where we came, and we rode a while longer.

I was a little disappointed when, at last, I saw the compound come into view.

He turned into the entrance but didn't stop at the bar. Instead, he drove right past it, toward the furthest building on the lot. When he finally stopped and killed the engine, I let him go reluctantly. He held out a hand, the only signal I needed that it was time for me to dismount, so I did.

"Why didn't you park closer to the bar?" I forced the words out of my mouth, needing to get my brain to focus on something other than the longing that beckoned between my legs. With my feet on the ground, I felt almost desperate for a release.

"We're not going back to the bar," he stated as he dismounted and turned to face me.

"We're not?"

I barely finished my question before Mustang took hold of the side of my neck, held me steady, then crushed his mouth against mine.

My knees were instantly useless.

I grasped either side of his kutte and held on.

I knew he didn't mind when he licked my lips open.

Reckless as it was, I moaned and pressed myself closer.

He kissed me deep and greedy.

It was *heaven*.

It was also exactly what I needed after our ride.

Except, if he didn't give me more, I was going to combust.

As if he could read my mind, he broke our kiss and asked, "You still want to go back to the bar?"

I shook my head, tightening my grip on his kutte.

We understood each other.

I knew this because he got my purse out of his saddlebag and held it with one hand, taking one of mine in his other; then he started for what I would soon learn was the Wild Stallions clubhouse.

Still very turned on, I didn't have the wherewithal to truly take in the details of the place. I noticed brick walls, cement floors, lots of leather couches, and a bar.

As Mustang pulled me along, I thought I saw two women making out while one guy watched. I looked away only to spot another man getting head across the room. When I shifted my eyes again and saw a couple getting dangerously close to having sex right there on the pool table, I squeezed Mustang's hand and stared at the Wild Stallions patch on his back.

Then I remembered the tattoo on his knuckles.

I twisted our hands until I could see K-A-T-E spelled out across the knuckles of his left fingers.

I didn't have a chance to think about what that could imply before Mustang pulled me down a hallway and through the fourth door on the left. It was a private room. *His* room.

I knew this because I could make out the faint traces of his scent in the air.

He slammed the door behind us, dropped my purse on the floor, flipped on the overhead light, then hauled me into his arms.

I gasped in excitement, and he took advantage, plunging his tongue into my mouth.

At the beginning of the night, I promised myself I was going to keep my clothes on.

There was no way I was going to be able to keep that promise now.

I wanted Mustang more than I could remember wanting any-one—*ever*.

When he broke our kiss again, a soft whine escaped my lips.

He flashed me his half-smile, then reached down to grab one of my butt-cheeks in a non-verbal reassurance we were just getting started.

Mustang backed away from me and shrugged off his kutte. He moved to hang it on a hook mounted to the back of the door—and I just knew nothing touched that hook other than his kutte.

As if that was the only thing holding him back, I had his fingers in my hair a second later. He gripped a fistful and angled my head where he wanted it before he gave me his mouth. I got another greedy, wet kiss as he snaked his other arm around my waist, pulling me close.

He then walked me backwards across the room.

As we went, he started tugging at my shirt.

Before I knew it, my top was on the floor.

We were still inching backwards when I pulled at the hem of his shirt, and he was quick to reach between his shoulders and yank it over his head. I drank him in, a small voice in the back of my head telling me *his* body was incredible, and mine wasn't quite so fine.

He had a patch of chest hair between his pecs—and more tattoos on either side.

On his right was an image of a galloping mustang, depicted like it was coming at me.

Over his heart were two little footprints.

I didn't read into those because my eyes kept going.

He had a six pack. Like an *actual* six pack.

My god—he was hot.

So hot, that small voice in my head was drowned out by a much louder one—this one telling me Mustang was turning me on to heights I'd never traversed, and if I didn't come soon, I might die.

Then the back of my knees hit the edge of a bed, and I quickly found myself no longer vertical.

Mustang wasted not a second before sliding off my shoes then reaching for the buttons of my jeans. He peeled them off, taking my soaked panties with them, and then I was in nothing but my bra.

As soon as he caught sight of my sex, he descended—with his mouth.

I was so primed—no joke—he licked me once, twirled his tongue around my clit, and I was coming.

After our ride and all my built-up arousal, my quick-hitting orgasm felt so good, I wasn't even embarrassed.

He kept at me until I grabbed a fistful of his hair and squeezed my thighs together.

Mustang freed his head in order to look up at me, and he did this grinning.

He nipped the inside of my thigh, then stood and proceeded to unbutton his jeans. As he freed the zipper, he walked toward the top of the bed, pulled open the drawer of a nightstand, and extracted a condom.

I started panting, my first orgasm barely scratching the surface of my need.

On his way back to the foot of the bed, he shoved down the waist of his jeans and boxer briefs only far enough to free his hard length.

I swallowed and squirmed at the sight of him.

He looked glorious—and I wanted all of that inside of me.

I ached for it. Desperately. Pathetically.

Thankfully, I didn't have to wait for long.

Mustang made quick work of the condom, then took hold of me behind my knees, spreading my legs wide before he thrust in deep.

All the way in. Until I was full. So blissfully full.

Then he took me hard and fast.

I moaned, reaching over my head for anything I could grab hold of. I caught a fistful of sheets just as the promise of another orgasm began to bloom inside of me.

"Oh, *god*," I cried.

I felt wild with desire, unable to control my body in the slightest.

Then I was coming. Again. Just like that.

Mustang stilled inside of me, my sex constricting repeatedly around his length.

That's when I heard it.

He was laughing.

I righted my head and frowned in confusion.

Breathless, I asked, "Are you—are you laughing at me?"

He let go of my legs and lowered himself until he was propped on his forearms, resting on either side of me. Still smiling, he shook his head and muttered, "Enjoyin' the ride, sugar."

Then he kissed me.

Deep and wet.

I circled my arms around his neck, burying my fingers in his hair, luxuriating in his kiss—him still inside of me.

The thought of more of him had me rolling my hips up, and he grunted before he broke our kiss, gently tugging my bottom lip between his teeth.

"Meet me in the middle of the bed, baby. Bra off," he told me before he stood.

I obeyed, first unhooking my bra and discarding it before I crawled on my backside to the middle of the bed, not interested in a scenario where I lost sight of him. I watched as he removed his boots so he could rid himself of the rest of his clothing.

Once he was completely naked, I gaped at him.

He'd been inside of me thirty seconds ago, and I couldn't believe I'd had *all of that*.

Better yet—he wasn't done.

He met me in the middle of the bed.

He was on his knees when he reached for my hips and yanked my lower body up off the bed. He slid inside of me, then guided my legs around his hips before grazing his hands down my sides, until he had me at my waist.

As he began to thrust in and out of me, his eyes locked in on our connection.

Somehow—remarkably—that turned me on even more.

Like the first time, he took me hard and fast.

Unlike the first time, I got to enjoy it for a while longer.

I didn't normally come three times during a single round of sex, but something told me Mustang was a different breed of man, and he was going to get me there. I was still high from the thrill of our ride, and I felt ultra-sensitive *everywhere*.

When he moved to press his thumb against my swollen clit, I started to lose control again.

He rubbed in firm circles, thrusting inside of me faster, making me crazy.

"Almost there, Tess. You're gonna come again—so you best get to it."

He was not wrong.

I was on the verge.

His command to *get to it* got me that much closer.

I took my breasts in my hands and tugged at my nipples.

Then it hit me. It hit me huge. My whole body was trembling as I came undone.

I cried out with every breath as I writhed.

Just when I thought it couldn't get better...

"Fuck," Mustang growled.

He abandoned my clit and slapped the side of my ass before he held on and lost himself in me. I watched as he forsook his rhythm, the muscles in his neck and shoulders tensed, and he threw his head back while he came.

Obviously—it was incredibly. Flipping. Hot.

When he was spent, he froze inside of me while he worked to catch his breath.

He righted his head, and his hazel-blue eyes found mine.

They were vibrant and *wild*.

This time, I felt it down to my bones.

He'd break my heart if I let him.

I just couldn't let him.

After a few breaths, he broke our connection, gently lowering my hips onto the bed. He then leaned down and kissed me—deep and greedy.

When I reached up to dive my fingers into his hair, he cupped my left breast and squeezed.

Before I was ready, he pulled away and mumbled, "Don't move. Be right back."

He got off the bed, then snatched up his jeans from the floor. He tugged them on and over his hips, worked the zipper closed, but didn't bother with the top button as he made his way barefoot toward the door. He then slipped into the hallway and closed me inside.

Feeling both incredibly naked and slightly chilly, I found my way between the sheets I finally noticed were dark gray. Taking advantage of my moment alone, I looked around to see what other details I could find in the room. There wasn't much to it. The bed was on a frame, but there was no headboard or footboard, it was just pressed up against the back wall. Above it was a giant, faded, American flag.

There was a plain, wooden nightstand to the right, and across the room, on the wall beside the door, was a matching dresser. There was clutter scattered across both surfaces, and a lamp on the nightstand.

The floors were cement, but he had a giant area rug that took up a good portion of the room.

The blanket I assumed belonged on the bed was in a dark green puddle on the floor.

Littered in various spots on the rug were discarded items of clothing.

It was messy, but I'd seen worse.

Not to mention, some of that clothing was mine.

That thought had me flat on my back.

My head hit the pillow, and I stared up at the ceiling.

I couldn't even last one night.

Curling up onto my side, I closed my eyes and tried to assess how much I'd given him just now.

It was the Harley. I couldn't resist.

I rewound the night in my mind, taking myself back to the open road—the wind in my hair, the vibration of the bike's engine between my legs, Mustang the anchor that kept me from flying away.

That was freedom, like I'd never known it before.

Out there on the road, I let go of everything, just because I could.

And I loved it.

That was the last thought I remembered before sleep pulled me under.

I didn't hear it when Mustang came back.

I didn't feel it when he crawled into bed with me.

But I slept all night wrapped in his arms.

CHAPTER Six

I WOKE WITH A start and immediately panicked.

First, because I knew I'd slept soundly, and I hadn't checked my phone in *hours*.

Second, because I'd slept soundly in a bed that wasn't my own.

Third, because I'd made a huge mistake I couldn't take back.

I felt Mustang behind me. He wasn't wrapped around me, but I still felt cocooned by him. One of his hands was resting on my hip, and his opposite arm was stretched out over my head. I knew this because I could see the fingers of his right hand dangling off the pillow.

I wanted to stay.

No, I wanted to roll over and catch a glimpse of him while he slept—then I wanted to burrow myself into his chest and stay a while.

But I knew all too well I couldn't always have what I wanted.

I'd taken what I wanted the previous night, and it was going to cost me.

I needed to get out of there before he woke up.

I also needed to get to my phone and pray no one had called me during the night.

I really didn't feel like being fired that day, on top of everything else.

When I was sure Mustang was definitely still asleep, I carefully rolled out from underneath his hand and quietly slipped out of bed. There wasn't much light in the room, but there was a small window above his American flag that let in a bit of sun—enough that I could see my bra on the floor where I'd tossed it.

I put it on, my eyes on Mustang as I did so. I told myself I watched him to make sure he stayed asleep, but that wasn't true.

I just wanted to see his face.

He was sexy even when lost in a dream.

Before I hurried to find the rest of my clothing, I saw the last of his tattoos.

M-A-R-Y was inked across his right knuckles.

Mary Kate.

I wondered who she was.

I doubted I'd ever find out.

Two minutes later, I was mostly dressed, my pink heels in my hands.

Freaking concrete floors everywhere were going to make it impossible for me to sneak out with my shoes on.

In bare feet, I raced to my purse and immediately went hunting for my phone. The relief that washed over me when I saw I had no missed calls was immense.

With one last look across the room, I strapped my purse over my shoulder and ever so slowly opened the door. I closed it just as carefully, then tucked my feet into my Jimmy Choos. Walking on tiptoes, I retraced my steps from the night before, hoping I didn't run into anyone.

The clubhouse was quiet. Then again, it wasn't even eight in the morning. Unless some of the guys were still up partying, I figured my chances were good I'd get out of there unseen.

I looked both ways when I got to the end of the hallway. When I saw no one, I hurried through the main room toward the exit. As I went, I noticed Mustang wasn't the only one with an affinity for area rugs. They were scattered strategically, under couches, tables, and chairs—furniture that was well worn, but not ratty.

Furniture that was also not all empty.

I spotted a couple naked women passed out on one couch, reminding me I didn't have time for a thorough look around. Not sure who else might have been sleeping it off in the room, I picked up my pace, holding my breath as I went.

The last thing I saw before I stepped out into the light of day was the Wild Stallions flag pinned above the double doors.

I made my trek back to my car unhurriedly, letting my mind process all that had happened as I went.

I'd crossed a line, and it was reckless.

I didn't regret it, but I knew I should.

It had been years since I slept with a guy on the first date. I was usually a third date kind of gal. Three dates let me know he wasn't just going to bail after he got me in bed. It wasn't fool proof, but it was a safeguard I was good at implementing—and when it came to dating, I didn't have many of those.

Mustang hadn't even bought me dinner.

He did, however, put me on the back of his bike, and that was way better.

Now, the tables had turned, and I was the one bailing.

What sucked more than anything was that I knew I wanted Mustang the moment I laid eyes on him. Then he came to Ed's house, he told me he wanted a third look, and I couldn't resist. Fully aware he was out of bounds, I walked into that bar in my favorite jeans anyway. And before the night was over, I let him take them off.

I fell asleep not sure how much of myself I'd given, but I woke up certain I'd given away too much.

The walk to my car wasn't full of shame. I might have been in last night's clothes, but there wasn't one thing I'd done I wished I could take back. Rather than shame, I carried a heavy dose of disappointment knowing I couldn't have him again.

Mustang was more than the embodiment of everything I was trying to keep out of my bed. He was sexy and rough and daring, sure—but he was also interesting and gentle and smart. I fell asleep in his bed, and rather than wake me up, he curled himself around me and drifted off himself.

I'd crossed a line, definitely.

Whether or not he wanted to admit it, Mustang was the son of one of my patients.

That was part of my mistake—but not the whole of it.

The whole of it was, I needed to reestablish that boundary with a man I knew I could fall for in a heartbeat.

When I got back to my car, the only one left in the bar's parking lot, I didn't hesitate to get inside and start it up. I knew I wouldn't be back. Not for a while. Not until I could forget what it felt like to ride wild and roam free at Mustang's back.

Sadly, I wondered if I'd ever return.

I hopped in the shower when I got home, hardly looking at myself in the mirror before I did. A thorough cleanse of my night at Steel Mustang with the man himself was needed. Once I was clean, I made some coffee and distracted myself by paying bills. I thought about making breakfast, but remembered it'd been a few days since I'd hit the grocery store. I settled for a yogurt, then went to get ready for my pedicure with Jenna.

Wishing to be out of the house with some much-needed company, I left ten minutes earlier than I normally did. When I arrived at the nail salon, I didn't stay in my car, but stepped outside and paced around the small parking lot.

I hadn't told Jenna about Mustang the last time she'd called. Now I needed to, but there was so much to say. While I waited, I tried to pack it all into a quick and dirty version of the truth.

She pulled into the lot right on time, taking the spot next to mine.

Jenna was a honey-brunette, her hair grown out a few inches past her shoulders and styled in a layered cut. She complained about how straight it was, but it was thick, so she had that going for her. That and so much else.

Aside from the adorable smattering of freckles sprinkled across her nose, she had dark hazel-green eyes and great eyebrows. She also had a beautiful smile. When she got out of her car, she aimed it right at me.

"Hey, you're early. You're also pacing around like a caged animal, what's up?" she asked on a laugh.

I swept a bit of hair behind my ears and met her in the space between our vehicles.

"I have a confession to make. And I don't really want to talk about it, but I do need to tell you, because if I don't, I'll just think about telling you the entire time we're in there, and it'll ruin our whole conversation, so I'm getting it out of the way now."

"Okay," she said, nonplused. "Let's hear it."

"I got a new patient this week. His name is Ed, and he's all alone—as in, the only people who come in and out of his house are the woman who does his laundry and me. And his house is sad. No pictures anywhere.

"When I asked him about any loved ones, he told me his wife was dead and his son didn't even know he was sick. Then I found out his son is local. He's the owner of Steel Mustang."

Jenna's eyebrows shot up at this new revelation.

"Yeah, I know. So, I got this wild hare of an idea to stop by and see if I could get him to visit his dying father. Well, turns out, he's not interested in that. Not even a little bit. But what he is interested in is *me*."

Jenna tried, and failed, to hide her smile. Still, she didn't interrupt.

"Get this—he meets me at his dad's house Friday night, and he tells me maybe he'll think about talking to the man if I go out with him. So, like an idiot, I say yes.

"Now, here's the part where I have to tell you—this man is not even a little bit ugly. And he smells really great. He also has a mom tattoo I am fairly certain is not the least bit ironic, which is *very* sweet."

Jenna was now grinning.

I sighed.

"I slept with him. I broke my number one rule. And then I snuck out this morning like a jack-hole." I smacked my palm against my forehead and held it there for a moment. After I gathered myself, I finished, "Anyway—the truth is, I'm kind of bummed about it, but it's probably for the best that I got out of there, because he's exactly the kind of guy I'd fall in love with, and we both know I need to stop picking the same guy over and over again.

"Okay. That's it. That's all. Let's go."

I turned to head inside, but she called, "Wait, wait, wait!" so I stopped.

"Just one question."

I nodded.

"How was the sex?"

My shoulders sank, the memory still very fresh in my mind.

"We went one round. I came three times."

I didn't look at her response but made my way into the salon.

It took her a couple seconds, but she followed me inside.

We browsed polish color options for a good ten minutes before we were both happy with our selections. She chose white. I picked blue, then told myself it had nothing to do with the fact that Mustang's Harley was almost the exact same shade.

The salon wasn't too busy, so we were seated in our massage chairs in no time. While they filled the soaking tubs with water, Jenna filled me in on a bit of hospital gossip. She always liked to tell me the latest, and I usually got a good laugh or gasp at it.

When we reached our first lull in the conversation, our technicians busy scrubbing at our feet, Jenna asked, "Tess, what if he never goes to talk to his dad? Does that put him back in bounds?"

There'd been no segue, but I was quick to follow her anyway.

"What? No, Jen, that's not the point."

"It is *totally* the point. In fact—" She twisted so she was leaning against the armrest closest to me. "I understand your boundaries. Ninety-nine percent of the time, they are absolutely necessary. You can't get mixed up with a grieving family member. You just can't. Even if he's the perfect guy, it ends up being a right place/wrong time sort of situation. Then by the time things could work, they just don't."

"But in this case—he's not grieving. He doesn't seem to care at all."

"Right, okay, so shouldn't that be a red flag?" I argued, leaning against my own armrest.

"I don't know. There are two sides to every story, and it kind of sounds like you haven't gotten either one."

'Lived with an alcoholic the first sixteen years of my life. Just in case that shit's hereditary, never touched the stuff.'

Jenna was kind of right. I still only had fragments of their story pieced together. But from the sounds of it, Mustang had his reasons as to why he'd cut his dad out of his life. I still wasn't sure if that was enough to justify my actions.

"It just seems messy. Like—sorry your son won't talk to you, and you're probably going to die all alone, but I did meet him and now we're sleeping together."

With a nod, Jenna conceded, "That's fair. But, honey…"

She paused long enough for me to realize she hadn't conceded after all.

"This is going to sound heartless, but it's the truth. Their relationship is not your responsibility. It's your job to make sure Ed is cared for and comfortable as he journeys through his last stage of life. In the meantime, you have to take care of yourself, too. If this guy wants you, and you want him, and you think it might go somewhere…"

"What about the fact that he's a Wild Stallion? He's like a bad boy on steroids."

"So, you have a type. Who cares? You're consistent. You like him, right? I mean, what are you supposed to do, walk into a bank and chat up a loan officer until he asks you out?"

I grinned, and she laughed, knowing she had a point.

"And is it so crazy to think that if he never talks to his dad, but you get the chance to know him a little bit, you could share what you learn about him with Ed? Maybe that could be enough."

I leaned back in my chair and considered what she said. It felt like a fairytale of an idea.

In a lot of ways, Jenna and I were opposites, but we weren't always perfect at balancing each other out. We both drew our hope from the same well, and I kind of liked her perspective of my situation.

But I'd snuck out that morning, likely ruining my chances of anything with Mustang.

"We don't even have each other's phone numbers. Maybe last night was the start and the end of it."

"He managed to ask you out the first time without your number…" She shrugged. "All I'm saying is, don't be so quick to close the door on it."

"Yeah, and what about you?" I asked, ready to change the subject. "What kind of guy are we going to get to check all your boxes?"

She scrunched her face at me. "Dating is *so* overrated."

I couldn't argue with that.

Except, it wasn't so bad when it involved a badass biker who owned a badass biker bar and a blue Harley.

CHAPTER *Seven*

Mustang

H E WOKE IN BED alone, and he was not happy about it.

He didn't even have her number, and that pissed him off even more. It made him the cat and her the mouse. There was only one place he knew he could go to catch her, and he didn't relish the idea of going back there.

If it were anyone else, he wouldn't have bothered.

But he'd had his third look, and she blew his damn mind.

He thought about the way she rested her cheek on his shoulder, melting into him as he pushed ninety on the highway, like she'd done it a million times.

Then he remembered how turned on she'd been when they got back. All he had to do was *breathe* on her, and she was coming. It made him hard just thinking about it.

No way was he done with her. Not by a longshot.

Nevertheless, it was Sunday morning. He needed to get showered and changed before he went to pick up his girl.

He'd deal with Tess later.

Mustang got out of bed, gathered what he needed, then headed down the hall to the communal bathroom to get a shower. He wasn't in there two minutes before he heard the door open.

"Mustang—that you in there?"

He recognized her voice. Charity, a club sheep. She'd been around for a couple years, hoping to be claimed as someone's ol' lady. Pretty as she was, he knew her chances were low. She'd fucked half the guys in the club—including him when she first started hanging around—but now she was used up. Hard for a man to claim a woman after he'd seen her take more than a few brothers' dicks.

"What do you want, Charity?" Mustang called from the stall.

"Just wondered if you wanted some company is all?"

Tess rushed to the forefront of his mind.

Her dirty blonde hair, more dirty than blonde, that he liked a whole lot out of a clip.

Her gorgeous golden-brown eyes, and that perfect mouth.

He reheard her moan when he'd kissed her beside his hog.

He shook his head, mad all over again he'd woke in bed alone.

"No," he grumbled in response.

"Alright," said Charity on a sigh. "Holler when you're done, I guess. I'm up on bathroom duty."

He finished his shower, wrapped a towel about his waist, and didn't holler anything on his way back to his room. Five minutes later, in fresh underwear, a clean shirt, and the jeans he'd worn the night before, he tightened his boots, grabbed his kutte, and was out the door.

He couldn't help but think of Tess as he started his hog.

When he pulled into his garage only to hop off and climb into his truck, he was actually relieved for the reprieve. He told himself the next time he got on his hog he was going after Tess.

It only took him five minutes to get to Trix's place. She lived on the second floor of a quadplex. It was old, if not yet rundown, and he knew she could afford better. He paid enough child support. The only reason he didn't bitch about it was because she was conveniently close to his house. He'd learned the smart thing to do with Trix was pick the right battles, and that wasn't one of them.

He took the stairs two at a time. When he reached her door, he rapped his knuckles against it and waited. He stood there long enough he was considering another knock when he heard the lock give way. One look at Trix, and he knew she was high.

He didn't even waste his breath but brushed her aside as he crossed the threshold. He got two steps and saw someone on the couch lighting up a joint. Mustang paused, glared back at Trix, then made his way around to the front of the couch. The man sitting there barely had a chance to register him before Mustang had him on his feet, his shirt balled up in his fist.

Startled, he dropped the joint, and Mustang crushed it with the toe of his boot.

"Hey!" he muttered.

"What the fuck?!" cried Trix.

"I don't know who the fuck you are, but you're gonna know me." Mustang ignored Trix even as she came to stand right next to him. "If I ever catch you smokin', getting' high again when my little girl is here, I'll see to it you don't inhale without excruciating pain for the rest of your pathetic fuckin' life. You understand me?"

"What are you doing?" Trix pounded her fists against his shoulders. "You son-of-a-bitch. Let him go!"

Mustang shoved the man back onto the seat, then used his forearm to brush Trix out of his way a second time. She called after him but didn't follow as he headed for the back of the unit, and he ignored her.

He popped his head into MK's open door but found her room empty. He saw Trix's door was closed, and he stomped down the hallway, opening it without delay.

MK was sitting cross-legged on the bed, her attention glued to the television.

At the sound of the door, she turned to see who it was. As soon as it registered, she was on her feet, bouncing up and down with her arms spread wide.

"Daddy!"

Instantly, his anger was assuaged.

"Hey, baby," he said with a smile.

He ate up the distance between them, and she leapt at him as soon as he was close. He caught her, like she knew he would, and she wrapped her arms around his neck even as she wiggled in excitement.

"Let's grab your shoes and get out of here. You hungry?"

As he carried her to her bedroom she answered, "Yeah. Can we have pancakes?"

"How 'bout eggs?"

"Hmmm," she hummed as they worked together to get her shoes on. "How 'bout pancakes *and* eggs? And bacon!"

"Now you're talkin'."

On their way out, he took her by the hand and let her walk. When they made it to the living room, Trix looked ready to pounce. Mustang gave her a single glare of warning and she snapped her lips shut.

"Tell mommy bye."

Without dropping his hand, MK waved. "Bye, mommy."

"Bye, sweet pea."

Mustang didn't bother closing the front door after they'd passed through it. The apartment needed a good airing out. He knew the chances of that happening were low, especially with MK gone.

He was tired of Trix and her mess. He wasn't a fool. He was well aware she could access harder, more lethal drugs. Hell, the club used to be in the business of helping to smuggle that shit across the border. Weed was child's play—except for when it came to *his* child.

He didn't give a shit what Trix did when MK wasn't around; but the last thing he wanted was for his little girl to grow up in a house like he did, with a parent constantly inebriated.

When they reached his truck, he lifted her up into the car seat he kept in the back on the passenger side. After she was buckled in, he didn't move to get behind the wheel. He got her attention so they could have a chat.

"Smells like grass in there, doesn't it?"

She shrugged. "It always smells like that when mommy's friend comes over. She makes me stay in her room. But I can watch cartoons!"

Mustang tamped down his anger before he next spoke.

"I need you to listen to me, princess. If it ever smells like that, you call me. You get the phone in the kitchen, you take it to your room, and you call me," he instructed, speaking of the landline he'd been paying for since MK's third birthday. He wanted access to his girl, and he didn't trust Trix. "You ever get scared, and you want daddy to come get you, you call me. You understand?"

"Okay, daddy."

"What's my phone number?"

She rattled off the digits he'd drilled into her head, and he nodded.

"And what do you do when it smells like grass?"

"Get the phone to my room and call you."

"That's right."

He pressed a kiss into her hair then finally moved to close her in and take his seat behind the wheel.

He hadn't forgotten about Tess. She was still there in the back of his mind. Now that he had MK, that's where she'd have to stay—until Wednesday afternoon, when he mounted his hog.

CHAPTER *Eight*

Tess

Three Days Later

I WAS MORE TIRED than usual. I couldn't remember how long it had been since I'd struggled through a double this much. It wasn't the work itself. For the most part, my patients were stable. I simply hadn't been sleeping well.

Not since Saturday night.

I tried not to think about Mustang.

We'd had one night together—that couldn't have been enough to mess with my sleep.

I hoped, after working twenty hours straight, I could get in a decent few hours.

When I turned onto Ramshorn Avenue, I groaned when I saw Lance's car and not Mitchell's parked in front of Sharon's house. I knew I needed to have a better attitude about him, but the thought of pretending I liked him for the duration of my visit wore me out just thinking about it.

I was grateful he didn't meet me at my car door.

I downed the rest of the coffee I'd had time to pick up on the way, then gathered my things to head inside.

Lance was quick to answer the door.

"Hey, Tess," he said in greeting.

"Hi, Lance. How you doin'? How's your mom?"

Respecting the routine, Lance filled me in on how Sharon had been fairing since my last visit. When I was up to speed, I went to spend some time with my patient. I had about forty-five minutes alone with her before I felt Lance hovering at the door. Unfortunately, Sharon was pretty tired that day. When she drifted to sleep, it felt silly to stay, which meant clocking in a few more minutes with Lance before I left.

I packed my supplies into my bag, then looped the straps over my shoulder as I made my way toward him. "Did you want to talk?"

"Yeah. That'd be great." He led the way into the kitchen and asked, "Can I get you anything?"

"I'm good. Thank you." I leaned against the kitchen island. "How you holdin' up? Really?"

With some family members and loved ones, it was difficult to maintain a healthy emotional distance. With Lance, it was no struggle at all. He spoke and I listened, responding at the appropriate times. I tried to be a comfort, knowing he deserved compassion as much as the next person.

When our conversation drew to a close, he hugged me. It didn't feel like a friendly hug, his large hands splayed across my sides. I was immediately uncomfortable. I patted his back, in an effort to signal he could let go, but he held on a moment longer.

"Lance, I should be going," I told him, gently pushing my way out of his arms. "I don't want to be late for my next patient."

"Sure. I understand."

"You hang in there," I said with a wave.

Once on the other side of Sharon's front door, I freed a heavy sigh and wiped off my fake smile.

I had one more patient, and then I could go home.

Much as I wanted a quick ten-minute nap, I was not hanging out in Sharon's driveway with Lance inside. I'd squeeze it in after I reached Thornhill Road.

Except, twenty minutes later, when I turned down Ed's street, I got a jolt of energy that completely eradicated any possibility of a nap.

This was because, parked on the far side of Ed's driveway, was a blue Harley.

And leaned up against it, in his usual attire, but with the addition of aviator sunglasses, was Mustang.

I wondered why he was there.

Was it for me? Or Ed?

It seemed safer to hope it was for the latter.

Unfortunately, my heart rarely played it safe.

Anxious to learn of his intentions, I didn't dally after I pulled in next to him and put my car in park. Grabbing my things, I stepped out, closed my door and murmured, "Hi."

He didn't speak right away.

I couldn't see his eyes, but I didn't think I imagined the heat which traveled across my body following his gaze as he looked me up and down.

A zing sparked in my belly.

Finally, he asked, "You think I let just any bitch on the back of my hog?"

My spine stiffened, having expected a different kind of hello.

Clearly, he was there for me.

I had to admit, I hadn't left in the best way on Sunday morning—but I didn't particularly like being called a *bitch*. Suddenly, I was way too tired for this conversation.

"I don't know," I snapped.

"Well, I don't, Tess. My hog is not a carnival ride, and I sure as fuck don't use it to get laid. Got a patch on my kutte that'll get me all the pussy I want. I put you at my back, I take you to my bed, I wake up and you're gone—no note, no nothin'—I take offense to that."

I couldn't fault him for what he'd said. All of that was very fair. Even badass bikers had feelings, and I understood how he might have thought I'd used him.

Feeling deflated, I told him honestly, "I'm sorry."

"Gonna have to do better than that, sugar."

"Mustang, I didn't know, okay? I didn't know it was such a big deal to go for a ride. You don't even know me, so why did you offer in the first place?"

"Tess, I've been inside you. You're no stranger."

I huffed, flustered by the reminder—especially in light of the fact that, seeing him standing there by his bike, even though I knew I needed to redraw a boundary line between him and me, I couldn't stop thinking about how he'd first kissed me in front of the clubhouse.

"That was *after* the ride, so my point still stands," I argued.

He pushed away from his Harley and came toward me until we stood toe-to-toe. I had to tilt my head back to look at him as he said, "I know you sat at the bar, didn't say shit for forty-five minutes, just listened to the music like that was enough conversation for you, and that made me want you more than I already wanted you the second I caught a glimpse of those fuckin' pink heels. Then you got on the back of my hog and rode for an hour without signaling you wanted to get off—and somethin' tells me, I don't stop, we'd still be ridin', baby. So, I know enough to know we're not done."

Before I could draw in my next breath, his fingers were in my hair. He grabbed a fistful, held my head still, then crushed his lips against mine.

Just like the first time, my knees were instantly useless.

The only thing I could think to do was grab hold of his kutte, part my lips, and sigh.

He swept his tongue through my mouth, I was reminded of all that was Mustang, and I was powerless against my own desire.

When I was younger, my dad warned my brother and me to never do drugs.

Not even once.

All my life I'd listened to him—until Saturday night.

In that moment, Mustang kissing me deep and greedy, I understood it only took one hit to create an addict.

Before I was ready, he pulled his mouth away from mine.

"Let me take you to dinner tonight."

Still in a fog after that kiss, I shook my head and muttered, "Mustang—"

"What time do you work in the morning?" he asked, cutting me off.

"Um, six o'clock, which means I'm up at four."

"Fine. Early bird special it is."

"What? No." I regained my footing and pulled back a little as I told him, "I need to go home and sleep. This is my last stop. I've been awake for almost forty-eight hours and—"

He cut me off again. This time with a kiss.

The footing I regained was lost once more as he wrapped his free arm around my waist and hauled me closer.

Regrettably, this kiss was much shorter.

"Give me your address," he demanded, his lips still grazing mine. "I'll meet you there when you're done here, cook you dinner before I fuck you; then you can get that sleep you need."

Even in his hold, I still managed to fall a little.

His grip around me tightened as the corner of his mouth stretched into a half-smile.

Another zing ricocheted in my belly.

"Address, baby."

My address fell right out of my mouth.

He repeated it, then the hand that was in my hair let go in order to reach down and squeeze one side of my butt.

A thrill raced up my spine at that promise.

"What time will you be home?"

"Quarter after four, if Ed's okay," I breathed.

He jerked his chin in a nod. "Gonna let you go now, sugar. You good?"

"Mmhmm," I hummed, willing my legs to function.

Mustang let me go, then turned, mounted his bike and started her up.

Without another word, he was gone.

Apparently, I'd see him at a quarter after four.

Unless, maybe, I'd dreamed all of that.

I reached up and brushed my fingers across my lips, deliriously wondering if I'd just squeezed in a ten-minute nap.

Either way, I had a job to do.

One more patient, and then I could go home.

I shook my head clear and headed for the door.

Using the spare key Ed had given me, I let myself inside. Still, I knocked and called out, "Ed? It's Tess."

"Yup. In here," he replied.

I found him in his recliner in front of the television, the volume turned down low.

The first couple of visits, I'd pulled a chair into the room from the kitchen so I could sit while I charted after his physical exam. I noticed this time the chair was already there. This made me smile, and I sat my bag on it before I went to stand beside his recliner.

"How are you feeling today?"

He shifted his attention away from the TV and told me, "Like shit. Not much different than yesterday."

"Okay. How about we define *shit*," I suggested, half teasing, half serious.

We talked for a few minutes before I got on with his exam. When we were done, we went over his prescriptions, and I made note of a couple refills I'd need to call in soon. A fresh wave of exhaustion hit me when I sat down with my tablet, and I hummed softly as I charted, so as to keep myself awake.

"My Mary-Kate used to hum while she worked," said Ed.

My head jerked up, and I stopped humming.

That was the first personal information he'd given me without prompting.

Mary-Kate.

Another puzzle piece clicked into place.

"Your wife?" I asked, opening the door in case he felt like talking.

He frowned down at his lap and muttered, "Yeah."

Aware memories of his wife were obviously painful, I treaded lightly.

"How long has it been since you heard her hum?"

"Twenty years, now."

'All in—twenty years. Makes me more Stallion than anything else.'

It felt like cheating, extracting information from Ed to piece together the incomplete picture of what happened between father and son that kept Mustang out on the driveway rather the inside, on the chair I occupied. Even more so because Ed didn't know I knew his son.

"Miss it," said Ed, pulling me from my thoughts. "Wouldn't mind if you kept goin'."

I didn't even know what I'd been humming before. It was simply one of my tricks for when I got too tired. Yet, something told me it didn't matter what I hummed, he'd find some sort of comfort in it anyway—so, I started up again while I finished his chart.

I didn't ask anymore questions, and Ed didn't volunteer anymore information for the remainder of our visit. When it was time for me to go, I promised I'd see him in a couple days and reminded him to call me should he need to see me sooner.

I let myself out, locking up as I went, then got in my car and pointed it toward home.

I lived in a two bedroom, one and a half bath townhouse I'd purchased a couple years before. It was a bit of a fixer upper I hadn't yet done much to fix, but the price had been right. It was possible I might have had a new fridge or an upgraded stove if I hadn't spent over a thousand dollars on a new pair of jeans and a killer pair of red-sole Louboutin heeled sandals—the straps adorned with silver spikes—but I had my priorities. I didn't want a new stove for my birthday.

Auto-pilot got me home, my head in a fog as I drove. Then, for the second time that day, I turned down a familiar street, and I saw that blue Harley—Mustang leaned up against it. He was parked by the curb, since my driveway was only big enough to accommodate my single car garage.

Safe to say, I hadn't gotten that ten-minute nap after all.

He came. He actually came.

Mustang was staring down at his phone until he heard me as I approached. I saw him pocket it before I lost sight of him as I pulled into my garage. By the time I got out of my car, he was walking toward me with a sack of groceries dangling from his inked fingers.

"Hope you're not a vegan or some shit."

The tired laugh that bubbled out of me couldn't be helped.

"No. Not a vegan. What's in the bag?"

"Food. Sooner you let me inside, sooner it'll be edible, sooner we get you to bed."

Bed. I'd been thinking about my bed for hours now.

Tired as I was, all of a sudden, it wasn't sleep I was thinking about.

Still, I hesitated. I hadn't been expecting a guest when I left for my nightshift the day before.

"Um—I can't remember the state in which I left my place, so—"

"Tess? Sooner you let me inside, sooner food'll be edible, sooner we get you to bed. Inside, baby."

Excitement rippled through me as I murmured, "Right. Okay," then turned to head inside.

The door to my garage was located kitty-corner to my front door, both at the bottom of my staircase. When I walked inside, I hung my purse on the wooden bulb at the end of its railing, like I always did, then took a right through my narrow living room to my kitchen.

Even though the two rooms were pretty much adjoined, the previous owners tried to make a distinction between them by painting the living room a soft yellow while the kitchen was mint. It wasn't exactly my style, so my furniture didn't match. Needless to say, painting was another thing I hadn't gotten around to yet.

Though, I didn't concern myself with my home décor issues as I tried to keep ahead of Mustang enough to pick up or hide anything I may have left out that was potentially embarrassing.

Fortunately, I found nothing. At least, not on the first floor.

I stood at the mouth of my kitchen, beside my round table with the cozy, cushioned, wicker back chairs. Mustang breezed right by me, setting the groceries on the counter by the sink before hooking his sunglasses in the collar of his shirt.

"Point me to your spices and I need a skillet," he said as he went to wash his hands. "Anything else, I'll root around until I find it. You can hop in the shower or whatever you do to unwind while I work. Thirty minutes tops."

"Spices are in the cabinet to the left of the stove, and the skillet is to the bottom right."

He dried his hands with a couple paper towels, then I watched as he went for the spices first, hunting for the ones he was after and plucking them out when he found them.

To say it felt surreal to see Mustang at work in my kitchen would have been a massive understatement. It felt odd to just leave him there. I wasn't sure if I could *unwind* while he was busy cooking with my skillet on my stove. It all seemed backwards. So, I just stood there—staring.

When Mustang noticed, he stopped what he was doing and gave me his pretty, hazel-blue eyes as he assured me, "Tess, I got this."

Unsure what to say, but somehow certain he wasn't going to continue his task until I left him to it, I turned on my heel and headed for the stairs. Remembering my phone needed a charge, I dug it out of my purse along the way, then hooked a left when I reached the second level and hurried for my bedroom.

I hadn't made my bed, and my dirty clothes hamper was overflowing out of my closet. I did what I could to straighten up, then rifled through my dresser for something to wear post-shower.

I debated with myself about whether or not there was any point in putting on underwear—especially considering I was so clearly behind on laundry—and came to a swift conclusion. I plucked a pair of cotton shorts and an oversized tee out of a drawer, then left my some-what tidy room to take a shower.

Even though I skipped washing my hair, I was under the water for a solid fifteen minutes. I hadn't shaved in days, and I didn't want Mustang to know that. Once I was dried and dressed, I let my hair down and ran a brush through it a few times. Glancing at my reflection, I noted I'd habitually washed my face in the shower, which left me with no makeup. Deciding makeup was just as pointless as underwear, I abandoned my reflection in order to return to the kitchen.

The smell of food hit me halfway down the stairs, and my stomach growled.

It smelled good.

I took one step onto the linoleum, and Mustang asked, "You like cheese on your burger?"

He'd made hamburgers. Yum.

"Yes."

"Sit, baby."

I pulled out a chair and did what I was told.

Not five minutes later, I had a plate with a cheeseburger and potato chips in front of me. He'd even brought over ketchup, mustard, and mayo so I could dress my bun the way I liked.

I was a bit beside myself.

I'd never had a man cook me dinner before. Certainly not in my kitchen.

It hardly made sense that a member of the Wild Stallions MC would be the first.

Mustang took the seat next to mine, dressed his bun, then dove right in.

My stomach growled a second time, and I followed his lead.

"Thank you," I murmured before I took my first bite.

His mouth full as he chewed, he answered with a jerk of his chin.

Something told me he probably would have answered the same way even if his mouth was empty.

After I was done with my first bite—which was delicious—I asked, "Are burgers your thing? Or do you cook anything else?"

"Burgers are fast and easy. Cook other shit, too. Take-out is garbage. Unless I'm on the road for an extended period, home cooked is my preference."

I was as impressed as I was surprised. At every turn, he was proving to be equal parts badass and interesting.

"That's very health conscious of you," I said before I took another bite.

"Ate garbage for a few years when I was broke. Metabolism kept up with me. Not worried about me. Got a kid. Don't want her growin' up with some whack relationship with food."

For a moment, my jaw stopped working. I had to make a conscious effort to keep chewing as I processed what he'd said.

He had child.

Then I remembered the two little footprints over his heart.

I spoke around my food as I murmured, "The feet on your chest..."

"MK's."

At this rate, it was questionable whether or not I'd ever get through my burger.

I forced myself to swallow before I inquired, "MK?"

"Mary-Kate. She's four. And before you ask, her mother and I are cordial—*barely*. MK was not planned. Least, not by me."

"But you love her," I blurted, my brain still trying to piece together the significance of everything he was saying.

He lowered his burger, looked me straight in the eye and answered, "More than life."

Oh, god.

He'd named his daughter after his mom. A daughter he loved more than life.

This told me three things.

First, he likely loved his mother more than life, too—and she was dead.

Second, he found out he was going to be a father to a kid he did not plan for, and rather than bail, he staked his claim on her by naming her after a woman he'd loved and lost.

Third, I was in over my head.

Mustang wasn't just a badass biker.

He was everything I knew I wanted in a man.

He was hard on the outside and sweet on the inside. Any man who preferred home cooked meals because he had a little girl he didn't want to grow up with a whack relationship with food couldn't be categorized as anything less than sweet and fatherly, and I totally loved that.

I loved it too much.

I was going to have to find a way out of this.

I didn't know how, but I knew if I didn't act soon, I'd fall so hard for him, he wouldn't just break my heart.

He'd *wreck* it.

Certain I couldn't handle any further revelations, I stopped asking questions and focused on eating my dinner. Mustang was not the least bit bothered by this. I knew because he cleaned his plate without saying another word. When he was done, he leaned back against his chair, kicked out one foot, and waited patiently for me to finish. As soon as my plate was empty, he got up, took our dishes, and deposited them in the sink.

Then, as cool as a cucumber, he came back to the table, removed his kutte, hung it on the back of his chair, looked down at me and inquired, "Bedroom?"

We hadn't gone for a ride on his Harley. I wasn't buzzing with a desperate need for a release. Yet somehow, this time felt just as reckless as the first time.

This truth didn't stop me from getting out of my chair and leading Mustang to my bedroom.

While the rest of my house still needed a bit of work, my bedroom was the one space I had managed to fix up the way I wanted.

The walls were painted a subtle cream eggshell, and I had a beautiful, scenic mountain scape framed above my bed. My bed that I loved. It had a simple, upholstered light beige headboard, and it sat high enough off the ground, my feet barely reached the floor if I sat on the edge. The nightstands on either side of my queen-sized bed had matching lamps, and there were decorative nick-nacks on the side of the bed I never used.

My duvet comforter was beige, and my accent pillows—which hadn't made it back onto the bed in my hurried attempt to straighten up—were tan, cream, white, with a couple sage green pops of color to match the gorgeous chunky knit blanket I always kept at the foot of my bed, regardless of the season.

The house was mine, but this room was *me*, and I felt a bit on display when Mustang followed me over the threshold.

The feeling didn't last long.

When I stopped by the side of the bed and turned to face him, he wasn't taking in the details of my room. He was removing his boots. Once his feet were bare, he straightened, unhooked his sunglasses from his collar, tossed them onto my dresser, then reached behind his head and yanked off his shirt.

He was just as sexy as I remembered.

No sooner had the garment hit the floor than he was on me.

He ate the distance between us in one step.

He sank the fingers of one hand into my hair—a habit I was already kind of obsessed with—and reached down to grab my butt with his other, hauling me into him as he descended for a kiss.

It was wet, and deep, and sensational.

His hold on me was so relentless, all I could manage to do was circle my arms around his back and try my damnedest to give as good as I got.

I wasn't wearing any panties, which meant I was soon on the verge of damp shorts when he slid the fingers at my backside up, around my hip, then under the waistband of said shorts.

Two fingers hit my sweet spot, swirled, then continued their decent and plunged.

Oh, god.

It took everything I had to stay upright as he kept at me. Adjusting my grip, I threw an arm over his shoulder and held on to the back of his neck. Then it was too much. I could barely breathe as he stoked the spark he'd ignited within me into a warmth that was beginning to grow.

"Mustang," I gasped, tilting my head back and breaking our kiss.

The desperation in my voice triggered something in him, because I lost his fingers from inside of me a second after I'd spoken. Then my shorts were falling to my ankles, and all at once I was half naked.

The abrupt shift brought me back to where we were—in my room—in the light of day.

My hands pressed against his hot, perfect body made me feel self-conscious about mine. He'd seen me naked, but that had been more frantic and unstoppable. This time, I wasn't high from a motor-cycle ride, so the voice in my head telling me to stop comparing what I had going on with what he had going on was not louder than the voice that told me I was a six to his twelve. Eight, if I was in kickass jeans and killer heels, but no higher than a six whilst completely naked.

This was why, when he reached for the hem of my tee, I dropped my hands in order to stop him.

"Uh—maybe this time I'll just—"

"Like fuck," he muttered, a scowl furrowing his brow.

"I'm not saying let's stop, I just—"

"Explain," he demanded before I could even finish.

"You, well—you obviously spend a decent amount of time in the gym, and that totally does it for me. But I—"

I didn't get the chance to finish. Again.

Mustang grabbed my wrist, pressed my hand against the bulge in his jeans, got in my face and said, "This is me just thinkin' about your naked body writhing underneath mine. Only had you once, but sure as fuck haven't forgotten what you look like. Hard at the thought of havin' you again. You don't lift your arms and let me strip you naked, I'll rip that damn shirt right down the middle."

For a fraction of a second, I contemplated letting him rip the damn shirt.

But I kind of liked it, so I lifted my arms instead.

I was completely naked a second later.

He took hold of my hips, lifted me off my feet, and plopped me on the edge of the bed the second after that.

Fingertips to my sternum, he pushed me until I was flat on my back.

Then I had his fingers again.

Only this time—his tongue played with one of my nipples while he worked.

Yeah, that felt good. *Really* good.

He didn't even have time to show attention to my opposite nipple before I was coming.

As my orgasm subsided, I watched as he extracted a condom from his wallet and then proceeded to get as naked as I was. He sheathed himself, and I squirmed a little in excitement.

"On your knees, sugar," he instructed with a twirl of his finger.

Knowing better than to deny him, I flipped over and got on my knees, my feet at the edge of the bed, and my torso leaning against my forearms. When I felt his hands on my behind, spreading my cheeks, I pressed my forehead against the mattress and tried not to overthink it.

Then he rammed himself inside of my sex, and my breath caught.

A moan spilled from my lips when he began to thrust in and out of me.

He rode me hard and steady, filling me just right. It wasn't long before I had my comforter balled up in both fists as I held on and rocked back, meeting him each time he came back to me.

I was so wet I could hear how drenched he was as our skin slapped together.

Somehow, that turned me on even more, and I felt my second orgasm start to bud at the center of my core.

Then I had the heat of Mustang across my back, and I felt the whiskers of his beard and his panting breath at my shoulder as he bent over me and bucked his hips harder. Faster.

"Oh, god," I moaned.

He reached underneath me, fondling my left breast, and the bud inside of me began to bloom.

"Yes, yes!" I cried, the muscles in my body already tensing in preparation for my unbridled climax.

He grunted his response, never breaking his pace as he brought me to the brink.

When I felt his teeth nip at my shoulder, I lost it, shuddering underneath him as my sex clamped down hard around his length while I cried out in pleasure.

"That's it, baby—fuckin' come for me," he growled as I continued to moan.

I was still trembling when his body locked up around mine, his arm across my chest plastering me against his as he came, bucking his hips in short, hard spurts until he was spent.

Heaven.

Or so I thought, until he pulled out of me, flipped me on my back, and sealed his lips with mine. He kissed me greedily, and I reached up and sank all my fingers in his hair as his body lay heavy between my legs.

That was heaven, too.

I was dazed when he broke our kiss. Lazily, I opened my eyes in search of his.

Hazel-blue stared down at me as he said, "Be right back."

I nodded, missing the weight of him just as soon as I'd lost it.

I watched him walk out of my bedroom, headed for the bathroom, completely naked. When I heard the soft click of the door shutting behind him, I moved to crawl between the sheets. I closed my eyes, meaning only to relax and enjoy the aftereffects of what we'd just done.

But I didn't hear it when Mustang came back, sleep having pulled me under.

CHAPTER *Nine*

MY ALARM CLOCK SOUNDED, and I jolted upright.

I was immediately aware of two things.

First, I was still naked.

Second, I had slept soundly. *Again.*

I reached for my phone, silenced the alarm, then held my breath as I looked to see if I'd slept through any emergencies. When I found only a text from Jenna, I sighed and fell back against my pillow.

I'd never missed a call in the middle of the night before. I kept my ringer really loud. Still, I couldn't help but to feel paranoid anytime I woke up feeling certain I'd slept hard. It wasn't until I was assured no one had suffered while I slept that I could luxuriate in my state of well rested-ness.

Then I remembered I was naked.

I jolted upright again, this time reaching for the lamp on my night-stand.

The warm, golden glow of the light splashed around my room, and I saw no traces of Mustang. This didn't come as a shock. It was four in the morning. I'd fallen asleep right after sex, which meant the summer sun hadn't even begun to set as I drifted into dreamland.

Of course, he'd left.

It wasn't disappointment I felt. It was better that he had gone. I needed the space to think.

Except, with him gone, I had no idea when I'd see him again or what I'd say to him when I did. I didn't know what we were doing, but it still seemed like a bad idea.

A bad idea that felt *incredible*, but a bad idea, nonetheless.

Aware I was never going to come up with any answers before coffee, I threw my covers aside and got out of bed. I snatched my discarded tee from off the floor and pulled it on, then went to my dresser for a pair of panties. I made a pitstop in the bathroom, then descended the stairs, headed for my coffee pot.

I frowned in confusion when I hit the living room and saw the light on in the kitchen. When I heard movement, my belly dropped, and my feet stopped. Nervous and completely at a loss as to what to do, I went to the window and peeked outside. My spine straightened, and my anxiety was replaced by shock when I saw Mustang's Harley at the curb.

He stayed?

I turned on my heel and marched to the kitchen, still not entirely sure I could believe it until I saw it.

Then there he was. At the stove. Putting sliced bacon in a skillet.

Somewhere, in the back of my mind, I knew I didn't have any bacon.

But I could only focus on one thing at a time.

"What—um—did you stay the whole night?" I stammered.

Mustang looked over at me, his eyes giving me a thorough once over before a half-smile tugged at the corner of his mouth. "Tess, you sleep like the dead."

I blinked hard once, then reached up to run my fingers through my hair as I tried to make sense of what was happening. "Um, yeah—only when I'm really tried. It happens once every few weeks or so. But, back to my thing. Did you? Were you here all night?"

"No," he answered, his attention back on the bacon. "Went to work. Hit the house to raid the fridge. Came back."

"Came back," I repeated on a whisper.

He left the bacon to cook, then shifted his attention to a skillet full of scrambled eggs.

Did I have eggs?

"Locked up when I left. Used your spare key. Found it in the first drawer I looked." He paused, shot me a warning glance with those hazel-blue eyes and said, "Not a safe place to hide a key, sugar." His attention back on the eggs, he assured me, "Don't worry. Found a better spot for it."

I was still too distracted to ask where. Instead, I begged to know, "Why? Why did you come back?"

"Fridge was scarce, Tess. You needed breakfast."

"You're—you're making me breakfast," I processed aloud.

Mustang frowned at me. "Baby, you need coffee to make sense in the morning or what?"

I gaped at him.

I didn't understand how he thought I was the one not making sense.

He was the one who'd left, gone to work, raided a fridge, only to come back to make me breakfast. Except, I didn't understand why—at four in the morning—he was in my kitchen making breakfast.

"What is happening?"

The timer on my stove sounded. He switched off the burner under the eggs, flipped the bacon, then used the tea towel that hung on the oven door to pull out a sheet of biscuits.

I was dreaming. There was no way in hell I was awake.

Badass bikers didn't make breakfast at four in the morning. They just didn't.

"You got jam? Only had syrup at my place."

For a moment, I stood there and said nothing. Then, simply to test out my theory, I went to my fridge and took out a jar of strawberry jelly. I held it against my chest, the chill of the glass seeping through my shirt, alerting me to the reality that I was truly awake.

Having come to this conclusion, I asked again, "Mustang, what is happening? Why did you come back? Why are you making me breakfast?"

He looked at me from over his shoulder. "You take care of people all day. Who's takin' care of you?"

The air in my lungs left me in a whoosh.

I was in deep shit. No doubt about it.

Five words, and I was already falling.

Only, that was par for the course for me.

That didn't explain *him*.

I managed to recapture just enough breath in my lungs to murmur, "You...you hardly know me."

Mustang scowled. "We back at that?"

"Well, it's true!"

He turned toward me and asked, "I need to fuck you right here to remind you of our previous conversation?"

"No—no, Mustang," I replied, exasperated. "I don't need you to remind me how good you are at making me come. Fantastic sex aside, that doesn't explain biscuits and eggs!"

"I know enough to know I want more, Tess. Cookin' burgers in your kitchen before I fuck you 'til you pass out, followed by biscuits and eggs for breakfast before more fucking gets me that. I get your number in my phone, you get mine in yours, we'll keep doing this until you stop tellin' me I don't know you."

I liked all of that. A lot. Too much.

I could barely catch my breath, my chest swelling with a dangerous amount of hope.

I needed a way out of this. I needed him to want to leave before it was too late.

"What about Ed?" I blurted, grasping at the only ammo I had.

"Already established, he's got nothin' to do with this."

"He's my patient."

He quirked an eyebrow at me. "So, you're supposed to be celibate because you're a nurse with patients?"

This time, I wasn't so quick with a rebuttal. What he said reminded me of my conversation with Jenna just a few days before.

I was losing my resolve to fight.

I switched tactics and asked, "Why do you hate him so much?"

"Don't hate him, sugar. He doesn't get that from me. He gets nothing."

"But why?"

"Because the only person he's ever cared about in his entire god-forsaken life is himself," he began, his face harder than I'd ever seen it, and his eyes cold—like they were the first time I mentioned his father. "The nicest thing he ever did for me was give me my first bike—after he bought it for himself and fuckin *wrecked* it drivin' drunk.

"If he wasn't calling me a sorry ass waste of space, he was pickin' my mom apart piece by piece. Don't know why she stayed. Loved him, I guess. And that love got her dead. So, I don't hate him, Tess. If I did, I might be dead now, too—but I plan on livin' long and free in spite of that jackass.

"Now are you going to eat your damn eggs before they get cold or what?"

A great wave of resolve washed over me, and all the muscles in my body relaxed as I stared into those hazel-blue eyes; eyes that were the picture by which I could piece together the puzzle that was Ed and Mustang; the puzzle that just became a little clearer.

Mustang had said he knew enough about me to know he wanted more.

I knew enough about him to be sure I couldn't fix what was broken between father and son. More than that, I knew I wanted the man who made me biscuits and eggs at four in the morning, whether his father was my patient or not—so I stopped pretending otherwise.

I'd deal with the fall out later.

Pointing at the drawer behind him, I simply replied, "I'll need silverware."

Not five minutes later, we were both at my kitchen table eating breakfast.

Mustang's plate was half empty when he asked, "You off at four?"

I nodded. "Yeah."

"You work the day shift tomorrow?"

"No. Friday is my night shift. If my patients remain stable, I won't have to start work until eight."

"Good. Dinner. Tonight. Pick you up at six."

A zing sparked in my belly as I filled my fork with the last of my eggs.

"You'll pick me up at six...on your bike?"

"Yeah, sugar, we're on the hog tonight."

I wasn't sure if I was hiding my smile from Mustang or myself as I shoveled my fork into my mouth.

When I was finished with my bite, I reached for the remainder of my biscuit and confessed, "If you keep feeding me bread at every meal, I will soon no longer fit into my clothes. I don't exercise. I know that I should, but after a day at work, going to the gym is the last thing I want to do."

In spite of what I'd said, as soon as I was finished speaking, I bit a chunk out of my butter and jelly smothered biscuit.

Mustang, having consumed his last bite, pushed his plate away from him. Mumbling around the food in his mouth, he said, "Exercise won't be a problem, Tess." He finished chewing, swallowed, then added, "You hurry up and finish that plate, we'll squeeze in a round of cardio before I go."

I looked down at my plate.

I had a bite of biscuit left and a strip of bacon.

With my mouth full of biscuit, I pushed my plate toward him and insisted, "You can have the bacon."

He grinned, and excitement rippled through me, warming me from the inside out.

This time—I didn't bother hiding my smile.

He didn't eat the bacon.

But we did get in a round of cardio.

After we both came, we exchanged phone numbers.

Then before he left, he kissed me deep and greedy.

I wasn't sure where we were going, but I was sure *dinner* with Mustang warranted my iconic, "hot chick," four-inch, Louboutin heels. I wore them with a pair of black jeans, and a flowy, white, crisscross halter top. I swapped out the studs in my ears for my small, gold hoop earrings, and put on my usual amount of makeup. I felt pretty certain Mustang was a fan of my wavy hair down, plus I liked it free to fly in the wind on the bike, so I let it be.

I grabbed my denim jacket, just in case, all the while making note that if this thing with Mustang really did go anywhere, that would be justification enough to splurge on a new leather jacket.

I was ready to go and pacing back and forth across my living room a few minutes before six o'clock. This wasn't our first date. Technically it was our second; though, one could make a strong case in saying it was our *fourth* if dinner followed by breakfast in my kitchen could be counted as dates. I wasn't so sure. But he *had* taken me to bed after each meal.

In any case, this somehow *felt* like a first date—and I was filled with that jittery, excited nervousness associated with such an occasion.

When I heard his Harley rumbling toward my driveway, I froze.

That sound alone caused an ache between my legs.

I wasn't sure if Mustang was the kind of guy to pick up his date at the door or not, and I contemplated meeting him outside. It was the gentlemanly thing to do to meet a woman at her door—but with the type of guy I tended to attract, it was never a guarantee.

I was still debating when there was a knock at my door.

I came unstuck and went to answer it.

My heart swelled when I found Mustang had dressed up.

To the casual observer, he still appeared dressed down—but I wasn't a casual observer.

He had on his kutte, but that was a given. He was also wearing a pair of dark-washed jeans and a short sleeved, charcoal gray henley that was fitted across the chest and tight around his biceps. It wasn't exactly a button-up, but it was a shirt with buttons, which he'd also tucked in, revealing the belt her wore.

He was so totally dressed up for me.

I smiled big, unable to help myself.

Then, in the blink of an eye, his hand was in my hair and his mouth was pressed to mine, kissing my smile clean away.

I took this to mean he appreciated what I had on, too.

The scent of leather, fresh air, and pine mingled with the taste of him, and it was sublime.

I was breathless when he broke our connection and asked, "You got sunglasses in that bag?"

Dazed from the contact high I'd just received, all I could manage was a nod.

"Good. Lock up, baby. Time to ride."

He didn't have to tell me twice.

Once at his Harley, Mustang stowed my jacket and my purse in one of his saddlebags before mounting his hog. This time, I managed to climb on a little more gracefully. Also, he didn't have to pull me into him. I melted against his back, snaking my arms around him, needing to hold tight to his solid body as I was already starting to feel turned on at the promise of our ride.

He reached down and gave my thigh a squeeze, as if he understood, then started his engine.

Ten minutes later, we were back on I-90. I still had no idea where we were going, but as he picked up speed along the highway, I didn't care. I just wanted to ride.

And we rode.

We rode for more than an hour.

We rode across state lines.

When we hit South Dakota, ridiculous as it sounded, I felt pretty certain I'd let him take me all the way to Florida if he wanted.

We finally slowed down when we reached Deadwood, and he parked us on Main Street, across the street from the Franklin Hotel. I spotted the Legends Steakhouse sign hanging off to the side and assumed that was our final destination. I'd never been to Deadwood, or to Legends Steakhouse, but something told me I'd like both.

As I sat up, I fussed with my hair a little, making sure it was still parted just off the middle and free of tangles, needing to do anything to distract myself from the longing that pulsed at my center.

When Mustang held out his hand, my signal it was time to climb off, I took hold of it and carefully dismounted. He didn't let me go when I was on my feet but pulled me toward him, close enough to wrap his arm around my waist. This meant I was straddling his leg, and I had to bite my lip to stop myself from moaning.

He removed his aviators, hooking them over the neck of his shirt, his eyes on my lips the entire time. After an extended moment, he reached up, pulled my sunglasses off, lifted his eyes to find mine, then asked, "You good, sugar?"

"Mmhmm," I hummed, not trusting my voice.

Mustang smiled, as if he saw right through me. "You'll get used to it."

I shook my head slightly and confessed, "I'm not sure I want to."

He furrowed his brow in confusion, and I knew he misunderstood what I'd said. To clear things up, I took hold of either side of his face and brought my lips to his. I knew my message had been received when the hand at my waist descended to take hold of one side of my butt, pulling me even closer before he completely took over our kiss.

I moaned, all consumed by him, and entirely uncaring as to where we were or who might see.

He did that to me.

I was in so much trouble.

He slowed down our exchange, then swatted at my backside before he promised, "Fuck you when we get back. Let's eat, baby."

I nodded, my initial arousal assuaged a little after that kiss, then stepped back so he could dismount. He gave me my purse and my sunglasses, then took me by the hand and led me across the street and inside the restaurant.

Even though no one was particularly dressed up, it still felt like a fancy place—at least, fancy for our neck of the woods. Rather than sit at a table, Mustang spotted a couple open seats at the bar and opted to take those. I didn't mind this, as it put him in closer proximity.

After the bartender offered us our menus and left us to peruse, I jokingly asked, "Are you ashamed to be seen with me or something? We traveled an awfully long way for a date."

His body already angled toward mine, he looked up from his menu, then painted me up and down with those hazel-blue irises. "Tess, even in jeans, you're classier than fuckin' Ruby Tuesday's."

I lost a little of my humor, too busy trying to keep a death grip around my will in an effort keep myself from falling in love with a man who hadn't yet even bought me dinner.

Not sure how to respond, I didn't. He didn't seem to mind as he went back to looking at his menu. I followed his lead. When the bartender returned, I ordered a glass of cabernet and the filet. Mustang stuck with water and got the ribeye.

Another glance around the restaurant alerted me to the fact that Mustang was the only one in there with a branded, leather kutte and tattooed arms on display. These characteristics had been what drew me to him in the first place, so I didn't feel strange sitting next to him in my red-soled heels. Though, I was still trying to figure out the man beneath all that swagger—the man, I was sure, who could walk into any establishment he pleased without caring a lick what anyone thought of him or his affiliation with the Wild Stallions MC.

That was the thing about motorcycle clubs. The real ones. Loyalty ran deep. He'd told me himself. He was more Stallion than anything else.

Having decided that I was going to do this—whatever it was—with Mustang, and acknowledging a dinner date meant I could pry a little, I asked, "What made you want to be a Stallion? I know you told me Bull took you under his wing when you were younger, but how'd you meet Bull in the first place?"

Mustang propped an elbow on the bar, extending his other arm across the back of my chair as he considered me for a moment. Then he said, "Told you about my first bike. Was a hunk of shit when I got it. Only place I knew to go get help fixing it up was the garage. Had some money from workin' odd jobs around the neighborhood. Mowin' lawns, rakin' leaves, that sorta shit. I was only sixteen, so I didn't know what the hell I was doin', but I'd borrow mom's car and drive over there asking questions about parts and whatnot. Kept comin' around. Guess you could say Bull was the first one who didn't think I was an annoying pain in the ass. He saw how much I wanted it. The escape. The freedom."

He paused when our bartender came back with my wine. I thanked him, looking to Mustang as soon as he was gone. I was learning a lot, but I wanted more.

Mustang didn't disappoint. He continued, "After mom died a few months later, I ran away. Couldn't stand to be in that house. I even left the bike. It wasn't road worthy by a longshot. Didn't know where to go, so I found myself on the compound. I'd break into the garage after closing for a warm place to sleep at night.

"Bull and Winona weren't married yet, but he'd made her his ol' lady and they were living together. Winnie was already workin' in the office, and she found me one morning. Scared the shit out of her at first, but it didn't take her long to read the situation. That night, and every night until I turned seventeen, I crashed on their couch. I was allowed to stay under two conditions—I put in my time at the garage, and I work to get my GED. Even back then, Bull was a hard-ass, thinkin' ten steps ahead."

Mustang paused again; this time lost in a reverie he didn't share. I watched him, not daring to pull him from where he'd gone. Finally, his eyes cleared, and he told me, "Closest thing I've got to a father is Bull, but he's my brother, too. He helped me haul that bike to the garage, and we worked on it together in my spare time.

"Nothin' else made sense by then. The Stallions were already family, even if I wasn't officially one of them. When I turned seventeen, I became a prospect and moved into the clubhouse. I was voted in on my eighteenth birthday. Youngest to ever become a Wild Stallion."

I didn't respond right away, not sure what to say.

There was so much there, and a few more puzzle pieces fit into place.

He let me have a minute, allowing all that he'd said to settle in my mind.

"I thought Bull was kinda cool when I met him, but now I know he's the shit," I said, completely serious.

Mustang grinned at me.

A zing sparked in my belly, then ricocheted like crazy.

Mustang was hot all the time, but he was downright handsome when he grinned.

"Yeah, sugar," he spoke in reply. "No doubt about it."

I was sipping at my wine when he asked, "What about you? How'd you end up a nurse?"

Right. It was my turn.

I set my glass down and laced my fingers together in my lap.

"I was eleven when my mom was diagnosed with colon cancer. For a short while, we thought maybe she had the chance to beat it, but she didn't. Near the end, she was so tired of hospitals and doctors, she just wanted to be at home with my brother and my dad and me. I was twelve when we got to that point, and it had become really hard for me, losing my mom so slowly and yet way too soon.

"Anyway, her hospice nurse, Debbie—she was incredible. Somehow, she took care of all of us. She didn't make it easier. There was nothing easy about my mom dying. But she made it seem possible to bear. And I remember after my mom passed—I remember her hugging me and sitting with me for hours while my dad wept in the room with my mom."

I dropped my gaze into my lap as I pictured Debbie as I first knew her.

She was around my age back then.

"In retrospect, I understand she let herself get closer to my family than she probably should have. She'd never admit it to me now, but I know. Not that I could blame her. I get how hard it is to draw emotional boundaries in my job. But with Debbie—sometimes I think it was meant to be. We still keep in touch. She's retired now, but still living in Casper. I consider her my greatest mentor." With a sigh, I sought out Mustang's eyes and concluded, "Debbie's the reason I decided to become a hospice nurse. I wanted to be able to take care of people the way she took care of us."

Our roles reversed, Mustang looked at me for a long moment without saying a word.

"Sorry to hear about your mom, baby."

Warmth washed over me like a tidal wave.

It had been twenty years, but it still touched me to hear him say it.

Wanting him to share the feeling, I murmured, "Sorry about yours, too."

"What about your dad? He still in Casper?"

I shook my head, the reminder of this loss a little closer to the surface than the other.

"He died when I was twenty-one. Brain aneurysm."

"Fuck, Tess," he muttered with a scowl.

"It's funny—I had months to say goodbye to my mom and no time at all to say goodbye to dad, but either way, they both sucked the same."

"And your brother?" he asked, still scowling.

Happy to talk about the living, I shifted in my seat and reached up to sweep a bit of hair behind my ear as I answered, "Andy. He's a pilot in the Air Force and currently stationed in Abilene, Texas. It might be totally naïve, but I like to think being a pilot in the military is marginally safer than any other job out in the field. And if I'm wrong, I don't want to know because I can't imagine losing him in the line of duty, and I'd rather just be proud than worried about him all the time. We're all each other has left."

He was *still* scowling, as if he really didn't like it that I'd endured so much loss, but I didn't want to talk about death anymore.

Glancing at the hand that was rested casually on the bar, I brazenly grazed my fingers across the ink on his knuckles and insisted, "Tell me about Mary-Kate."

Finally, he un-furrowed his brow.

"Don't know how the fuck she's so sweet, but she is. She sees the good in everyone, especially me."

"Can I see a picture?"

He didn't hesitate to pull his phone from out of his pocket.

He didn't even have to open it.

Mary-Kate was his lock screen.

She was sitting on his Harley, in a pair of pink denim overalls, her gorgeous curly hair everywhere, her eyes hidden behind sunglasses in the shape of stars, and she was smiling huge.

"She's adorable, Mustang."

"No doubt about it," he said, pocking his phone once more.

I smiled, enthralled by the father in him. "Do you want more kids?"

"Didn't used to want any. After MK, I changed my mind. Not for me, but for her. I don't want her to be alone. Anything ever happens to me she'll always be taken care of by the club, but she's a girl. It's different. So—yeah. I think about claimin' an ol' lady and poppin' out at least one more."

That was a good answer.

I liked it. A lot.

Too much.

Fortunately, before I could dwell on it, our dinner arrived.

Our food steered the conversation in a different direction. I wondered how he'd discovered the steakhouse, and he told me he made trips to South Dakota regularly. For a decent ride or a good band, and for Sturgis every August. He also rode to Montana and Idaho every so often, as there were other chapters of the Wild Stallions MC in Missoula and Boise.

I'd been to Bozeman, Montana, on a weekend trip with Jenna a couple years back; and my parents took my brother and me to see Mount Rushmore when we were kids, but there was so much outside of Wyoming I hadn't experienced.

I shared this with him, and his simple reply was, "Always down for a ride, sugar."

I couldn't say how I'd become *sugar*, but it was sticking, and I liked it.

I also pocketed the promise his statement implied.

When we finished our dinner and the bartender asked if we wanted dessert, Mustang hit me with the same question using only those beautiful eyes. Remembering the New York style cheesecake with peaches in bourbon cream I'd seen on the menu earlier, I couldn't resist.

We split it, then Mustang picked up the check, and we were out of there.

I double checked my phone before we got on his hog and was happy to see no new notifications. This meant I was free to enjoy our ride to the fullest.

On the open road, I cleared my mind and let everything go, just because I could.

Well—everything but Mustang.

I luxuriated in the feel of my body wrapped around his, and the rumble of his bike underneath us. The power of his hog was a reminder of his own prowess, and I looked forward to our next ride—where I was sure he'd take me to new heights of pleasure.

It was after ten when Mustang pulled into my driveway, and neither of us pretended we had a mind to do anything other than to go inside and rip each other's clothes off.

Metaphorically speaking, at least.

I hoped he wouldn't rip my top. I liked it far more than the tee I'd spared from a shredding the previous evening.

We were two steps beyond my door when Mustang hooked his arm around my middle and hauled my back against his front. I shivered at the feel of his beard hairs tickling my ear as he spoke.

"Bedroom, baby. Everything off—except the shoes."

I shivered again. Bigger this time. Then nodded.

He let me go and I hurried up the stairs. I heard him slide home the deadbolt on my front door, but I hardly registered it. I was primed and ready to go. Even the act of walking was a tease, my clit so swollen with desire, one touch and I knew I'd detonate.

I dropped my purse on the floor the moment I stepped over the threshold of my room and flicked on the overhead light. My top was gone a second later, my bra soon to follow. I was stepping out of my shoes in order to remove my jeans when Mustang filled my empty doorframe. His kutte was already gone, and he made quick work of yanking off his shirt. While I shimmied out of my jeans and panties, he tugged his feet free of his boots. When I slipped my blue nail-polished pedicured feet back into my Louboutins, Mustang stopped undressing himself and bathed me with his eyes.

If it was possible to come from a look, I would have.

He practically growled as he ate up the distance between us. One hand splayed open at the small of my back, the other buried in my hair, he brought me close, so close my nipples tingled pleasurably as my breasts smashed against his bare chest, and he kissed me.

No. He *drank* from me—and it was heaven.

My hands were everywhere. Up his sides, across his back, over one shoulder, along his neck. I felt crazed with desire, like more than two hours on his Harley with no release had turned me into an unhinged version of myself.

"Mustang," I whimpered between kisses. "I need you. To. Fuck me. Now. Please."

He tugged my bottom lip between his teeth before he let me go, reaching for his wallet.

"Belt," he muttered, extracting a condom.

My hands got to work without delay. I unhooked his belt, then freed his top button and lowered his zipper before he took over. He shoved his jeans and his boxer briefs down past his hips before he rolled on the condom, and then he reached for me.

His hands skimmed the back of my thighs before he took hold, and I understood. I circled my arms around his shoulders as he lifted me off the floor, and we both worked to get my legs wrapped around him. My back hit the wall, his eyes locked with mine, and I felt the tip of his length a second before he impaled me.

He rocked his hips twice.

That's all it took.

"*Oh, god—yes,*" I moaned as pleasure ripped through me.

I was still coming when he shifted one of his hands, bringing his thumb to massage my clit. He kept thrusting, and I couldn't tell if my first orgasm was growing bigger, or if he was already making me come again, but I dug my nails into his back as I squeezed my thighs tight at his sides, my toes curling in my shoes and my back arching as I cried out in ecstasy.

I was panting, my insides still quivering when he readjusted his grip around my thighs and moved me away from the wall. He sat me on the edge of the bed, wrapped a hand around the back of my neck, and the other behind my right knee before he demanded, "Other leg, sugar."

I let go of his shoulders, spreading my legs wide as I pulled back my left knee with one hand, and used my other to help stabilize myself as he began to pound in and out of me. His thrusts were hard and relentless, and I never wanted him to stop.

My head lulled as he continued to support my neck, and my eyelids fell closed as I got lost in all he was giving me.

Friction had never felt so good.

Not anywhere in the history of the world.

I was sure of this.

When I felt another orgasm coming on, the sound that crawled up my throat was almost guttural.

"*Mustang!*"

"Fuck, yes, baby. Touch yourself. Come for me."

I didn't hesitate. I surrendered myself to his hold and reached for my clit. We both groaned when my sex clamped tightly around his length. He pulled out of me, and my core continued to flutter in his absence.

Then I was on my back, Mustang's lips grazing mine as he panted, "Pretty in pink, and wild like the wind, my Tess."

I was fairly certain I was delirious and hadn't heard him correctly, which was why I didn't read into what he'd said before he completely distracted me with a long, hard, deep, wet kiss.

With that kiss, there was no denying, I was an addict, high on all that was Mustang.

"Shoes off, baby," he told me when he lifted his mouth from mine. "Meet me in the middle of the bed."

I took off my shoes as he rid himself of the rest of his clothing, and we met in the middle of my bed.

His body on top of mine, he asked, "You got one more in you, or do you want my dick in your mouth?"

I considered his question for a moment. I'd come twice already, maybe three times—I still wasn't sure. I couldn't say whether or not he would be able to make me come again, as I'd never been with a man who could make me come as often and consistently as he could.

But I'd also yet to have his dick in my mouth.

"Mouth," I told him without second guessing myself.

He rolled onto his back and reached down to remove the condom. When he was bare, he met my gaze and said, "You want my dick, you got it. Give me that pussy."

Yeah—I definitely made the right call.

I positioned myself appropriately, then sucked while he ate, and it was *sublime*.

It wasn't long before I realized I *did* have another one in me. As I drew closer to yet another orgasm, I sucked and stroked his length with all I had, wanting him to come with me. This was why, when he jerked his hips and smacked the side of my ass as he began to come in my mouth, it pushed me over the edge, and I writhed with my own climax right along with him.

I licked him clean then collapsed onto the bed beside him, more sated than I ever had been in my life.

For a few minutes, neither of us spoke as we worked to catch our breath.

Finally, Mustang propped himself up on his forearms, looked over at me and muttered, "Fuckin' hell."

I didn't know why, but that made me giggle.

My giggle got me a lazy grin, and a zing shot through my belly.

"Between the sheets, baby."

I nodded, then mustered the energy to move and meet him under the covers. He lay against my pillow, an arm lifted in invitation, and I stretched out along his side, resting my cheek on his chest. As soon as we were settled, he started grazing his knuckles back and forth across my waist, and I sighed contentedly.

"You gonna pass out before I get a chance to recuperate?"

My eyes widened at the possibility of more sex, but the reaction was only temporary, counterbalanced by his gentle, repetitive touch.

"Chances are high I pass out if you don't stop touching me like that," I warned him. Though, hoping he wouldn't stop, I added, "Unless you keep me talking."

His knuckles continued their journey back and forth across my skin.

"Why are all the walls in your house painted a different color?" he asked.

My body shook with my laughter. "It came like that when I bought it." A yawn interrupted me before I went on to tell him, "I moved in a couple years ago with all these grand plans of remodeling it. I have the cans of paint in the garage and everything. I got as far as my bedroom and then was too tired or busy to keep going."

He didn't miss a beat before he replied, "Tell me what color in what room. Brothers and I'll come finish the job one day while you're at work."

I frowned, taken aback by the offer. "I—I couldn't ask you to do that."

"You're not askin', I'm tellin'. You got a man now, sugar, which means you don't have to live in a place resembling a box of skittles."

This time, I knew I was not delirious.

I propped myself up on my elbow, and my eyes caught hazel-blue as I blurted, "I've got a man?"

"Yeah, Tess. You're lookin' at him," he told me matter-of-factly.

My eyebrows shot up my forehead. "Mustang, you—"

He didn't let me finish. Instead, he said, "Tess, I like where this is goin'. I swear, if you spout some shit about how I don't know you, I'll spank your ass. I know enough. I know the thought of someone else's hands on you—or worse, you on the back of some other fucker's bike—pisses me right the hell off. So, yeah, you got a man. Not ten minutes ago, he came in your mouth, and you came in his."

My mouth fell open but no words came out, all of them stuck in my throat. I then watched as Mustang's gaze drifted down to my lips and a thrill raced up and down my spine.

I shut my mouth, forced a swallow, then found my words.

"What I was going to say is—you can't say stuff like that to a woman like me. I fall hard and fast. Every time. Too hard and too fast, *every time*, Mustang. And every time, I'm the one who gets hurt because I come on too strong too soon. I—I can't help it.

"I spend all day protecting my heart. When I leave my patients and their families, I no longer have the capacity to do that in any other area of my life. If you say stuff like that to me—"

He cut me off, again, rolling toward me and pinning me beneath his body as he said, "Sugar, you fall as fast and as hard as you're going to. Rate we're goin'? I'll be there at the bottom to break your fall."

My breath caught, and my chest felt heavy as my eyes grew glassy with tears.

I was in so, so, so much trouble.

"Mustang..." I barely managed on a whisper.

"Done talkin' about it, baby," he said.

Then he kissed me.

I let go and began my free fall.

He explored my mouth with his tongue and my body with his hands until he was hard again. He then diligently sought after my last orgasm of the night and enjoyed my body until he was spent.

When he left me in bed to go dispose of his condom, I passed out before he even reached the hallway.

I didn't hear it when my man came back.

I didn't feel it when he crawled into bed with me.

But I slept all night wrapped in my man's arms.

And that's who Mustang was.

Mine.

CHAPTER
Ten

W HEN I WOKE FRIDAY morning, I was on the wrong side of the bed.

I was bewildered by this only until I felt Mustang at my back, his hand resting heavy on my hip.

I remembered the first time I woke up in bed with the man and how I'd snuck away. The last thing I wanted to do was leave him in bed again, but I needed to check my phone—the phone I'd left in my purse while we went at each other after our date.

Only, this time, when I began to carefully roll away from him, his fingers tightened their hold before he grumbled, "Where do you think you're goin'?"

I smiled, in love with his voice first thing in the morning—low and rumbly from lack of use.

"I need to check my phone, babe. It's in my purse. I'll be right back."

Satisfied with my answer, he gave me another squeeze and then released me.

I found my phone with ease. As I began my return trip to the bed, I saw I had a couple unread text messages, but nothing urgent. I also noted it was a few minutes after eight before I discarded the device on the nightstand I never used and crawled between the sheets with my man.

My man.

The thought made me want to burrow in his chest and stay a while—so I burrowed in his chest, biting down on my lower lip to contain my grin when he immediately engulfed me in his arms.

"Got shit to do today," he told me, his eyes still closed.

With plenty I'd been neglecting since I left work on Wednesday, I could relate, so I simply replied, "Okay."

"I'll make breakfast before I go."

I reached for his bearded cheek as I said, "Mustang, you don't have to do that."

He peeked open one eye and met my gaze. "You gonna eat breakfast if I don't?"

My smile couldn't be helped. He'd seen my fridge. It wasn't always as desolate as it had been the last few days, but I didn't make a habit of concocting a full spread first thing in the morning.

"Eventually," I answered honestly, trying to remember if I still had any yogurt left.

He studied me a moment longer, then closed his eye and repeated, "I'll make breakfast before I go."

I didn't argue.

Fifteen minutes later, we got out of bed and Mustang made us eggs and bacon.

My contribution had been the coffee, whereupon I learned my man liked his with two sugars but no cream.

When we were finished eating, he didn't linger.

I did, however, get a delicious kiss goodbye.

Alone, awake, and not on the clock, I found myself with some real time to process everything that had transpired since I found Mustang on Thornhill Road Wednesday afternoon. It didn't take long for me to admit I was happy. It all still felt a bit reckless, given the circumstances, but I wanted him, and he wanted me, and I didn't have any desire to deny either of us.

However, it did seem like a smart idea to get an outside perspective.

I needed to speak with Jenna.

After cleaning up in the kitchen, I headed upstairs for a shower. While I bathed, I thought of the chores I should do and the errands I should run. Mustang and I hadn't exactly made plans, but I hoped we'd see each other again the next day, which meant I needed to be productive in the present.

As soon as I was out of the shower, I shot Jenna a text.

Best friend emergency. Not life or death. Just can't wait.

I had time to get dressed and make my bed—with all the pillows this time—before I got a reply.

If you can make it to the hospital, I might be able to take 15 minutes for a coffee break.

I knew right away I was not going to show up at the hospital empty handed, which meant a trip to our favorite coffee shop for two lattes and a chocolate croissant, Jenna's favorite. Factoring in the time this would take, I was quick to send my reply.

ETA 10:30.

At two minutes past the half hour, I was strolling into the emergency room, looking for Jenna. She spotted me from where she stood behind the nurses' station, smiled, then waved me over.

"Your timing is perfect. Just give me two minutes," she insisted.

Two minutes later, each of us with our lattes and Jenna already biting into her croissant, we were headed outside. It was a beautiful morning, and she wanted the fresh air. We found an empty bench and sat.

"Alright, what's going on? To what do I owe this pleasure?" she asked before taking another bite of her treat.

"Well, you were right about Mustang. He didn't need my number to get in touch."

Speaking around her bite, Jenna shielded her mouth and asked, "Mustang? That's his name?"

"Oh, yeah," I muttered, having forgotten I'd left that detail out last we spoke. "That's his road name. His real name is Sully, but he doesn't like people to call him that. After having spent some time with him, I understand he is one-hundred-percent Wild Stallion. That's his family, so he's Mustang."

"Got it. I'm with you now. So, he got in touch?"

"Mmhmm," I hummed with a nod. "We're officially *on*."

Jenna lowered her coffee from her lips and smiled.

Before she could say a word, I added, "But you know how I get..."

"You mean, off the deep end after the third date?"

I nodded and said, "I think I met my match."

Her eyebrows shot up her forehead in excitement. "Yeah?"

"Last night, we were in bed, and he called himself *my man*. Just like that, he said—*you got a man now, sugar*," I said in a poor imitation of his deep voice.

Jenna's brow relaxed as her smile stretched into a grin. "He calls you sugar?"

"Jen, focus, that's not the point. I'm officially in uncharted territory now. I don't know what to do."

"Honey, you enjoy the ride."

I coughed out a laugh, unconsciously squeezing my thighs together. I was already enjoying *many* rides, and I had the sore bits to prove it. But that wasn't what I meant.

"I'm talking about Ed. I didn't go looking for his son thinking any of this would happen. Now Mustang's calling himself my man—which, by the way, is my exact brand of crazy—and it feels unfair somehow.

"There are still parts of their story I haven't pieced together yet, but I'm coming around to the idea that there's a reason Ed is alone in that house. He was not the greatest father or husband. Mustang is not entirely unjustified in his refusal to speak to the man, and I'm not holding my breath waiting for him to change his mind. But do I tell him?"

Jenna thought for a moment. "Well, I wouldn't tell him you're sleeping together. I would tread lightly. Like you said, you've still only got part of the story, and it sounds like Mustang's side. Not saying that he's wrong," she was quick to add. "Just saying—you didn't go looking for Mustang at Ed's request."

I knit my eyebrows together in concern. "I had the best intentions."

"I know you did. Don't beat yourself up over it, either. Now, you have to give it time to play out."

"Yeah," I murmured noncommittally.

"So, when do I get to meet this Mustang?" asked Jenna, playfully kicking at my leg.

The thought of introducing the two of them instantly brightened my mood.

"When's your next Saturday night off?"

"I don't know—but I'll find out."

Just then, my phone rang from inside my purse. I was quick to reach for it and found a patient was calling. That could only mean one thing.

"I'm going to have to go."

Jenna needed no further explanation. "Go. Thanks for my breakfast. I'll text you when I'm free."

I slid my thumb across the screen, picked up the call, then jammed my phone between my ear and my shoulder. I waved at Jenna as I greeted my caller, then stood and hurried toward my car.

Friday wasn't as personally productive as I'd hoped it would be.

My unexpected patient visit lasted several hours. By the time I was finished, I managed to squeeze in a couple quick errands before I ran home to throw together a late dinner, and then I was right back out the door for my night shift.

I hadn't had the time to think of what to tell Ed, so I didn't tell him anything during my visit. This was made easier given he was usually prone to be less chatty at my night drop-ins.

Since I didn't have time for a nap before my shift, I fell into bed almost as soon as I got home.

My sheets smelled like leather, fresh air, and pine—and I went to sleep smiling.

I woke naturally Saturday afternoon and immediately reached for my phone. I had a text from Jenna, but no other notifications. I rolled onto my back and frowned up at the ceiling, allowing myself a moment to wallow in my disappointment.

I hadn't heard from Mustang since he left the previous morning.

Things between us were moving fast, but in some ways totally out of order.

We'd slept together three times before we exchanged numbers. Even though we'd gone on a couple dates and shared a handful of meals, neither of us had ever texted or called the other. That said, I didn't know what it meant to go more than twenty-four hours without hearing from my man—but I knew I didn't like it.

Fully aware I was equally culpable for our shared silence, I unlocked my screen, searched for his contact info, and started a text thread. I hesitated, wishing to say something less lame than *hi*. Finally, I decided to simply ask what I wanted to know.

Do I get to see you today?

His reply came less than thirty seconds later.

Depends. You ever gonna come downstairs?

I gasped and sat upright.

He's here?

'Used your spare key. Found it in the first drawer I looked. Not a safe place to hide a key, sugar. Don't worry. Found a better spot for it.'

I'd never asked him where that better spot was.

Now I understood—it was on his keyring.

It probably made me certifiable, but this realization brought a grin to my face.

I jumped out of bed, hurried for my door, and swung it wide open.

Immediately, the smell of food hit me, and my stomach growled.

I already had all the motivation I needed to get my happy butt down the stairs, but the promise of food was a welcome bonus.

When I stepped foot into my kitchen, Mustang was there in his usual attire—only, rather than a full tee, he had on a white tank top underneath his kutte, a subtle difference that made my sex clench. That, plus he was filling a plate with something that smelled delicious.

"Hi," I breathed, still taking him in.

He cut his eyes at me, quirked an eyebrow and asked, "That's the best you got?"

I was pretty sure before, but I was certain then—I'd definitely met my match.

Fighting a huge smile, I closed the distance between us, then snaked my arms under his kutte and around his waist as I leaned into him and semi-repeated, "Hi, babe," before I pressed up on my toes and kissed the underside of his bearded chin.

The hand not holding my plate reached down until he had a palm full of my butt.

"Better."

No longer hiding my smile, I asked, "What's for lunch?"

"Bone-in chicken thighs and sauteed green beans. Was going to make sandwiches, but don't know what we're doin' for dinner. Likely will involve bread. Had the time, so we're eatin' chicken now."

I liked that. All of that. A *lot*.

I must have said as much with my face, because Mustang's next words were, "Like that look in your eyes, baby, but food's ready now. It's time to eat. I'll fuck you after."

I shivered in response.

He felt it and grinned.

The grin was too much to resist, so I let him go, turned to grab the plate in his hand, snagged some silverware, and headed for the table.

"Are you going to be here every time I wake up?" I asked as I sat.

He filled a second plate and informed me, "Got MK tomorrow 'til Wednesday."

I nodded as my brain made quick work of his answer.

I'd snuck out of his bed the previous Sunday, and I didn't see him again until Wednesday afternoon. I didn't see him because he had his daughter.

This made sense.

I also gathered that he hadn't said *no* to my question, only that he needed to focus on his fatherly duties the next few days. I interpreted this to mean next Thursday, he *would* let himself into my house and be there when I woke up.

I looked forward to that.

I also couldn't help but wonder when I might get to meet his

Mary-Kate.

I'd never dated anyone with a child before. Obviously, it wasn't a deal breaker—but there were boundaries when it came to kids I'd never before traversed.

As if he was in my head, after Mustang dropped into his now usual spot, he asked, "You free Monday night?"

I picked up my fork and murmured, "Yes."

"We'll go to dinner. MK likes Railyard. Their food's not total shit."

Nervous excitement sparked in my belly as I watched him take his first bite.

"Are you sure? If it's too soon, I'll under—"

"Tess?" he interrupted.

We held each other's gaze, and I said nothing as he finished chewing.

"You like where this is goin'?"

I nodded my head *yes*.

"You plan on bailin' any time soon?"

I shook my head *no*.

"Then Monday night, I'm takin' my girl and my woman to Railyard for dinner."

"Okay," I agreed.

My stomach reminded me of the food I'd yet to try. I dropped my attention to my plate and filled my fork with my first bite.

"You got shit you need to do today?"

The chicken was good. The green beans even more so.

It took me a second to think of the things I needed to do.

"Uh, I should probably do a couple loads of laundry, and I need to go to the grocery store."

"Let me rephrase that. You got shit you need to do today that can't wait 'til tomorrow? Fridge is already full, sugar."

I stopped chewing, tilted my head in confusion and asked, "I'm sorry, what?"

"Was getting old, havin' to stop by the store or my house to get grub. You're stocked up. Anything you don't like, you let me know. I miss somethin', you let me know that, too."

I had to force my jaw to move so I could finish chewing and swallow my bite.

It was proving to be a consistent challenge to *eat* and *converse* with Mustang at the same time.

"Mustang, I can afford my own groceries."

"Seen your shoes, Tess. Know you can. But if you're not workin' you're sleepin', and if you're not sleepin' you're doin' what you got to do or you're with me. Seeing as I prefer you with me, and I had some time on my hands, I checked off an item on your to-do list."

He finished his statement as if it was nothing, then took another bite.

I was too distracted by all he'd said to follow suit.

"That's—that's really sweet," I murmured.

Speaking around his food, he said, "Get used to it, sugar."

I was a little afraid of getting used to something that seemed too good to be true.

"I've never met a badass biker so...*domesticated*."

Almost as soon as the words fell out of my mouth, I wished I could shovel them back in and swallow them whole. That was because, as soon as they landed, I learned what Mustang looked like when he was annoyed. While it might have been a look I could appreciate when directed at someone who wasn't me—or, better yet, pointed at someone on *behalf* of me—when that irritated, hazel-blue stare was aimed my way, it made me want to tuck tail.

"Man's got to eat. Got a kid, and I've got to feed her, too. Now I got a woman with a whack schedule which means, I want to see her,

I've got to do my part. Not a dick, baby, and I've got more than shit for brains." His gaze softened a little before he demanded, "Now eat. You ain't got shit to do, we'll get in a round of cardio before we head to the clubhouse. Workin' the bar tonight, but the lineup is stacked. You can hang. You get tired before I'm done, you can pass out in my room at the clubhouse."

I sort of didn't regret my comment anymore. Mostly because he'd admitted he intended to do his part to make sure we'd see each other in spite of my whack schedule, and I liked that.

"Okay," I conceded.

He filled his fork again and I just sat there, replaying all the nice things he'd said since I woke up and came downstairs.

"Baby," he called gently.

I offered him my undivided attention, and he gave me a half-smile.

"Eat."

Nodding, I proceeded to do as I was told.

Twenty minutes later, Mustang got my heart rate up.

We went one round. On the couch. I came twice.

I was beginning to wonder if he was more than he appeared.

Perhaps he was a sex god *disguised* as a badass biker.

Or maybe he was merely a generous lover who got off on getting me off.

I was happy either way.

Because either way—he was mine.

After our highly pleasurable workout, I got in the shower while Mustang got dressed and then kicked back in front of my TV so he could wait for me to get ready. In an effort not to take forever, while I bathed, I mentally sorted through my closet, piecing together an outfit that could transition from an afternoon at the clubhouse to a night at the bar.

By the time I'd dried myself off, I knew I was going with my fitted, single-shoulder, burgundy, sleeveless top with my light-wash, high-waisted, wide-leg distressed jeans. They had a hole in each knee, and a cut across the left thigh.

I didn't have a pair of designer heels that would work exceptionally well with the look, but I did have some nude, peep-toe, booties with three-inch chunky heels I liked.

I kept Mustang waiting forty minutes, and then I finally descended the stairs, ready to go. After a really hot, greedy kiss—Mustang's way of telling me he thought I was worth the wait—we were on our way to the compound.

It was the shortest distance we'd ever ridden together, but I thought that was for the best. When we parked in front of the clubhouse, I didn't feel wild with desire—just a manageable amount.

Then a thrill danced up my spine when Mustang grabbed my hand possessively and led me inside.

The door was barely closed behind us before a little ball of energy came racing our direction. A boy, no older than five or six, crashed into Mustang's leg and greeted, "Uncle Stang! Where's MK?"

"Hey, Otto," said Mustang, rustling the boy's hair. "She's not with me today. Next time."

Momentarily disappointed, he frowned and said, "Okay." The very next second, he ran back across the room. He stopped at the pool tables, where two teenage boys were playing a round. He stood beside another boy, who looked just a couple years older, and both of them watched on in vague interest.

"Hey, Uncle Mustang."

This greeting had come from the bar, where a girl sat cross-legged on the counter, reading a book in her lap. She wasn't quite a teenager, but she looked to be well on her way. She also looked an awful lot like

Mustache—sans mustache, of course—who sat in a chair at the bar next to her.

"Hey, Marlowe," greeted Mustang with a chin lift.

In approximately thirty seconds, I'd learned two very fascinating things.

First, the clubhouse appeared to be kid friendly when the sun was up.

Second, Bull and Mustang weren't the only Stallions with kids.

Mustang escorted me further into the room, toward the others. There were two men behind the bar, and another bellied up to it with a woman occupying the seat next to him. Bull and Winnie were close by, Bull on the couch with a bottle of beer in his hand, and Winnie on its arm.

When Winnie turned and saw me, she smiled. "Hey. Good to see you again."

I returned the sentiment, then Mustang did a quick round of introductions.

"You know Bull, Winnie, and Wrangler. That's Marlowe, his oldest," he said, whereupon I learned *Mustache* was *Wrangler*. I glanced at his kutte and also learned he held the office of *Enforcer*.

That wasn't at all intimidating...

Then again, I knew him to be not scary but flirty.

"That's Buck and Maverick," he continued, pulling me from my thoughts. The two men behind the bar dipped their chins at me. "And this is Twister and Lyla."

Twister, whose kutte identified him as the Vice President of the Gillette chapter, raised his bottle of beer, but Lyla looked me up and down and barely contained a sneer. I wasn't sure what that was about, but it didn't go unnoticed how she'd been introduced as neither Twister's woman nor his ol' lady.

"Hi," I said with a blanket wave. "I'm Tess."

As soon as I said it, Mustang let go of my hand and draped his arm around my shoulders, pulling me into his side. A zing shot through my belly as I smiled up at him.

He'd just made a statement without speaking a word, and it felt good.

Really good.

"Over there are Miles, Jett, Otto, and Axel," added Winnie, speaking of the boys. "Axel is Wrangler's youngest. The rest are the hellions I was telling you about."

"Don't worry, darlin'. We won't test you on names until next week," teased Wrangler.

I laughed as Buck asked, "Somethin' to drink?"

"No, thank you. I'm good for now."

Maverick's lips curled slowly into a smirk as he looked between Mustang and me.

I noticed his *Road Captain* patch and wondered what that rank entailed. He was wearing a backwards trucker style baseball cap over his long, curly hair. It was grown out halfway down his back, and it was beautiful. I was sure Jenna would kill for a fraction of his hair's texture.

"Interesting," he muttered, folding his arms across his chest.

"Won't last long if you don't know how to party, sweetie," piped in Lyla snidely.

"Don't be thick, sheep. It's unbecoming. You see whose arm she's on," drawled Wrangler.

Lyla rolled her eyes as Twister chuckled.

I was on the verge of an explanatory reply when I felt the vibration of Mustang's phone from inside his front pocket. He let me go in order to reach for it, then cursed under his breath when he saw who was calling. As he answered, he turned his back on the group.

"Hey, baby. You okay?"

I tried not to react to him calling someone else *baby*, but I still stood frozen as I stared at his profile while I waited with bated breath for his next words.

"Okay. Stay in mommy's room, princess. Daddy'll be there in a bit."

I let out a quiet sigh at the same time I felt all my organs turn to mush.

Mary-Kate was his princess.

My man was hard on the outside and sweet on the inside.

I loved that.

I barely had a chance to recover from my reaction before Mustang turned and I caught a glimpse of his hardened features. Whatever warm and fuzzy feelings I'd felt a second ago were gone in an instant.

"We gotta go," he told me. He then looked to Winnie and said, "Might need a favor tonight."

"Whatever you need, Mustang. You know that," she assured him.

He jerked his chin in acknowledgment then grabbed my hand and started for the door.

I didn't know what was going on, but I knew from the grip he had around my fingers it was not good.

I didn't ask any questions.

I merely followed his lead.

CHAPTER *Eleven*

Mustang

'D*ADDY, IT SMELLS LIKE grass again. Mommy says I can't come out of her room until her friend leaves, but I'm hungry.'*

His daughter's call was like a track set on repeat in his head.

His blood had gone from cool to boiling in a matter of ten seconds.

He was so mad he could hardly see straight.

He was pulling into his garage in under three minutes—a new record.

He'd barely killed the engine on his Road King before he held out his hand and barked, "Off."

He didn't need to say it at all, his woman already in motion.

"In the truck."

She nodded and was reaching for the passenger door as he got off his hog and stomped his way around to the driver's side.

He was peeling out of his driveway without his seatbelt seconds later.

As he drove, Tess didn't say a word. Didn't ask a question. Didn't even flinch.

Mustang added that to the list of reasons why he thought he might just ride with her forever.

The five minutes it usually took for him to get to Trix's place took three in his rage. He came to a screeching halt in the parking lot, his truck filling two vacant spots, and him not the least bit concerned about it.

"Out," he growled before he bolted from his seat.

It took Tess a second longer to meet him in front of his truck, but she kept pace with him when he took her hand and dragged her behind him to Trix's second story unit, her heels clicking to the beat of her hurried steps.

When he was in front of the door he wanted, he pounded his fist loudly against it then immediately reached for the handle. It was locked, so he pounded again. He was two seconds away from striking it with his heel when he heard the deadbolt slide free before the door was opened.

"What the fuck?" Trix scoffed in greeting.

Mustang looked at Tess and demanded, "Stay right here."

She nodded and he let go of her hand as he stepped toward Trix and caught hold of her chin. He gripped her hard as he searched her eyes, and she tried but failed to fight against him.

"Mustang, let me go! You're such an asshole!"

She wasn't high. At least not yet.

This did not calm him down.

He freed her chin and brushed past her as she cried, "What are you doing? And who is she? Who are *you*?"

Mustang stopped dead in his tracks, twisted until he had line of sight to those gorgeous golden-brown eyes and said, "Not a fuckin' word."

She stared back at him, keeping those perfect lips closed, and he continued through the apartment.

The apartment that wreaked of weed.

Trix's bedroom door was cracked. He pushed it open, spotted MK on the bed, her eyes glued to the doorway, and headed straight for her. She was ready, arms extended in anticipation. As he scooped her up and against his chest, he said, "We're leavin', baby. Let's get some shoes on."

They hit her room just as Trix started down the hallway.

"You can't take her. It's Saturday! You don't get her until tomorrow," she hollered.

Mustang ignored her as he helped MK into the first pair of shoes he saw. When her feet were covered, he picked her up a second time, brushing Trix out of the way as he headed for the front door.

"Hey! I'm talking to you!"

Still ignoring her, he stopped in the still open doorway, his eyes on Tess as he said, "MK, this is my friend, Tess. She's gonna take you to the truck, alright?"

Tess nodded as MK murmured, "Okay, daddy."

He set his little girl on her feet, and Tess reached for her hand.

"Hi. I'm so glad to meet you," Tess said as they started for the truck.

MK looked back over her shoulder at Mustang, but Tess kept talking, recapturing her attention.

"Your dad always calls you MK when he talks about you. Do you mind if I call you Mary-Kate?"

Trix was still making a fuss behind him, but he tuned her out, blocking the exit as he watched his woman with his little girl. Seeing them hand in hand did something to him—something he felt down deep.

He'd known since the moment he laid eyes on Tess he wanted her.

After he'd had her, he knew he wanted more.

The more he learned about her, the more certain he became.

Without knowing it, she was who he'd been waiting for.

MK's hand tucked inside of hers, he admitted he didn't just want Tess for himself.

He wanted MK to have her, too.

Someone kind, nurturing, and beautiful inside and out.

There was plenty of him she hadn't yet seen—but he'd show her.

He'd make sure she accepted it. Accepted him.

He wouldn't have it any other way.

As soon as he'd lost sight of them on their trip down the stairs, he shifted his focus, turning his attention on the reason he was there.

He got in Trix's space, and her eyes got wide as she backed into the door.

"You? Shut the fuck up," he yelled.

He then looked into the living room. Trix's *friend* was on his feet—his blunt abandoned on the coffee table as he stared at Mustang in a dazed uncertainty.

"What'd I tell you?" sneered Mustang as he barreled toward the man. "What'd I tell you, motherfucker?!"

This time, when he had him by the shirt, Mustang didn't hold back. He slugged him hard across the cheek. Once. Twice. Three times.

Trix started yelling as the man tried to cower away from Mustang. He couldn't get small enough, Mustang's grip on his shirt preventing him from crumbling to the floor.

"Fuck, man. It's just weed!" he cried pathetically.

"I warned you, you dumb fuck. Did I not? Pretty sure I did."

Mustang punched him in the nose, until he heard it crack, then punched him once in the throat before he finally let go. The man collapsed in a heap on the floor, choking for air.

"What the hell is wrong with you?! Who do you think you are? Get out of here, you jackass!" screeched Trix.

Mustang turned on her then. She lost most of her bravado when she caught sight of his face, and she took two steps back.

"If I ever hear you tell my girl to stay behind a closed door while you or anyone else is out here gettin' high, I will relieve you of your duties as her mother," he warned.

She huffed, squaring her shoulders with new confidence as she argued, "You won't. I'll take you to court. I know shit—shit on you and the club. You won't get her."

"Try me, bitch. I *tolerate* you for her. I follow our court ordered custody agreement for *her*. But you *fuck* with my girl, I will go above the law. You want her? Fuckin' act like it, or she's mine."

He stormed out, buzzing with rage—MK's call still playing on repeat in his head.

When he reached the truck, he knew he needed to calm down.

He didn't get behind the wheel but stood outside the door and forced himself to breathe.

Glancing through the window, he locked eyes with Tess. He could see her worry, and he felt her fear—fear he could tell she was trying to hide.

It took him a minute, but when he felt in control, he opened the door and climbed into his seat.

He didn't look at Tess as he started the engine and began to back out of the parking space. When he pointed his truck toward home, he heard her breath catch, and he knew why. He could already feel his right hand starting to swell.

"Daddy?" MK called softly.

Mustang caught her hazel-blue eyes in her reflection of his rearview mirror.

"Can I have some strawberries and goldfish when we get home?"

"Yeah, baby," he said, refocusing his attention on the road. "I think we still have some berries."

It was then Tess reached over and gently coaxed his right hand off the steering wheel. He let her have it, and she brought it into her lap, carefully lacing her fingers between his with one hand, covering his bruised knuckles with his other.

He glanced at her, and he felt her fear had subsided.

Her golden-brown eyes were calm, and he saw all he needed to see.

His Tess, pretty in pink and wild like the wind, stared back at him unwaveringly.

Never before had he invited a woman he'd taken to bed into his home.

That was about to change.

CHAPTER *Twelve*

Tess

H is knuckles were swollen and bloody.

Whether or not it was his blood I couldn't tell.

It was obvious he'd beaten the shit out of someone.

My guess was the guy I'd seen in the apartment who appeared to be terrified as he watched Mustang's every move.

I hoped it wasn't the woman who was clearly Mary-Kate's mother. I prayed my man wasn't capable of laying hands on the mother of his child.

In a way, she was beautiful. One look at her and I could tell she didn't take great care of herself, but I also saw a woman who would have no trouble catching a man if she wanted.

Mary-Kate had inherited her curly hair and her nose.

But she had Mustang's eyes.

Ed's eyes.

I had so many questions—questions I knew I couldn't ask in the moment.

Mustang was still calming down, and the last thing I wanted to do was poke the bear.

We were mostly silent as we rode back to his house. It wasn't until we pulled into the driveway that I got a proper look at it.

We'd been in such a rush before, I was too distracted to notice the big, ranch style home on a spacious lot. He had a small deck that extended off his front porch. There was a built-in bench and two, cushioned Adirondack chairs in front of two large windows on the center of the house.

We pulled into his garage and Mustang extracted his hand from mine. I looked over at him just as he murmured, "Out, sugar."

I was *sugar* again, and I knew that meant he was coming back to himself.

We both got out and Mustang walked around the back of his truck to the rear passenger door. He had Mary-Kate propped against his chest in short order. I watched her cling to his neck with her temple pressed against his, and I saw how connected with one another they were. It wasn't just Mustang in his adult wisdom with the knowledge of his child—it was Mary-Kate, in her innocence, in tune with her father.

He caught my hand with his free one, and I trailed behind them into the house.

The door from the garage opened into a generous open floor plan. The kitchen and dining area were right in front of us, and his living room was toward the front of the house. As he led me into the belly of the kitchen, we passed a sliding glass door off the back of the house, and I glimpsed his screened-in porch and an absolutely gorgeous view.

He sat Mary-Kate down on the island counter and let go of my hand on his way to the fridge.

"Daddy, are you bleeding?" she asked, sounding worried.

He pulled a carton of strawberries out of the fridge with his unaffected hand, then paused to look down at his other—as if for the first time.

"Babe, let me help," I insisted, reaching for the fruit. "You need to ice that. Just, uh, point me in the direction of a cutting board."

I glanced around the room. He had about a million cabinets and drawers. I wondered if he'd managed to fill them all. If so, I was sure he was roughing it in my kitchen.

"Second drawer down. Right side of the stove," he told me. "Knives are in the block. I cut 'em in half."

"Got it," I assured him as I went about my task.

I heard him open up his freezer drawer and glanced back at him as he took out a bag of peas and unceremoniously plopped them over his knuckles. This was apparently all the attention he was going to give his hand, as he then went straight to the tall cabinet next to the fridge and pulled out a container of goldfish. I rinsed strawberries and listened as he poured out a few into a bowl.

"More, daddy!" Mary-Kate insisted on a giggle.

"We'll see about that. You eat those and your strawberries first."

After I'd halved a few, I carried the cutting board over to the island. Mary-Kate hummed her delight and immediately reached for one.

"Thank you," she said politely.

"You're welcome."

Mustang popped a strawberry in his mouth too, eliciting a gasp from his little one.

"Hey!"

Smiling, he muttered, "You can share, princess."

"Yeah, okay," she conceded, kicking her feet as she reached for another berry. "You can have one, too," she told me.

"Oh, thank you. That's so nice of you."

As I accepted her offer, Mustang pulled his phone from his pocket. He tapped the screen a few times, and Mary-Kate and I both watched him as he brought the device to his ear and waited. He didn't have to wait long.

"Yeah," he said, answering a question we couldn't hear. "Need to be at the bar tonight. Can she stay at your place?"

Uninterested in her father's conversation, Mary-Kate grabbed a goldfish, then looked at me and said, "You're pretty. How come I never met you before?"

I might not have had any children, but I knew they had a tendency to speak their mind, so her compliment felt like an invitation into their world I wouldn't dare take for granted.

"Thank you, Mary-Kate. I think you're pretty, too."

"Hey, what do you say?" asked Mustang, already pocketing his phone once more.

Mary-Kate, obviously familiar with his tone, looked up at him to find he was, indeed, speaking to her. This made her grin before she murmured, "Thank you." Looking to me again, she repeated, "How come I never met you before?"

"I only met her a few days ago, babe," Mustang interjected. "Hey, listen to me."

He waited until he had her attention before he continued.

"I've got to work tonight. You're gonna stay the night with Aunt Winnie and Uncle Roy."

Her whole body jolted in excitement before she cried, "Yay!"

Mustang chuckled. "Yeah. Figured as much." Jerking his chin, he instructed, "Finish up. I'm gonna go pack you a bag." To me he asked, "You okay here?"

"Yeah, of course."

I watched him walk out of the kitchen and disappear down a hallway between the kitchen and the living room. As I looked in that direction, I took in a few more details. He had a leather sectional couch in front of a big screen television he'd mounted to the wall. Behind the sitting area, to the right of the front door, he had a long narrow table with drawers and a shelf at the bottom. On the shelf were a pair of boots and tennis shoes that obviously belonged to him; and beside them were at least four pairs of little girl shoes in different colors and styles.

It was remarkable to me to be inside of Mustang's house which was so clearly a home. It lacked a feminine touch—it wasn't decorated, per say—but it had a certain lived-in comfort.

"Do you know my Aunt Winnie?" asked Mary-Kate, pulling me from my thoughts.

"I do, actually."

"She's Otto's mommy. Otto is my best friend. Whenever I stay with Aunt Winnie and Uncle Roy, we get to play all the time!"

"You know what? I saw Otto today. He was asking about you."

"You saw Otto? Where?!" she asked, those hazel-blue eyes wide in excitement.

She was adorable in a photograph—but she was radiant sitting in front of me.

"Your dad and I were at the clubhouse," I told her, speaking through a smile. "He was there with his brothers."

"Sometimes daddy takes me to the clubhouse, but not all the time," she said before consuming her last strawberry. "And sometimes I see Uncle Jed there, and he brings Lowe and Ax. They're my friends, too. But not like Otto. Otto is my *bestest* friend."

I noted how in the last two minutes, I'd learned the badass bikers I knew as Bull and Wrangler were also affectionally known as Uncle Roy and Uncle Jed—and I sort of loved that.

"Well, Otto missed not having you there today. I bet he'll be so excited to see you."

Just as I finished speaking, Mustang reappeared. He had a little pink backpack with multi-colored hearts scribbled in a pattern held in one hand, the bag of peas in his other. He went straight for the freezer and discarded the latter before turning to address me.

"Winnie was rounding up her crew. Should be here any minute now. I'll get MK's car seat loaded up in their cage, then we're back on the hog."

"Okay, babe."

As if right on cue, a knock sounded at the door.

"Down, daddy! I want to get it," insisted Mary-Kate.

Mustang helped her off the counter, and she took off the second her feet hit the floor.

"You wait for me before you open that door," he called out to her.

His words were for his daughter, but he was still looking at me.

I wasn't sure what he was saying as he stared, but I stared right back.

A second later, his fingers were in my hair and his lips were on mine for a short, hard kiss.

It was over before I knew it, and then he was halfway across the room, headed toward his daughter, who was bouncing in excitement.

The last hour had been a whirlwind—but as I watched him from where I stood at his kitchen island, I grappled with not a single doubt.

Father. Protector. Badass biker. Wild Stallion.

That was my man.

Mustang hadn't exaggerated. The lineup of bands that night was *awesome*. I was glad I'd been at the bar early to snag a seat, because it was standing room only by ten o'clock.

There was no way the crowd wasn't a fire-safety hazard.

There was also no way everyone in the crowd lived in Gillette.

Judging by the number of Wild Stallions patches I saw, I ventured to guess that a good number of that night's attendees had made the journey from Cheyenne or the chapters in our neighboring states.

Earlier on in the night, one such Stallion sidled up next to me at the bar. The patch on his chest let me know his road name was Pistol. He was, apparently, an enforcer—his final patch cluing me in that he belonged to the Missoula chapter. He ordered a drink, then proceeded to strike up a conversation with me. This lasted all of about ten seconds before Mustang hollered, "That one's not on the menu."

No sooner had he said it than Buck was at my back. He was younger than the other Stallion, but that didn't stop him from tapping him on the shoulder and suggesting he scram. The warning glare that came from behind the bar helped, too.

From that point on, Buck stayed close to keep me company.

Or, more accurately, mark me as off limits—but I preferred to consider him company.

I even made him talk to me a little, which was how I came to know he was a prospect with the club. He'd been working on earning his patches for the last nine months. He had one more to go before he was a fully patched member.

I wondered what all that entailed.

Obviously, babysitting wasn't off the table.

While a normal bar might have started to empty out after one A.M., Steel Mustang felt like the party was just getting started. Even though my phone hadn't rung all night, I cut myself off after my first ranch water. Experience told me I'd regret staying up into the wee hours, but I didn't want to leave. Not without Mustang.

At two in the morning, he and his bar manager—the redhead I'd learned was Phoenix—shut down alcohol service, which was reason enough for the revelers to go looking for a change of scenery.

Lucky for them, they didn't have to go far.

After the bar was emptied, when Mustang pulled me behind him through the clubhouse, I caught a glimpse of just how wild the Wild Stallions could get after dark. What I saw was nothing in comparison to what I'd seen the first night Mustang brought me there. Part of me wanted to stay and watch it all unfold—but a bigger part of me wanted to focus all my attention on just one man.

Mine.

Seeing as he didn't stop until he had me alone in his room, I knew we were on the same page.

We made quick work of removing each other's clothing, and it wasn't long before he had me flat across his bed.

He made me come with his fingers first.

A while later, a fistful of my hair in his grip, I came on my hands and knees with him inside of me.

Not long after that, he found his own climax before we both collapsed, panting for breath.

This time, when he left me to go deal with his condom, I didn't fall asleep.

My moment alone brought back the events of the day, and all the questions I hadn't yet had the chance to ask.

I was sitting with his top sheet tucked underneath my arms, my knees pulled up to my chest when Mustang returned. Whatever party was going on in the main room didn't sound like it was even close to dying down.

"Would've lost that bet," said Mustang as he dropped trou.

"What bet?" I murmured, admiring his nakedness as he came to join me between the sheets.

"Never fucked a woman capable of crashing as fast as you do after sex. Least not a sober one."

I hummed a laugh as I rested my cheek atop my knee.

He sat with his back propped against the wall behind the bed.

He was in a good mood, and my body still felt relaxed and sated, but there was a reason I was still awake—and I didn't want to keep it from him.

I dropped my gaze to look at his hand. The blood had long since been washed away, but bruises had started to form on the skin across his knuckles. Before we left his house earlier, he'd let me look at it. Begrudgingly. As soon as I was sure he hadn't broken anything, he wouldn't let me fuss over him anymore.

"Mustang?" I whispered, lifting my eyes to find his.

"Right here, sugar."

"What happened today? With Mary-Kate's mother?"

His demeanor shifted in the second it took me to blink.

It wasn't a chill I felt at the visible change I saw in his eyes, more like a silent warning to brace myself. So, I did. I sat up straight, hugging the sheet to my chest as I let my knees drop to the bed, angling my body toward his.

I was open. I was ready, and I wanted him to know that.

He received my message and started sharing.

"The only reason I don't have MK full time is because I've got a dick, not a pussy. I can't be her mom, and I know she needs one. I know because I did, and I've got a dick. When I lost mine, I felt it. Trix is a selfish bitch, but MK loves her, and I know I gotta respect that.

"She also knows shit about me and the club she shouldn't know. Met her when the Stallions were in a different place. Stuff she knows could get a brother popped if she played her cards right. Not sure she's smart enough to play those cards right, but she threatens me with that shit all the time.

"Trix walks a fine line. I tolerate her for my girl, but I sure as fuck don't need to tolerate the shit company she keeps—especially if it means they're gettin' high with MK closed up in another room. I don't have a stick up my ass. Trix wants to find an escape from her miserable life, all the power to her—just not when she's got MK.

"I grew up with an abusive parent who was hooked on his own drug, and I'll do what I've got to, to make sure my girl doesn't endure the same fate. I can't win every battle, but I will win this one. I'm prepared to fall on my sword if I have to. Trix keeps goin' down this road, I will get full custody, even if that means my MK hates me for it one day."

He'd laid it all out there, plain and simple. It was a lot to absorb, but he'd definitely filled in the blanks. He didn't mess around when it came to the safety and wellbeing of his daughter. I got that. I admired it, even. His tactics were a bit rough, but so was he.

He was a Stallion.

It was *that* realization which hit me anew.

I'd known since the moment I met him he was part of a motorcycle club—and not one of those clubs that got together just to ride for fun. It wasn't like the Wild Stallions were in the news for stirring up trouble—but it seemed unlikely they weren't the kind that stirred the pot every now and again. I'd just never seriously considered what that could look like.

I reached up and swept a bit of hair behind my ear, ignoring the nervous pang in my belly as I asked, "Um—what do you mean when you say *the Stallions were in a different place?*"

He studied me for a full minute, then warned, "Baby, you open this door—it don't shut."

I could feel my chest rising and falling as my breaths grew shallow. He was giving me the chance to change my mind—to keep my eyes closed and just enjoy the ride.

But I was his woman. I *wanted* to be his woman. I couldn't do that in a state of blind ignorance. I wouldn't. Moreover, if there was any chance the truth could break us, I needed to know before it was too late.

Before such a truth could destroy me.

"Mustang, I want to know."

He hesitated a minute longer, then gave it to me straight.

"Bull's the president of the Wild Stallions MC. Not just the Gillette chapter—the whole organization. He's a good man. A family man. He's business savvy, always thinkin' ten steps ahead. He was one of the founding members twenty-seven years ago—but he's only been our leader the last four, and he didn't earn his title simply by puttin' in the time. He fought for it. Lost blood and brothers for it. It was a hostile takeover during the club's darkest time."

My heart was pounding as he spoke.

I feared any attempts to brace myself for what was coming wouldn't be enough.

"Stallions have always been in the business of protection. The garage and the shop are legit—but we've got other ways of lining our pockets."

Protection seemed promising. Maybe even safe-ish. I could get on board with that.

"For a long time, we aided in the transport of drugs and guns across the Canadian border."

Okay—that part didn't seem so safe.

"Club rule stated we saw the drugs to where they needed to go, but we did not buy or sell them. We did not partake. None of the hard stuff. It was strictly for profit. We didn't want the hassle of any addicts in our ranks. The money was good, the work was consistent, we were reliable and therefore sought after. At least, that's how it was when I joined.

"I was nearly a decade in when we started expanding. Started multiple chapters and opened up garages in other towns. Things started to get messy. Fuckers started to get greedy. Brothers started using—including the highest ranked among us. Scorpion, our former prez, let shit slide. He wanted to start a stable. Prostitutes brought in drugs. That shit spread like a virus—and he was the worst infected.

"Six years ago, we weren't transporting only drugs and guns, we were trafficking people—mostly women, but sometimes girls. It was fucked, and not all of us were down to do that shit. A couple brothers left, some just took a hit in pay, refusing to take certain jobs—but Bull was the first among us to make a stand.

"Took nearly a year to recruit enough of us on his side. He was patient, smart. He didn't want an all-out civil war, but that didn't mean there wasn't a battle. We lost one of the best among us, but we won. In the end, we won."

He stopped his story, and I stared at him, feeling like he'd left out the most important part.

"But what does that mean? How are you different now?"

"No women. No trafficking, no stable—none of that. A woman shows up here wanting Stallion dick, she earns her keep, but we don't sell her pussy."

I nodded, still trying to absorb it all.

No women. No human trafficking. That was a marked improvement.

Holy hell, how was I even having this conversation?

"And, um, what about the drugs and the guns?"

"No drugs. That was a harder sell—but that's part of the reason I opened Steel Mustang, as another source of income for the club."

No human trafficking. No drugs.

"And the guns?"

"Still move guns, baby. Protect the right people for the right cash, too."

I shook my head in confusion. "What does that mean?"

"Means someone needs to get from point A to point B, we don't ask questions, we just get them there."

I pulled my bottom lip between my teeth and gnawed on it a little.

I wasn't sure my brain had the energy to fully process most of what he'd shared, but I felt pretty clear on what they *weren't* doing. Mostly. They'd been into some dangerous, very illegal activities—but I didn't know what a *battle* amongst his brothers entailed. Not to mention, I didn't imagine one could be in the *guns* and *drug* business without meeting some very questionable people.

"But you don't, like..." I stopped myself and frowned, uncertain if I could finish the question.

"Spit it out, sugar. You opened the door. You best walk through it."

I licked my lips anxiously then blurted, "You don't kill people, do you?"

It wasn't until I said it that I realized that was my line. I didn't have the capacity right then to figure out what that said about me, but nothing he'd said made me want to run. Not yet, anyway.

He quirked an eyebrow, but there was no humor in his expression.

"We're not hired assassins and the Stallions aren't a gang—but we're not martyrs, either. We're outlaws. In a kill or be killed situation, we do what we have to."

I felt short of breath, suddenly worried about the prospect of Mustang in a kill or be killed situation.

"Does that—does that happen a lot? To you? I mean—how often is that a choice you have to make?"

"No, baby. There's a reason the patch on the front of my kutte says Sergeant-at-Arms and not VP or Enforcer. Bull wanted me to be his right hand, but it wasn't a job I wanted. We made a compromise. I lean in where I'm needed, I keep my brothers in line, but Steel Mustang is my bread and butter."

For the first time since we started down this line of conversation, I pulled in a deep breath, filling my lungs completely before letting it all out on a sigh.

Mustang watched me, his hazel-blue irises painting every inch of my face.

"Any of that change this?" he asked, motioning between us.

For a second, I thought about how I would feel if I got up, got dressed, and walked out of his door for good. Even after everything he'd told me, just the thought of that made me ache all over—and not in a good way.

We'd known each other for a matter of *days*, and we'd just discussed the circumstances under which he or one of his kind might kill someone—which would likely involve gun trafficking, or some shady protection run. Yet, as crazy as it sounded, it wasn't altogether unbelievable. He was a Wild Stallion. I wasn't under the impression they garnered their reputation around town by selling candy bars door to door.

What was more unfathomable was my desire to stay.

Except, that didn't seem to fit my current circumstance, either.

We were in a relationship. Not twenty-four hours ago, I told him I had no plans of bailing on said relationship any time soon.

We hadn't known each other long, but Mustang was the one constantly reminding me how we knew *enough*. We knew enough to want more. He knew enough to trust me with the truth, and I knew enough to be sure he wasn't a monster. He was far more complicated than that.

I dropped the sheet I held around my chest and crawled toward him, until I was straddling his lap. I took his hands in mine, lacing our fingers together as I tried to think of the words to say.

"I won't lie to you. I don't know what to do with most of what you just said. And, honestly, seeing you this afternoon—how angry you were—it caught me off guard, and it scared me a little. But I'm not so naïve as to think you didn't have it in you. You're a Stallion, not a Boy Scout."

"Should go without sayin', I'd never lay a hand on you, sugar."

"I know, I know," I insisted on a whisper.

I leaned toward him, touching my forehead to his as I let my eyes fall closed.

I pictured him, holding Mary-Kate against his chest, her temple pressed to his.

I remembered our first ride—me holding onto him as we sped down the highway on his Harley in the dark of night.

He was wild, but he wasn't reckless, and he was mine if I wanted him.

And I still wanted him.

"I understand you are a man who will do whatever you have to in order to protect your brothers and your family. You said Stallions have always been in the business of protection and—babe?" I pulled way enough to see into his eyes. "I've never been with a man who's made me feel safer."

I meant that. In more ways than one.

"Fuck," he muttered a second before he crushed his lips against mine.

He extracted one of his hands from my grip, then reached up and buried his fingers in my hair. I hummed into his mouth as he swept his tongue through mine, kissing me deep and greedy—the Mustang way.

He pulled back abruptly, my hair in his fist, and his lips still grazing mine when he said, "I'm gonna need you to put my dick in your mouth. Get me hard, baby, 'cause I plan on fuckin' you again as soon as I am."

My lips spread into a smile and a thrill rushed up my spine.

That was my man.

I pressed a soft kiss against the corner of his mouth—then I did as I was told.

He fucked me again.

It was out of this world.

When he went to discard his condom, I was out like a light when he got back.

CHAPTER *Thirteen*

One Week Later

L ATE ON SUNDAY MORNING, Mustang had dropped me off at home, and I spent the rest of the day doing laundry and preparing for the week ahead—which included a nap.

On Monday I got through my day shift with the anticipation of my dinner plans. Mustang and Mary-Kate picked me up at six, and we went to Railyard. Just as excited as I was, Mary-Kate had *insisted* she needed to dress up for the occasion, which meant Mustang had been dragged to the store so she could pick out her new sleeveless, cotton summer dress covered in watermelon print.

I loved it.

I loved it more that she'd dragged Mustang to the store to buy it.

Even more than that, I loved knowing my man didn't get dragged anywhere, which meant he wanted her to have the dress she insisted she needed.

After waking up without Mustang Tuesday morning, I was actually relieved I had a double shift to work. In a matter of days, the man had barged into my life so completely, I found it took hardly any time at all for me to miss him.

I was still lost in a free fall.

He promised to catch me, so I did nothing to stop it.

Wednesday afternoon, I came home to find a Harley parked on the curb and my man in the kitchen. I took this to mean there was no drama with Trix, which he confirmed.

He fed me. He fucked me. I passed out and he left for work.

Thursday morning, he was back making me breakfast, and I continued my fall.

Mustang took me back to Deadwood that night, and we had Italian for dinner.

When we got back to my place—we didn't even make it to the bedroom.

I'd never look at my stairs without thinking of him again.

Friday night, before I left for work, I taped a note on my fridge.

It read: *It's my turn to feed you. You'll just have to hold your horses until I wake up.*

Now it was Saturday afternoon. I checked my phone to make sure I hadn't missed anything, and then I made a quick trip to the bathroom. I handled my business then brushed my teeth, running my fingers through my hair a few times before I decided it was good enough. I didn't bother getting fully dressed, certain my nightshirt would suffice for the meal I had in mind.

When I reached the bottom of the stairs, I found Mustang on the couch, his feet on my coffee table, the TV on with the volume turned down low, and his phone in his hand.

He'd held his horses.

I grinned.

His eyes found mine and I said, "Hi, babe."

He set his phone down and replied, "That's the best you got?"

I crossed the room, pressed a knee onto the couch, kicked my opposite leg over his, and settled down on his lap. Then I sank my fingers in his hair, tilting his head back slightly, and gave him my mouth.

He took over from there, caging me in his arms as he kissed me greedy.

It was marvelous.

When he pulled away, his hazel-blue eyes were vibrant and warm.

"Better," he muttered.

I laughed softly before I asked, "You hungry?"

"Yeah, baby."

"'Kay. We're having breakfast for lunch," I told him. Then I frowned, considering what I'd said. "Wait—that's brunch. We're having brunch," I amended, maneuvering myself off the couch.

"Whatever you call it, get to it, sugar," he replied, a half-smile tugging at his lips.

Twenty minutes later, I was practically giddy watching him shovel my banana pancakes into his mouth.

"MK would devour this," he told me, pointing his fork at his plate.

I finished my bite then offered, "Maybe I could make them for her some time."

"How 'bout tomorrow?"

I smiled huge. "Okay."

"Pack a bag. You'll stay at my place tonight. We'll pick her up mid-morning, spend the day. You've got dinner duty—or whatever the hell you call breakfast for dinner."

My smile softened as he stuck his fork through a triple-stacked bite of pancake.

"Your place, as in—your house?"

It hadn't escaped me that while he had constant access to my home, I'd only been to his place once—and that had been an emergency situation. He lived less than five minutes from Steel Mustang, but if we weren't in my bed, we slept in his room at the clubhouse.

I'd never really read into it, until after I met Mary-Kate. Even then, I understood his home wasn't just *his* place, it was *theirs*. I respected that boundary wholeheartedly.

That also meant I felt the significance of his invitation now.

He quirked an eyebrow at me, his pending bite waiting in a puddle of syrup.

"Only room in the clubhouse I want you naked is mine. You want a shower you'll do it at my place. No point in sleepin' at the clubhouse if we'll wind up under my roof anyway."

Practicality aside, I still reveled in what our plans implied.

Before he could take his next bite, I dropped my fork, placed my hand at the back of his neck, and drew him to me for a kiss.

He didn't resist.

He tasted like banana and maple syrup.

I had half a mind to abandon the rest of my meal in order to feast on him when he pulled away and said, "Gotta get that, sugar."

It wasn't until he spoke that I heard the vibration of his phone in his pocket.

I nodded as I let him go.

"Yeah?" he answered shortly.

I took my next bite, chewing slowly as I felt the shift in his demeanor.

He reached up and raked his fingers through his hair as he replied, "Need twenty minutes."

Whoever he was speaking to responded, then Mustang disconnected without even a grunt of goodbye.

"Everything okay?"

"Club business. I've got to go." Even after he said it, he shoveled another bite of pancakes into his mouth and immediately started spearing the last of what was on his plate onto his fork.

"Oh. Alright."

Armed with my new awareness of what *club business* might be, I wasn't so sure I wanted anymore of my lunch.

"Should I—"

"Pack that bag. We'll meet at the bar later. Not sure how long this'll take, so plan on after dinner. I'll let you know if any of that changes."

He took his last bite, and my uncertainty increased.

As if he could sense my mood as easily as I'd felt his, he slowed down enough to look at me and say, "Tess, what'd I tell you?"

I shook my head, not sure what he was referencing. "About what?"

"I lean in where I'm needed—don't find myself on the wrong end of a barrel every time there's club business to be handled. You need peace, that's what I've got to give. I'm not givin' you a play-by-play every time I walk out that door. You know what you know, and that's enough. You're just gonna have to trust me."

It would have been a lie to say I'd wrapped my head around all he'd shared the previous weekend. It was more of a work in progress. Still, I reminded myself he'd been a Wild Stallion for almost twenty years, then I reminded myself he'd trusted *me* with the truth of what that meant.

He was right. I'd made my choice. I needed to trust him.

"Tonight. Meet at the bar," I murmured.

He jerked his chin in a nod, stood and pocketed his phone, then leaned down to press a quick, hard kiss against my lips.

"Later, baby."

"Bye, Mustang," I said as he went.

I didn't finish my plate, but I did work on being okay with the fact that my man was off doing *club business* while I cleaned the kitchen. This was the first time he'd been called away to do such a thing when he was with me, but it wasn't going to be the last. I wanted to be his woman, not his weak link. I was going to have to get used to this part of our relationship, so I made it a point to do more than sit around and worry.

After I was finished with the dishes, I went to pack an overnight bag. Then I hopped in the shower, taking extra time to shave and wash my hair. I was dressed and getting ready to power on my blow drier when I heard my phone ring. I hurried back to my room, hoping it was Mustang.

It wasn't him.

But it wasn't disappointment I felt when I read the name on my screen.

A different sort of worry twisted my stomach when I answered Mitchell's call.

I'd been to see Sharon less than twenty-four hours ago, and she slept the entire visit. That week, she'd been significantly frailer and more lethargic with no appetite. We all knew she was getting close.

"Hi, Mitch," I answered gently.

"Tess—will you come? Please?"

Even though he couldn't see me do it, I nodded.

"Of course. I'll be there as soon as I can."

We disconnected without further discussion, and I went to grab a fresh pair of scrubs.

Ten minutes later, on my way out the door, I shot Mustang a text.

I got called into work. Not sure how long I'll be. Will keep you posted.

Three hours later, Sharon breathed her last, surrounded by the ones she loved most in the world. It was a couple of hours after that before they were ready to say goodbye. I gave them the space they needed, helping with little Emilia until she fell asleep next to me on the couch. Around eight o'clock, Renee came out to switch places with me, informing me both Mitchell and Lance were ready for me to make the necessary calls to have Sharon's body picked up and taken to the funeral home.

I stepped out onto the porch to make my calls and to get a little fresh air. The sun was starting to set, and the sky was painted in orange and pink hues. It was peaceful, just as Sharon's passing had been, and I found it incredibly comforting.

Having reached the people with whom I needed to speak, I decided to take advantage of my moment alone and call Mustang. I wasn't sure if he'd answer, but I wanted to try to hear his voice before I settled for a text.

He answered on the fourth ring.

"Hey, baby. You on your way?"

I could hear the muffled sounds of the bar in the background, and I was sure he'd stepped into the back hallway to take my call. I frowned, realizing I actually didn't feel up to hanging out at the bar until closing—even if Mustang was there.

"No, actually. I'll be a little while longer. But, babe, I'm not sure the bar is where I want to be tonight. My patient died, and I'm feeling a bit drained. Maybe we should just plan on meeting in the morning?"

He hesitated a couple seconds, then said, "Stop by the bar. I'll give you my key, you can let yourself in."

I dropped my gaze to my sneakers.

I liked that idea. A lot.

Still, I asked, "Are you sure?"

"Tess? Stop by the bar. I'll give you my key."

I could picture his face as he repeated himself, the same face he made every time he felt the need to drive his point home, and a small smile tugged at my lips.

"Okay. I'll text you when I'm on my way."

"Sugar?"

"Yeah?"

"You good?"

I brought my gaze back up to admire the colors streaked across the sky with the rapidly setting sun.

"Yeah. I'm good," I answered honestly.

"See you in a bit."

"Bye, babe."

He disconnected and I slipped my phone into my pocket but didn't turn to head back inside. I wanted to watch the sun disappear.

It was almost over the horizon when the front door opened, and Lance stepped outside.

His blond hair was tousled, as if he'd been running his fingers through it, and his eyes were red-rimmed. He'd been pretty quiet since I arrived, and I felt for him. I really did.

"Hey," he muttered softly, shutting the door behind him.

"Hi, Lance. Is there anything I can do for you?" I asked carefully.

He furrowed his brow, shoving his hands into the pockets of his jeans. He stared at me for a minute, and I didn't break his silence, sensitive to his state of mind.

Finally, he said, "It's strange. You've been a part of our lives for months. Now, what, I just won't see you anymore?"

"Well," I began, thinking fast in an effort to choose my words wisely. "Gillette isn't so big that we won't run into each other from time to time, I'm sure."

"And what if I want to see you more than that?"

"Oh, Lance, I—"

"We wouldn't have been able to get through this without you," he interrupted, taking a step closer to me. "I—*I* wouldn't have been able to get through this without you. The way you kept my brother and me from ripping each other's heads off? Reminding us of what was important."

"Lance," I tried once more.

I gasped in surprise when he yanked his hands from his pockets and pulled me into his arms. He held me so tightly my own arms were pinned to my sides. I froze and tried to assess exactly what was happening.

For a moment, he just hugged me. Thinking it was something he needed, I let him. When I felt his nose tickle my neck, I began to squirm in his hold.

"Lance? What are you—?"

"I don't want to leave it to chance," he said, his hands moving across my back, as if he was exploring me.

I was beginning to panic, my breaths coming short and fast as I continued to try and wriggle out of his hold. His lips touched my jaw just when I was able to yank my hands free and shove them against his chest.

"Lance!"

My tone and my touch were enough to get him to take a step back, and we stared at each other for what felt like ages, but was probably only ten seconds, as I tried to get my breathing under control.

When I had my wits about me, I calmly but firmly explained, "I understand this is a difficult time. You're hurting, and you're longing for comfort. I'm sorry, but I cannot be that for you. It's not appropriate. Please—please go back inside and be with your family."

He balled his hands into fists and released them a couple of times, then took a deep breath and let it out in a huff. "I'm sorry. Shit timing," he said, taking another step away from me. He ran his fingers through his hair, shook his head, then continued, "I—I can't go back in there. I think I'll go for a walk."

I watched him leave before I sank my fingers in my own hair, pulling it away from my face and clinching it into my fists as I tried to shake off what just happened. While Lance's behavior hadn't come as a total surprise, it still totally sucked, and I was definitely ready to get out of there. Preferring to be inside with the others and not alone when Lance returned, I went back into the house to wait for the funeral home staff to arrive.

It was another forty-five minutes before Sharon's body was collected. Sad as it was to say goodbye to Mitchell, Renee, and their daughters, I was relieved to close myself into the confines of my car, and happy I'd tossed my overnight bag in the backseat before I left home.

Lance had come back to see his mother taken away but didn't say a word to me before I left. I'd told him earlier that maybe we'd see each other around town, but as I pulled out of Sharon's driveway and onto Ramshorn Avenue for the last time, I hoped it wasn't true.

I headed straight to Steel Mustang. The parking lot looked like it usually did on a Saturday night just before the headline band took the stage—full. Nonetheless, guessing by the number of motorcycles parked out front, I assumed the crowd was a little smaller than it had been the week before, no out-of-town Stallions around to party hard all night. As I approached the entrance, I didn't feel a thrill of excitement at the prospect of going inside, but I did feel a longing I couldn't put into words.

When I stepped through the door, Wrangler was there, leaned

against the wall, his arms folded across his chest. He jerked his chin at me in greeting and I waved before making my way back toward the bar. The second my eyes landed on Mustang, that longing I felt intensified. He was busy, handing off a couple draft beers to a customer, but I didn't have to wait long before he noticed me.

When his hands were free, as if he felt my stare, he looked over at me, and those eyes of his made me stop dead in my tracks. He studied me a moment, then muttered something to Phoenix before making his way out from behind the bar. I watched him disappear behind one swinging door only to watch him prowl through another. I reached for him as he drew near, and he didn't stop until I was burrowed deep into his chest, one of his arms wrapped tight around my back, his other raised so he could bury his fingers in my hair. I slid my arms underneath his kutte, splaying my hands across the hard surface of his back.

I closed my eyes, breathed in deep, and held on tight.

The scent of leather, fresh air, and pine engulfed me.

Instantly, I felt safe and far from alone.

My man held me until I was ready to let go.

Right there, in the middle of his bar.

Like he didn't care where we were.

And I loved it.

When I pulled away enough to look up at him, he loosened his hold on me, then signaled with a tilt of his head toward the exit. I nodded, and he tucked me under his arm as we headed back toward the door I'd just entered. Once outside, he reached into his pocket and pulled out a key, dangling from an otherwise empty ring.

"Code to the garage is oh-four-two-five. MK's birthday, if that'll help you remember."

I took the key, repeating the number aloud.

"You remember how to get there?"

"Yeah, I'm pretty sure."

"Things taper off, I'll put Wrangler behind the bar, be home as soon as I can."

I didn't tell him how much I wanted that. I didn't want to be needy.

Death was part of my job. I was around it often enough, I knew how to handle myself when I lost a patient. It was what happened with Lance that had me feeling off—but I'd handled that, too. I just needed to let it go.

Rather than tell him what I was thinking, I merely said, "Do what you have to, babe. No rush. I'll probably just grab a shower and crawl into bed, if that's okay."

"Bedroom's not hard to find. Shower's not hard to operate. You want to watch TV, remote's either on the dresser or the nightstand."

"Okay."

His eyes searched my face before he dropped a hand and squeezed one side of my butt.

I couldn't help but to smile.

His mouth tipped in a smirk before he said, "See you in a bit, sugar."

I found Mustang's house with little trouble and let myself inside, fumbling for light switches as I moved from one room to the next. It felt a little bit like snooping, but I poked my head into every room I passed in search of his.

There were five doors down the hallway.

The first was a room, just behind the living area, which Mustang obviously used as a home gym. A Wild Stallions flag hung on one of the walls.

The second led to a bathroom. Like everything else I'd seen, it was clean and functional, but lacking any décor. Though, the shower curtain in there was pink, purple, and teal mermaid print, and Mary-Kate got credit for that.

Across the hallway from the bathroom was a linen closet. Pleased to have stumbled across his collection of towels, I grabbed one and proceeded with my exploration.

The third door to the left was Mary-Kate's room. I paused a moment to admire it. It really was a room fit for a princess. She had a simple, wooden canopy bed draped with sheer, cream linen across the top and down the sides. Her bedding was a rosy pink, and it matched the printed pink area rug situated in the middle of the room. There were low-hung shelves with books along one wall, and baskets stuffed with playthings along another. Above it, in pink painted wooden letters, her initials had been mounted. It was perfect.

Finally, I passed through the second door on the right side of the hall, knowing it was my final destination. I wasn't at all surprised to find a simple, masculine room—but I instantly loved it for all that made it different from his room at the clubhouse.

He had a large headboard made of dark, distressed wood. His nightstands and the dresser, which also served as his TV stand across from his bed, looked to match. His bedding was dark gray, and the large rug he had underneath the bed was patterned with beige, gray, and black. On the opposite side of the room from where I stood was a bay window, built into the wall to create a sort of bench. I was sure it offered an amazing view, out across his backyard and the horizon beyond.

That's where I set my overnight bag before I gathered what I needed for a shower. His master bathroom and adjoining closet were behind a sliding farmhouse door and easily twice the size of mine. His shower was awesome, and I let the water beat down on my neck and shoulders for a few minutes before I washed up and got out.

Since I tended to sleep naked with Mustang, I hadn't packed anything to wear to bed. Not in the mood to be naked in his bed without him, I decided to borrow something from his wardrobe. When I found a faded, black Harley Davidson tee, I knew I need search no further. I slipped into it, turned out the lights, then tucked myself between Mustang's sheets.

I was drained, but not exhausted, which meant I didn't crash as soon as my head hit the pillow. I thought about the events of the day—the good and the bad—and where I found myself. Then I remembered the first time I woke to find Mustang in my kitchen cooking me breakfast.

'You take care of people all day. Who's takin' care of you?'

He was. He was taking care of me in ways I never imagined a man could.

I'd always hoped I'd find a man who would at least appreciate what I did for a living—to the point that he wouldn't get upset if a patient called me away in the middle of the night or during a date; a man who understood why sometimes it took me a little longer to get to the grocery store or that I typically couldn't hit the town with the intention of getting drunk because I couldn't afford to be inebriated, just in case.

But Mustang didn't simply understand—he filled my fridge when he thought it looked empty. One time he dug my phone out of my purse and put it on the nightstand when I forgot and passed out after sex. He didn't get annoyed by my weird sleeping schedule; he worked around it so he could be with me as often as he wanted.

My badass biker was hard on the outside but sweet on the inside.

I wondered then about his mom. I wondered what she'd been like and how she'd loved. I knew Mustang had learned to love by her example, and I wished I could thank her for it.

How she died was still a mystery to me—still a part of the puzzle I hadn't pieced together. Neither father nor son had volunteered the information, and I wondered if they ever would or if I'd have to extract it myself.

It wasn't long before I started to doze, drifting in and out of my thoughts. I didn't hear it when Mustang got home, but I did feel it when he climbed into bed with me.

"Hi," I whispered into the darkness.

"You good, baby?"

He reached for me, his warm, calloused palm skimming my bare thigh. It made me want to kiss him. Everything about that moment made me want to kiss him—his touch, him asking if I was good, the fact that we were in his bed for the first time—all of it reignited the longing I'd felt when I walked into his bar hours earlier.

I leaned into him, searching for his mouth with my own. When I found it, I answered him with a kiss. Like always, he didn't disappoint. He reciprocated—deep and wet. Except, rather than completely take over, I could tell he was following my lead. That sent a spark of excitement right through me, turning me on.

I rolled into him, and he let me, putting him flat on his back with my legs straddling his hips. It dawned on me then, he'd taken me fast and hard a number of times, but I'd yet to ride him.

Suddenly, that's all I wanted to do.

Humming into his mouth, I ground my naked sex against the growing bulge in his boxer briefs, hinting at my desire. He jerked his hips up in response, submerging the fingers of one hand into my hair, keeping me close as he kissed me deeper still. When I felt his arm snake around my waist, I broke our kiss, afraid he'd have me on *my* back before I got my chance.

"I want to ride you, Mustang," I insisted breathlessly.

He shot upright, taking me with him, his lips grazing mine as he said, "You want a ride, you got it, sugar—but we do that shit with the light on so I can watch my Tess get wild."

I shivered in anticipation, and I was sure he felt it because the next thing I knew, I was no longer in his shirt. With his arm around my waist keeping me stable, he then reached toward his nightstand in order to switch on his lamp. That done, he pulled open the drawer and grabbed a condom. Working around me, he stretched out, lifted his hips, and shoved his underwear out of our way before he sheathed himself.

Finally, he sat up once more, crushed his lips against mine in a bruising kiss, then muttered, "Take what you want, baby."

I didn't hesitate.

Hand against his chest, I pushed him onto his back, then teased us both as I grazed my sex along his hard length, coating the condom. When I was ready, I grabbed hold of him, positioned him at my entrance, and took him inside me.

Then I rode.

I rocked my hips slowly at first, luxuriating in the feel of him filling me full. Soon, my need began to grow in intensity. With my hands spread open across Mustang's abs, I leaned forward and picked up the pace. As I stoked the fire of my own pleasure with his body, he never took his eyes off of me. I couldn't explain why, but that made me even more wanton.

I bucked my hips harder, chasing the high I only ever felt when I was with Mustang. When he reached up to fondle my breasts, I let my head fall back as I surrendered to the sensation of his touch.

"Oh, my god," I moaned.

I could feel the orgasm building inside of me and knew it was going to be huge—but I had to reach for it. So, I thrust faster, harder, panting in my desperation.

When Mustang pinched my nipples, he got to see his Tess get wild.

I righted my head and dug my fingertips into his belly as I cried out, giving him all I had.

"*Mustang*—oh, god! *More*," I begged, on the brink.

He abandoned my nipples, grabbing hold of my thigh with one hand as the thumb of his other made contact with my clit.

That did it.

And I was right.

My orgasm was huge.

All I could do was hold on, my hands gripping his sides as I trembled uncontrollably.

Mustang's groan mingled with my moan, but he wasn't done.

I was still coming when he grabbed hold of my hips and began pounding into me from below. It was too much, but it hurt so good.

Fortunately, he wasn't too far behind me.

"Fuck, baby," he grunted, his rhythm soon broken as he found his release.

He pummeled inside of me twice more, lingering each time as his muscles locked, pleasure washing over him.

After his last thrust, I collapsed onto his chest, my skin damp with a thin layer of sweat.

I didn't know it until I'd taken it—but that was exactly what I needed.

Neither of us moved as we caught our breath, and I could have stayed on top of him all night. Too soon, I lost him from inside of me before he reached down, grabbed one side of my butt and muttered, "Got to get out of this condom, sugar."

I kissed his neck in acknowledgment, then reluctantly dismounted, curling up beside him. It was when he sat up, and I found myself staring at his Stallions tattoo, that I remembered how he'd left me in my kitchen earlier. The day had gotten away from me, and I hadn't asked how things had gone on his end.

"Babe?" I called gently, just as his feet hit the ground.

He looked back at me from over his shoulder in reply.

"Um, how did it go today?" I stammered, not sure the best way to bring up the topic.

There was a chance it wasn't my place to bring it up at all—but I'd opened the door, and he'd pulled me through it.

"With club business, I mean," I clarified. "Is everything okay?"

"For now. Nothin' for you to worry about, baby."

When he didn't say more, but stood and disappeared into the bathroom, I understood. I needed to trust him. Moreover, I needed to learn to trust the Wild Stallions, as a whole, to protect each other. To protect my man. Whatever that looked like.

I wasn't entirely sure how I was going to do that, but I wasn't going anywhere, which meant I had time to figure it out.

For now, sated and content in a way I hadn't anticipated feeling after the events of my night, I closed my eyes and waited for Mustang's return. I was already drifting towards sleep when I heard him click off the lamp before climbing into bed. Without even looking, I reached for him, and I sensed him lifting his arm in invitation. Snuggled up against his warm, solid chest, I fell asleep in the safest place I'd ever known.

I woke the next morning on my belly, naked, Mustang's knuckles grazing gently up and down my spine. The sun was peeking through the blinds at his bay window, and I turned my head on the pillow, in search of my man. My eyes caught his hazel-blue ones already staring at me.

"How's this go?" he asked in lieu of good morning. "I need to treat you with kid gloves today or what?"

I smiled sleepily at my badass biker, reaching over to graze my fingers along his bearded cheek. "No, sweetheart. I'll be okay. She was ready to go, and I was ready to help her."

A slight frown tugged at my brow as memories of Lance flashed before my eyes.

"Yesterday was harder than normal because the family—well, one of her sons, he didn't take it well. He was hurting and didn't know what to do with his grief. But I handled it."

"So, you're good?"

My smile got bigger, and I fell a little harder before I replied, "Last night helped. And I think a day spent with my badass biker and his little princess will make me feel even better."

"Think I can manage that. You starved, or do you mind if we go get MK before we eat?"

"Wouldn't mind a coffee on our way out."

"I can manage that, too."

Thirty minutes later, we were in his truck, on our way to get Mary-Kate.

I couldn't remember a better Sunday than the one I had with the two of them.

We played, we laughed, and we ate way too many banana pancakes.

I'd been invited into their world, and I loved every minute of it.

That night, I went to bed alone in my own bed—but I did it feeling happy.

CHAPTER
Fourteen

I T WAS LATE THURSDAY afternoon, and I was on my way home after my last patient of the day. I planned on staying only long enough to freshen up and pack an overnight bag. My car needed an oil change. Seeing as I was dating a Stallion, it only made sense I take it to the garage on the compound.

The garage would close for the day shortly after I arrived, but Mustang had arranged for me to drop it off before they locked up so it could be a priority first thing the next morning. My overnight bag was needed on account of I was going to spend the night at his place, which solved the issue of being carless until the following day.

We'd also planned to stay in for the night.

Well—mostly.

He was going to cook me dinner, and after the sun went down, we were going to go for a ride.

We'd reached July, which meant the days were hot, but the evenings were cool, and the forecast was all but begging us to get out on his hog. I hadn't been on the back of his Harley in a week, and I was itching for a chance to feel the freedom I could only find wrapped around my man, out on the open road with the wind in my hair.

As I pulled into my garage, I was mentally going through my closet, trying to decide what I wanted to wear for a date night *in*. I hadn't yet made up my mind when I walked into my house and immediately forgot what I was thinking.

This was because it smelled like fresh paint.

A lot of fresh paint.

I dropped my purse at the foot of the stairs, my eyes staring at my walls, painted *natural linen*, a shade I'd so carefully selected ages ago. I walked further into my house to find that no longer were my living room and my kitchen—two rooms that shared a wall—different colors.

'Tell me what color in what room. Brothers and I'll come finish the job one day while you're at work.'

I coughed out a laugh of disbelief, shaking my head even though there was no one there to see me do it. Then I hurried for the stairs, curious to know if they got it all.

I smiled huge when I hit my bathroom and found it was painted a beautiful subtle green with gray undertones—the shade titled *sea salt*. For a moment, I just stood there, gaping.

In one day, Mustang and his brothers had done what I'd only dreamed of doing since I'd bought the house. I barely even remembered he'd made the offer. I'd seen him that morning before I left to start my shift, and I had no idea how he planned on spending his day.

Now I knew.

I still didn't have any idea what to wear for a date night in, but I hardly cared anymore. All that mattered was I get to him as soon as I possibly could.

I raced into my room, grabbed my overnight bag, and started chucking clothes inside. I stuffed it full, thinking I'd sort an outfit from the mess later. After a quick return trip to the bathroom for a few toiletries, I was bounding down the stairs. I snatched up my purse on my way out, and I was behind the wheel restarting my engine in no time.

It took me ten minutes too long to reach the compound. I parked on the side of the garage and left everything inside of my car, not even bothering to lock it as I headed for the clubhouse.

I was dating a Wild Stallion. I wasn't worried about leaving my car unlocked on Stallions property. I was on a mission, and it was quite urgent.

I took two steps into the clubhouse and stopped, my eyes hunting for Mustang.

When I clocked him, near the back of the room playing pool with Maverick, I started in his direction. I was still in my sneakers, which meant he couldn't hear my approach over the music that played through the sound system.

I was twenty feet away when I called, "Hey!"

Both he and Maverick looked my way, but my gaze collided with two pools of hazel-blue and held on—my feet carrying me straight to him without missing a beat.

I knew he understood what I was after when he set his pool cue down and braced. I took my last few steps at a run, then leapt toward him, daring him to catch me.

He didn't disappoint.

My legs wrapped around his waist, my arms circled around his neck, I brought my lips down on his for a long, hard, flipping *greedy* kiss.

Maverick laughed.

Someone whistled.

I didn't care who was watching—I was too busy thanking my man.

After I'd kissed him until I couldn't breathe, I pulled away only far enough for me to bring my hands to either side of his face and look him in the eye as I murmured, "I'm seconds from the bottom, babe. If you don't catch me, I'll die at the rate I'm falling."

I felt as much as I saw his face break out in a grin before he replied, "Sugar, you already fucked your man on the landing pad."

"What?" I asked in confusion, still trying to catch my breath.

"You think I let just any bitch in the bed under my roof?"

This time, I didn't bristle at his question.

Instead, my breath caught as a zing sparked in my belly.

He wasn't finished.

"Only you, baby," he muttered softly. "First and last, I get my way."

All the air in my lungs left me in a whoosh.

I no longer wanted to be in a room full of people anymore.

"Mustang?"

"Right here, Tess."

"I'm going to need you to take me down the hall. Like, right now."

He chuckled as he started for the hallway, and a thrill raced up my spine.

He made quick work of two orgasms, and I prayed no one heard me enjoy either of them.

Then again, if they did, they'd know only that my man knew how to get the job done.

Mustang was pulling his jeans up over his hips when he looked back at me and asked, "This the thanks I get when I paint, what do I get if I build you somethin'?"

I only grinned coyly in response before I got up in search of my scrubs.

"I'm gonna hit the can then pull your car in the garage."

"Oh, uh—I left my bags on the floor in the front passenger seat. Will you grab them for me?"

He jerked his chin in acknowledgment then instructed, "Meet me out front. When I'm back, we'll roll."

I nodded and he tagged his shirt off the floor, grabbing his kutte from its hook on his way to the door.

After I'd dressed and straightened myself out as best I could, I left to return to the main room. Maverick was now seated at the bar with a bottle of beer in his hand, Bull keeping him company while Twister sat with his own beer on the nearest couch. I hadn't noticed the other two when I'd arrived earlier—but I'd been distracted.

Playing it cool, I went to say hello.

Before I could say a word, Maverick teased, "He didn't do it alone."

Twister chuckled and added, "Yeah, what do we get as a sign of your appreciation?"

I felt myself grow flush, heat crawling up my neck as I smiled sheepishly. "Well, I, uh—"

"Don't pay them any mind," interrupted Bull, totally resucing me. "You've done your part."

Frowning in mild confusion, I stammered, "I—I have?"

Bull nodded slowly, piercing me with his blue eyes as he explained, "Known him a long time. Never seen him so content. Only girl who's ever made him happy is his own. Until you. That's not nothin', darlin. He's our brother, means a whole fuck of a lot. Woman like you comes along, makes one of us content, gives us something else to fight for—another reason to keep our shit clean—makes you one of us.

"As I said, you've done your part. You keep doin' it. No need to thank us. You're family now. Don't you forget it."

In a profound way, it felt like he'd just hugged me.

It felt nice. Better than nice.

I wanted to reciprocate the feeling, but I wasn't sure what to say.

I didn't get a chance to find my words before Mustang came back for me.

"Baby, we're out," he called from the door.

I glanced his way and nodded, then looked to Bull once more.

He didn't exactly strike me as a man who doled out hugs, but I couldn't help it. What he'd just given me was huge. Without second guessing myself, I took two quick steps toward him, wrapped my arms around him in a quick hug, then hurried for my man.

I didn't look back, but I was sure I hadn't imagined the low, soft rumble of his endearing laugh.

"What was that about?" asked Mustang as I reached for his hand.

"Just saying thanks. Come on—that cardio worked up my appetite."

He looked back at his brothers from over my head, squeezed my hand, and then we were gone.

We had steak, potatoes, and roasted broccoli for dinner.

Like everything Mustang cooked, it was delicious.

Soon after I helped him clean up the kitchen, we were on his hog.

We rode west for nearly an hour, making it all the way to the next town over before he turned around and pointed us home.

When he pulled into his garage, I was buzzing from my road high and aching for my man.

I thought for sure we were on the same page when, after we both dismounted, he leaned down, shoved his shoulder into my belly and hoisted me off of my feet, carrying me all the way to his bed.

But I was wrong.

We weren't on the same page.

His page was better.

Way better.

He laid me down gently across his mattress, making room for himself between my legs before he kissed me. He worked my mouth so well for so long, I thought I might come out of my skin if he didn't touch me. I moaned and tried to work him out of his kutte, but he caught my hands and pinned them to the bed.

Finally breaking our kiss, he gave me his eyes—vibrant and smoldering—and asked, "You on the pill?"

My sex clenched and I shivered at the promise held in that one question.

"Yes," I whispered.

"Been a month since I got checked, but you're the only pussy I've fucked since—that good enough for you?"

I was aching for him already, but now I was all but trembling with need, and I couldn't manage more than a nod.

That was all the answer he needed.

"Don't move," he demanded before he stood.

I watched as he stripped himself naked, squirming impatiently when I saw how hard he was for me already. He'd never made me wait to have him after a ride, and I could feel my arousal leaking out of me as I endured this slow torture.

Then he started undressing me. He took his time, exploring every inch of skin he uncovered with his hands and his lips.

That's when I knew—his page was better.

Way better.

When he finally sank himself inside of me, the only reason I didn't start crying was because I needed him too much. I was more turned on than I thought possible and blinded by desire.

His gaze locked with mine, he pulled out of me slowly then thrust in deep and hard. He did this only twice before my first orgasm tore threw me. My back arched away from the bed, my grip at his shoulders tightened, and he stayed buried inside of me as I constricted around his length.

When I began to relax, he started up again—slow and hard.

He was making love to me.

No. More than that.

He was making love to me, in his bed—on the landing pad.

That's when I hit the bottom.

"Mustang," I whispered, reaching up to sink my fingers into his hair.

"You got me, baby," he spoke softly in response. "I'm right here."

He cupped one of my breasts on a return thrust and gave me a squeeze in reiteration.

I wanted this heaven to last forever.

For a while, it did—his patient rhythm carefully stoking the passion within me.

As my second orgasm grew, I held on as long as I could. I didn't want to it to end.

I moaned in my desperation.

"Let go, baby," Mustang instructed, propping his forehead against mine.

"Not yet," I panted.

His thrusts were coming harder now, making it nearly impossible to hold on.

"Now, Tess."

Another moan spilled from my lips, but I wrapped my limbs around him tightly as I held on with everything I had.

"Sugar, I'm there, baby—let go," he demanded.

I surrendered, my pleasure like a wildfire that caught at my center, spreading to the top of my head and the tip of my toes.

As my sex clamped down around his, Mustang lost his rhythm, groaning deeply as he lost himself to his own climax, spilling his seed inside of me.

When we were both still, I tilted my head until my lips grazed his and breathed, "I love you, Mustang."

He didn't flinch.

He pulled away enough to look me in the eyes and stared at me for a moment.

Then he crushed his lips against mine, kissing me deep and wet.

He didn't stop until he was hard again.

He hadn't said the words, but when he made love to me a second time, I knew we were on the same page.

I'd met my match, and I was never letting go.

I was pulled from sleep the following morning when my phone rang. I rolled toward the nightstand and reached for my mobile blindly, bracing myself as I squinted at the screen. When I saw it was Andy calling, I smiled as I answered.

"Hi, big bro."

"Hey. Where are you?"

I frowned in confusion. I was still a little groggy, but conscious enough to know that question made more sense coming from me than him.

"Um, I'm just waking up."

"Okay. You're up now. Come answer your door."

I was upright in a second, clutching Mustang's sheets to my chest as I processed my brother's demand.

"You're—you're *here?*" I asked, suddenly brimming with excitement.

"Yeah, Tess. I've been knocking on your door for the last ten minutes."

Scrambling out of bed, I hunted around the floor for something to cover my nakedness. "I didn't know you were coming!"

"That's because if I told you it would ruin the surprise."

I laughed as I grabbed the tank top Mustang had on yesterday and quickly slipped it on.

"Oh, my gosh! I can't wait to see you. But I'm not at home right now," I told him, as I went to look for Mustang.

"Okay," he replied cautiously.

"Just hold on a second."

I found Mustang in the kitchen, dressed in a pair of gym shorts and a muscle tee, not surprisingly already making breakfast.

Pressing my phone against my belly, I hurried to stand beside him. "Babe, my brother's here. He's at my house right now. I haven't seen him in months! Will you take me home? He probably rented a car, so he can take me to pick mine up later."

He quirked an eyebrow at me, as if he thought I wasn't making sense. "Why doesn't he just come here?"

I thought I'd hit the bottom, but it suddenly felt like I was falling again.

"Really?"

He shook his head. "Baby—don't say shit I don't mean. I'm already makin' breakfast."

I reached for the back of his neck and drew him toward me, pressing up on my toes before I kissed him short but sweet.

"Thank you." On my return trip to the bedroom, I brought my phone back to my ear. "Andy, could you meet me here? Mustang's making breakfast. You could join us."

"I'm sorry—*Mustang?* You're seriously sleeping with a guy who refers to himself as Mustang?"

I rolled my eyes as I closed myself in the bedroom. "First of all, don't be a judgmental jerk. You know I hate it when you're like that. Second, he means a lot to me, and I really want you to meet him. Plus, my car's in the shop, my house smells like paint, and you'll be here in ten minutes if you leave now. Please just come."

"Fine. Text me the address. I'll see you in ten."

After a quick goodbye, I hung up and texted Mustang's address.

Ten minutes wasn't nearly enough time to get ready for the day, but I managed to hop in the shower long enough to rinse the remnants of last night's love making off of me before I washed my face and dressed in clothes that were mine. I was pulling my hair up in a little top knot when the doorbell rang.

"I'll get it!" I cried before rushing down the hallway, my bare feet clapping against the hardwood floors.

"Tess?" Mustang called, halting me as I reached to twist the locks free.

I looked back over my shoulder to see him doing the same at me.

"Peephole, sugar. It's not just for show."

His warning gave me pause.

I remembered how he hadn't allowed Mary-Kate to open the door without him when it had been Winnie on the other side. I figured he was just being a protective dad. Right then, I understood it was more than that. I didn't know if club business had ever found its way to his doorstep—but I did what I was told.

Before I twisted the locks, I checked the peephole.

The sight of my brother, in a crisp tee tucked into his fatigue pants, like he'd left the base and came straight to visit me, made me giddy.

I squealed as I opened the door and launched myself at him.

"Hi!"

Startled, he took a couple steps back so as not to lose his balance, then wrapped his arms around me with a chuckle.

"Hey, sis."

I breathed him in—closing my eyes at the familiar scent of fresh rain laundry detergent and Old Spice aftershave, just like dad used to wear.

"Missed you."

"Was only gone three weeks, Tess."

I pulled away from him with a scowl. "Overseas for three weeks, sure. But I haven't seen you since Thanksgiving."

Having said the words, I got a good look at him.

His hair was like mine, only more blond, and he wore it cropped short. He wasn't particularly tall, but he was taller than me, and he was still as toned and fit as ever. His dark brown eyes were smiling, and I knew he was only teasing.

"So, did you just get back? How are you here? I thought you'd call when you returned to the states."

"Got back last night. We were routed through Cheyenne. We'll take the plane back south Monday. Got permission to make the trek up here to see my baby sister."

I took hold of either side of his clean-shaven face and gushed, "Best surprise ever."

He only grinned and shook his head at me. "Drove up here without stopping. You mentioned breakfast?"

"Yeah. Come in." I turned to lead him inside then immediately changed my mind. Spinning back around, I stuck a finger in his chest, raised my eyebrows, and warned, "Be nice."

He smirked, I rolled my eyes, then turned to lead him inside.

Needless to say, I didn't have time to prepare either man for their introduction to one another. I didn't even feel quite prepared myself. Mustang knew I had a brother in the Air Force, and Andy knew I had a type when it came to the men I dated—but seeing the two of them occupy the same room was surreal.

When Andy and I reached the kitchen, Mustang had already filled three plates with scrambled eggs and bacon. Two of the plates included a double stack of toast. This made me smile, and I went to stand next to him as I began introductions.

"Andy, this is Mustang. Mustang, meet my brother."

"Hey," my man said as he extended his hand.

Andy accepted the gesture, clearly eyeing the extent of ink on display up the length of Mustang's arm. Honestly, I thought he had plenty of room to spare, and I wouldn't have complained if he felt inclined to fill the empty space. My brother, on the other hand, had not a drop of ink on him and was always quick to question why anyone would want something so permanent marring their skin. Even his years in the military hadn't changed his mind about tattoos.

"Hi," was his simple reply.

I nodded to myself as the realization struck that I was obviously going to have to carry the conversation.

"Who wants coffee?" I asked, headed for the cabinet which housed Mustang's small collection of mugs.

A couple minutes later, we sat together at the kitchen table, and I managed to steer the conversation while we ate. I asked how Andy's drive had been, and we talked about my schedule over the next couple of days. I wondered if there was anyone in Casper he might want to visit on his way back, and he told me he was thinking of grabbing a drink with a buddy on Sunday afternoon.

Mustang was the first to have an empty plate. Andy must have seen this as his opening, because that's when he asked, "What is it you do for a living?"

"I own a bar up the road."

"Hmm," Andy hummed noncommittally.

"He's totally downplaying it," I said. Mustang looked at me and I pressed, "It's true. Don't look at me like you don't know it."

My comment earned me a half-smile before he added, "It's a good spot for anyone who doesn't mind a bunch of bikers and some live rock-n-roll."

Andy pushed his empty plate away from him, casting his gaze my way as he asked, "Is that how you two met?"

"Uh, yeah. Essentially."

"And how long have you two been...whatever?"

Sensing my brother was now digging, the stubborn part of me replied vaguely, "We met last month."

Mustang reached for Andy's empty plate and stacked it on top of his own before pointing at mine. "You done?"

"Oh, babe, no—I'll clean up," I insisted with a frown.

"Was gonna hop in the shower, go check on your car, give you two some time."

I wasn't all that surprised Mustang wanted to skip the part of the conversation that involved our backstory. He wasn't a big talker to begin with, and I knew he wasn't going to sit around and talk about his feelings with a man he'd barely just met—regardless of who that man was.

"Okay. But leave the dishes. I'll do them."

He jerked his chin in a nod then excused himself.

Andy quirked an eyebrow at me.

"What?"

I didn't give him a chance to answer before I started clearing the table. He followed me to the kitchen, leaning against the island as I stood at the sink.

"You know what I never understood?" he asked.

I turned on the faucet and said, "Tell me."

"How you always go for the guy who's rough around the edges when dad was as average as they came."

Loading our plates in the dishwasher, I replied, "I don't know why you're bringing dad into this."

"Isn't that always the case with women? The relationship they have with their dad is the catalyst for all their romantic decisions?"

I couldn't help but to laugh. "Okay, Mr. Psychologist."

"I'm serious. A biker bar?" he asked, his voice hushed. "I just don't get it."

I dropped our silverware into the plastic basket, pushed in the bottom rack, then closed the door and turned to face my brother. "You want to go there, big bro? Because we can talk about me and my taste in men, or we could talk about *you* and how the only commitment you've ever made is to the military; or how you can fall in love with the sky, but not with a woman down here on the ground."

He coughed out a humorless laugh, folding his arms across his chest as he pointed his gaze at his boots. "Let's not make this about me, Tess."

"Mmhmm," I hummed teasingly.

Before either of us could say another word, the sound of Mustang's boots began to echo softly down the hall. I glanced over my shoulder to catch a glimpse of him as he emerged and saw his hair was damp from his shower, and he was dressed in a pair of black jeans with a white tee underneath his kutte.

He was also headed straight for me.

A zing shot through my belly when he stepped in front of me and kissed me boldly, like I was his and he wanted Andy to know it.

"Be back in a bit," he muttered against my lips.

"'Kay," I whispered before I watched him leave.

No sooner had the door shut behind him than Andy asked, "He's in a motorcycle club? And why do I get the feeling that the *wild* printed on the back of his vest is some indication the club he belongs to isn't merely recreational?"

I didn't get a chance to respond before Mustang's Harley revved to life, the rumble of his engine bouncing loudly off the walls of his garage.

"Seriously, Tess?"

"Andy, I love you, and I admire the hell out of you—but I'm a big girl, and I don't need you to protect me."

"You met this guy how long ago? And you're already here playing house with him. You do this, sis. You do it every time. And every time—"

"Mustang's different," I interrupted.

Andy pressed his lips together and tilted his chin skeptically. The look in his eyes was more communicative than any words he could say. He didn't trust Mustang. They'd spent barely twenty minutes in the same room, and he'd already decided I was making a mistake.

"I love him, Andy."

He looked at me like he thought I'd lost my mind. "I talked to you three weeks ago, you never even mentioned him."

I nodded. He was not wrong. Though, I wasn't going to tell him how right he was.

"I understand your skepticism, given my track record. I'll let you have that. But in return, I need you to give him a chance. There's more to him than meets the eye. I mean, look around you. He's not some loser living in a drug-riddled shit hole.

"Yes, he is a Wild Stallion, but he's also a business owner, and a dad. And you know what else? I *do* get like this, every time—and every time the guy bails, but he hasn't. He's different, Andy. I mean it."

My brother stared at me, and I could see the wheels in his head turning. He couldn't deny I had a point, not after he'd just eaten the breakfast my man made us and saw the way he'd kissed me before he left.

"I'm happy," I assured him. "I'm even happier now that you're here. Don't spoil it."

He hesitated then dipped his chin in agreement. We'd both endured enough loss that we knew the fickle nature of happiness, and we loved each other too much to rip it away from each other.

I closed the distance between us and wrapped my arms around his middle, resting my head on his shoulder. "I don't need you to protect me, but I love you for wanting to."

He grunted in response, and I smiled.

Looking up at him, I suggested, "Come with me to Steel Mustang. That's the name of his bar. We can go tomorrow night. Saturdays are when he brings in the best bands. He'd never say it, but around here—he's kind of a big deal."

"Okay, okay, alright," he chuckled. "If I say yes, will you stop gushing over the guy?"

My smile turned into a grin.

"No promises, but I'll try."

CHAPTER *Fifteen*

One Week Later

IN THE SPAN OF a month, I had become a Saturday night Steel Mustang regular.

The week prior had gone down in the books as a win.

Andy had indulged me, and we went together. As I suspected, it didn't take him long to admit the bar was awesome because the music was great. I convinced him to let me be his designated driver, and he cut loose enough to get a little drunk.

It was a blast.

When he left the next day, he and Mustang weren't besties, but there was a new level of respect there. I hoped, given time, that respect would grow into friendship.

Now, as was my new weekly ritual, I was getting ready to go out.

If I wasn't working, I could be found sitting at the bar in a pair of killer heels and kickass jeans.

Well—except for this Saturday.

This Saturday, I was going to the bar with my girl Jenna, which meant it was time to pull out my little black dress.

Emphasis on *little*—as in, I could wear very little underneath it.

It was a black, vegan leather, high neck, sleeveless dress with a double zipper down the front. It came just low enough over my thighs that I could sit in it—but barely. I wore a thong, but no bra—pulling the zipper halfway down my torso to show off a little cleavage.

It was easily the hottest item of clothing I had in my closet, which meant I had to wear it with my hottest shoes.

I finished my look with my black, four-inch stiletto, Louboutin leather sandals with the spike trim I'd purchased for my birthday.

Seriously badass.

I was in my bathroom, fussing with my hair, when my doorbell rang.

"Coming!" I yelled toward the stairs.

I had been looking forward to this Saturday since Jenna told me she had the night off. A biker bar wasn't exactly her scene, but she'd wanted to meet Mustang in his element, and I wanted the same. We agreed to ride together so she didn't have to show up alone.

When I was satisfied with my appearance, I hurried back to my room to grab my overnight bag and my clutch. I had no idea how I was going to climb on to the back of Mustang's hog in my dress, but I decided I'd worry about that later.

I carefully made my way down the stairs and was grinning in excitement when I swung open my front door.

Jenna took one look at me before her jaw dropped.

"Holy shit, you look *hot!* Do I need to go home and change?"

She had on a scoop-neck white tank top and a pair of tight leather pants with high-heeled ankle booties. Like me, she hadn't bothered with a ton of makeup, but wore just enough to enhance her best features, and she looked great.

"No way," I assured her, setting my bags at my feet. I reached for her hair and tousled it a little as I said, "You, my dear, are unattached. If you look too sexy in a place like this, you will not be left alone." I grinned mischievously as I pulled back and added, "Those pants on their own will buy you a drink or two."

She threw her head back and laughed. "What have I gotten myself into?"

"Trust me," I said, carefully bending down for my bags. "It's fun to walk on the wild side. You'll see."

As I locked up, she observed, "It's actually kind of remarkable we've been friends for years and this is the first time you're taking me to a place like this."

"Yeah, well, you're an overworked ER nurse."

"Good point."

"Plus, there was that one time we went to Montgomery's after the rodeo with all those cowboys. Remember that?"

We were getting into her car when she admitted, "I may have blocked that from my memory. That guy you were dating? *Awful*."

She wasn't wrong.

"Tonight won't be that. Promise."

It was a few minutes after nine when we turned onto the compound. The parking lot in front of the bar was already three-quarters of the way full. I was sure the headliner that night would mean a packed house in another hour.

As soon as we stepped foot inside, I headed straight for the bar, like always. I spotted Mustang right away. He was sitting with Maverick, both of them facing the door, an empty stool between them.

When my man spotted me, I swear I felt the heat of his gaze as I watched his eyes trail me up and down, and I fought the urge to smile huge.

By the time I'd reached him, he was on his feet. I was pressed against his side a second later, his lips grazing my ear, and one of his hands resting suggestively on my butt.

"Prefer my Tess naked—but, baby, you better believe I'm fuckin' you in this dress soon as we get home."

A low, victorious giggle bubbled out of me as I pressed into him deeper, my free hand gripping hold of his kutte as I turned my head to kiss the underside of his bearded chin. As if he had no tolerance for soft caresses, he buried his hand in my hair, gripping a fistful before pulling my head back enough to deliver a searing hot kiss.

It wasn't until he pulled away, leaving me breathless, that I understood that kiss wasn't just for me. I knew he'd been branding me when he continued, "Don't wear this dress again unless I'm takin' you out. Can't spare Buck tonight, need him behind the bar. Phoenix has the night off which means I gotta work, and I need Wrangler on the door. That leaves Mav. He'll keep an eye out, but he sees a pussy he likes, he'll leave you to chase that tail, which means I gotta have one eye on you all night. Not much of a hassle, aside from the fact that my dick is hard right now, and it's bound to be all night if I keep one eye on you. So, do me that favor, and warn me the next time you get a hankerin' to show off them legs."

Then and there I decided I was going to need to invest in a larger collection of LBDs.

I nodded as much as his hold would allow, the zing in my belly bouncing around like I was a pinball machine. "I hear you, sweetheart," I managed in reply.

"Good," he said with a jerk of his chin. He kissed me one more time, short and hard, then released my hair and demanded, "Introduce me to your friend."

I took me a second to compose myself. When I finally turned toward Jenna, I saw she was trying, and failing, to hide a grin.

This time, I couldn't fight it. I smiled huge as I introduced my man to my best friend.

"It's great to meet you. I've heard only good things," said Jenna.

"Sorry I have to be behind the bar tonight. I'll stop by as often as I can. You drinkin'?"

"Yeah. I can have a couple."

"What'll it be?"

"I'd love a ranch water."

Mustang looked down at me. "Make that two?"

"Yeah, babe. Thanks."

He winked at me then let me go, headed for the bar.

Jenna and I sat—me on the barstool Mustang had vacated, and Jenna on the empty one next to Maverick.

She leaned toward me, speaking only loud enough for me to hear her over the music as she said, "I don't know what he said to you, but that whole exchange was seriously hot. I kinda liked him before I got here, seeing as I know he makes you happy; but after what I just witnessed, I'm officially a fan."

"The night is still young. Maybe we'll find *you* one," I teased.

Right on cue, Maverick leaned against the bar, catching my attention before he asked, "Aren't you gonna introduce me?"

He wasn't wearing his trucker hat, his curly mane hanging loose down his chest and back.

No sooner had the words left his mouth than he was eyeing Jenna with interest.

"Jenna, this is Maverick. Maverick, my best friend, Jenna."

In spite of the fact that I'd just armed him with her name, he looked her in the eye and asked, "Hey, foxy. How 'bout you put that ranch water on my tab?"

Jenna looked at me, and we had an entire conversation in one glance.

Her pants had gotten her that first drink.

And just like that, our night was underway.

An hour later, I sat my empty glass on the bar. Jenna had just received her second drink, courtesy of Maverick, who hadn't found another tail to chase. I didn't think he had much of a chance with Jenna, but I was going to let him figure that out on his own.

We sat facing the band on stage. They had a few more songs left before the headliner that night. While the bar hadn't reached standing room only status, business had picked up, and the room was full. I was casually looking around when the door at the front entrance opened, and I jolted in surprise as he walked through it.

Lance Jones.

He was in a blue button-up and jeans, and I'd never seen someone look more out of place.

My thoughts were validated when Jenna leaned toward me and said, "What is this guy doing here? He looks more out of his element than I do."

"I—I know him," I stammered.

"What? You do?"

I knit my eyebrows together and sighed as I looked at Jenna and explained, "I had a patient. She died a couple weeks ago. *That* is her youngest son. I have no idea what he's doing here, but something tells me I have to go talk to him."

I watched as she peeked over at him before raising her eyebrows at me. "Um, something tells me you're right, because he just clocked you and he's headed this way."

"Shit," I whispered. I slid off my seat, leaving my clutch on the bar, and tugged my dress down as far as it would go—which wasn't far.

"Are you okay? Do you need me to go with you?"

"No. No, I got it. I'll be back in a minute."

I made my way around a couple tables, my belly twisting uncomfortably as the distance between us shrank. Lance's gaze never strayed from mine as I approached, and he wore a small, satisfied smile.

I didn't like that he knew where I was. I liked it even less that he'd come looking for me.

"Hi," I said when he was close enough to hear me. "What are you—what are you doing here?"

"I was looking for you. Was hoping we could talk."

I glanced back at the bar, searching for Mustang. He was busy with a customer, but both Jenna and Maverick were watching me. I reasoned that even if I stepped out for a minute, I had plenty of people at my back. Plus, the parking lot was well lit, and we wouldn't go far.

"Do you want to talk outside?" I asked him, pointing toward the door.

"Sure. That'd be great."

He turned, headed back that way, and I followed. Wrangler looked at Lance and then at me, a question in his eyes as we passed. I dipped my chin in a nod, signaling I was okay, and stepped out into the night.

As soon as the door shut, dampening the sound of the music and Steel Mustang's patrons, Lance put a hand to the small of my back, guiding me to walk along the front of the building. I took two steps in the direction he insisted, relaxing a little only when he dropped his hand.

"How did you know I'd be here, Lance?"

"Honestly? I followed you," he admitted, sounding embarrassed. "The night my mom passed we got in our cars at the same time. I didn't know where to go, and I don't even think I was fully conscious of it, but you came straight here. I watched you go inside. I didn't want to go in, so I left."

"Oh," I murmured.

"I keep thinking about that night. About how I knew she was going to die, but it still took me by surprise, somehow."

As we continued our slow walk, I peered up at him and said, "I understand what you mean. Really, I do. Maybe you should talk to someone about it."

He looked down at me and frowned. "I'm talking to you."

As gently as I could manage, I clarified, "I mean a professional. Someone who's trained to help in situations like these."

"You're a hospice nurse. You deal with this all the time. Besides, you were with my mom until the end. Some therapist can't compete with that."

We'd reached the end of the building, and I stopped walking, already feeling too far away from the door.

"Listen, Lance, I understand how you could think that; but it might be helpful, speaking to someone who is more objective."

"Well, the thing is—the kind of support I was hoping for? It's not the objective kind."

A tinge of fear began to course through my veins a second before he took a step toward me. But a second wasn't enough time to react, so I took a step back and tried to use my words.

"Lance, we talked about this."

He advanced another step, and I was startled to find myself backed against the wall.

"Yeah, we did. We did. But that was before. You were on the job. Now you're not. There's no need to be so professional, Tess," he said, drawing closer still.

"Lance, I'm not—"

I inhaled the last of my sentence on a gasp when he gripped one of his hands between my neck and my shoulder, pressing me back hard against the wall. I tried to wiggle out from underneath his hold, but he pinned me in place, his other hand shoved against my hip.

"I was surprised you came straight here that night."

He was so close, I could feel his breath on my face, and I cringed as I continued my attempt to shimmy free of his grasp, pushing my hands forcefully against his chest.

"Made me wonder," he continued, his tone darker than I'd ever heard it. "Sweet Tess at a place like this? Maybe underneath those pastel scrubs is a body that craves it rough."

I shook my head on a whimper, the facing of the building scraping abrasively at the skin of my bare shoulders as I continued to struggle. "No. Lance—let me go!"

He didn't let me go. Instead, he leaned down to kiss me. I was quick to jerk my head to the side, but he bit my cheek in retaliation, pressing his body flush against mine.

A sob clogged my throat as I panicked, unable to get him off of me. I tried to beat him with my fists, but to no avail. I felt weak in comparison with his strength, and I had a hard time gaining the right leverage in my stilettos.

"Lance—I will *scream* if you don't let me go right now."

It felt like a decent threat. He was outside of a Wild Stallions biker bar, and I wasn't alone.

It turned out, my threat fell on deaf ears. Rather than let me go, he slid the fingers at my shoulder around my throat and squeezed.

My hands immediately reached for his wrist, and I yanked as hard as I could. His grip only tightened, and then his other hand began to move. I felt his fingers graze the inside of my thigh, and I started to hyperventilate, momentarily frozen.

He pressed his forehead to mine as he muttered, "I see you in a whole new light now, Tess. You. Here. In this dress. You're just begging for a fuck, aren't you?"

When his fingers reached the zipper at the bottom of my dress,

I abandoned my attempts to free my throat, and started to claw at his face. He jerked his head back, his fingers at my throat digging in deeper—then, all at once, he was gone.

I sucked down a hungry breath. As my lungs filled with air, my knees gave out, and I began to sink down to the ground. I was trembling as I tried to make sense of what was happening. I saw Wrangler dragging Lance toward the parking lot, but I couldn't see what happened next, a row of motorcycles and a frenzy of shuffling feet in my way.

"Hey, hey—honey—are you okay?" Jenna cried, her voice shaking as she wrapped her thin arms around me.

I shook my head, feeling confused and disoriented, then tried to get to my feet. My knees, still a little useless, were no help.

I heard the first punch and tried again to stand.

Jenna, understanding what I wanted, helped me to my feet.

Then I saw him, lit by the streetlamp yards away, its halo stretching to meet him.

Mustang.

He landed a second punch. And a third. And a fourth.

Wrangler had Lance's arms pulled back, so all he could do was take the beating.

The crowd around them grew, most of them men in their Wild Stallions kuttes, and I lost sight of what was happening—but I heard Lance grunt in pain after the fifth punch and the sixth.

Even though I couldn't see, I knew when he hit the ground, and I flinched when I heard a boot make contact with his body. Once. Twice. Three times.

The beating stopped only when Maverick and Rodeo reached for Mustang and pulled him back. The men surrounding the scene parted as his brothers tried to drag him away, but Mustang resisted them as he yelled, "You sick *motherfucker*—you put those hands on *any* woman who doesn't want your limp dick, I'll find out, and I'll cut your fuckin' hands off. You put those fuckin' hands on *my* woman again—I will saw your dick off and feed it to you."

I looked from Mustang to Lance, and I knew Maverick and Rodeo were holding him back so he wouldn't beat Lance to death. As it was, he wasn't moving.

Then Mustang shrugged off his brothers and looked right at me.

I was still trying to gulp down air. Even without Lance's fingers wrapped around my neck, I was having a hard time catching my breath. As I stared back at Mustang, my vision grew blurry with tears.

It was one thing to see his bruised knuckles after a fight he'd won on behalf of his daughter. It was another thing entirely to see him beat the shit out of someone defending *me*.

The man I was calling mine talked with his fists. He wasn't passive or timid. He was a fighter—a violent one. And as scary as it was to see that part of him unleashed, I knew he would never hurt me. He was a Wild Stallion. They were in the business of protection—and I was his to protect.

In that moment, I knew I always would be.

When my first tear fell, he made his way toward me.

By the time my sob finally clawed its way out of my chest, I was burrowed in his, one of his arms around my waist, his other hand pressed gently against the back of my head. He held me for a couple minutes, until the initial shock of it all wore off and I was able to breathe deeply.

I tilted my chin up, and Mustang moved his hand around to my cheek before tracing his knuckles down my tear streaks.

"Tell me what you need, sugar," he muttered as he painted my face with his eyes.

Before I could answer, my attention was drawn to the parking lot.

Lance was on the ground, still not moving. The crowd had dispersed, but Maverick was standing in front of him, arguing with Jenna.

"Leave him, babe. He ain't dead."

"I don't expect you to understand, but I am a healthcare professional. I have an obligation—"

"He put his hands on your girl. Why the fuck do you even care what happens to him?"

She glanced my way, her fists clenched at her sides, and I could see the war in her eyes even through the darkness. With a huff, she craned her neck to meet Maverick's unwavering stare.

"I don't get a choice. I have to treat everyone—even sons-of-bitches like him. It doesn't excuse what he's done. Not even a little. But Tess is exactly where she needs to be right now, and if you would *move*, I could be where I need to be."

He didn't speak in reply, and Jenna took this to mean he'd conceded.

Jenna was wrong.

When she moved to step around him, Maverick bent down, hooked his arm around her thighs and hoisted her off her feet. She squealed, gravity pitching her forward until she was folded over his shoulder. I watched him carry her off, then frowned at Mustang's chest.

Maverick's chances with Jenna had already been low.

Now, they were non-existent.

"That's not going to end well," I muttered.

"She'll be alright. He's more of a gentle giant."

I lifted my gaze to find his hazel-blue eyes and clarified, "I meant for *him*."

A ghost of a smile played at his lips before he bent to touch his forehead to mine.

"Not worried about either of them, baby. You still haven't told me what you need."

There remained a slight tremble in my hands, and I'd barely begun to process everything that had just happened. I didn't know what I needed—but I knew what I wanted.

"I could use a drink. A stiff one."

"I can make that happen."

'You. Here. In this dress. You're just begging for a fuck, aren't you?'

I heard Lance in my head, and I sealed my eyes closed tight, balling my fists around Mustang's tee as I tried to shove him out of my thoughts.

He'd *followed* me.

That night two weeks ago, I hadn't come straight for the bar. I came straight to Mustang. I came to the man who'd been taking my back and picking up my slack since the moment I met him. And me, at a biker bar, in a little black dress, that was for *my* man—not anyone else. I couldn't let Lance take that from me.

I wouldn't.

"Tess?"

"I want a drink, and then I want you to take me for a ride," I said, peering up at him.

"I'll call Phoenix. Soon as she's here, we're gone."

On a deep exhale, I took a step back and asked, "How's your hand?"

"It'll heal."

I nodded then added, "And I want you to ice your hand."

This got me a half-smile before he threw his arm around my shoulders, and we started for the door.

"Okay, sugar. Whatever you need."

Phoenix arrived fifteen minutes later. I knew she'd been read in when she walked right up to me and asked, "You okay?"

After I answered with a nod, she cut her eyes at Mustang and asked, "You make it hurt?"

Mustang, who sat beside me—his right hand on the bar, a bag of ice covering his knuckles—merely looked at her like she couldn't have asked a dumber question.

I wondered how she'd missed the man lying in the middle of the parking lot unconscious.

She smirked, then made her way to the back.

After another ten minutes, Maverick stomped toward the bar with my overnight bag in his grip and a scowl on his face. He shoved the familiar duffle at my man.

Mustang took it just as Maverick looked at me and said, "She's a pain in my ass."

I shook my head in confusion. "Where's Jenna?"

"On her way to the hospital, I suspect. She was fuckin' bound and determined to get that punk-ass bitch some help. Like she could drag his dead weight into her car all on her own."

He rolled his eyes, and I quirked an eyebrow at him. "You helped put Lance in her car?"

"Like I said—pain in my ass."

He said nothing more before he stomped away.

I lifted what remained of the bourbon Buck had poured me to my lips, a strange sense of relief washing over me as the burn of the liquor raced down my throat.

Relief that Jenna had been there.

Relief that I had a friend who had relieved me of the burden of guilt I might have felt the next morning, picturing Lance abandoned, unconscious in the parking lot all night.

Given I could still feel the pressure of his fingers around my throat, I wasn't sure if I was capable of feeling that guilt—but now I'd never have to worry about it.

I told myself I'd call Jenna in the morning, then I downed the rest of my drink.

It was time for me to figure out how to mount Mustang's hog in my dress.

I only had to give him a look and we were out the door.

Fortunately, the parking lot was empty, so I didn't accidentally flash anyone as I situated myself on the back of the Road King.

I pressed myself tight against Mustang, and we took off—speeding down the road, headed nowhere.

My favorite destination.

I wasn't sure how long we rode before we slowed down along the familiar street to his house. Then he pulled into the garage, shut the door, and made good on his earlier promise.

With me propped on the seat of his Harley, he fucked me in my dress and heels.

Unbelievably turned on, we both came hard and fast.

It was *out of this world*.

Then he carried me inside and striped me naked.

After kissing every inch of me—branding me as his for the second time that night—we made love.

Like always, my man had seen to my needs.

So, when I finally closed my eyes to sleep, Lance was the furthest thing from my mind.

CHAPTER Sixteen

Four Days Later

I'D BEEN ASSIGNED A new patient, and our initial appointment ran long. I was late as I turned onto Thornhill Road, but I needed ten minutes. Ed was my last stop before the end of my double, but I didn't want him to *feel* like he was my last stop, so I was going to squeeze in a quick nap.

Ten minutes.

Ten minutes of sleep was going to carry me through.

It was all I needed.

Just ten minutes.

Except, when I parked my car in his driveway and leaned my head back against the seat, I closed my eyes and saw Mustang. It felt like every spare moment I had he was popping into my head. I hadn't seen him since Sunday, and I missed him.

I considered the fury I'd seen marring his pretty eyes when I woke up Sunday morning with bruises on my neck, and I had to admit, I didn't think it altogether bad we'd been apart long enough for the reminder of Saturday night to fade a little. I hardly had to apply any concealer while I was freshening up between the end of my last shift and the start of this one.

But it wasn't just my longing for him that prevented me from indulging in a quick nap.

It had been a month since the first time I laid eyes on him.

Not at Steel Mustang, but in a black and white newspaper clipping in a frame beside Ed's sickbed.

In a matter of weeks, Mustang had gone from being the subject of an old article to the man I loved, and I'd not breathed a word about him to Ed.

Ed was running out of time. I couldn't say for sure how much longer he had, but I would guess less than a person with the same condition surrounded by loved ones—people to hold onto until the very end. I was beginning to feel truly guilty about the fact that I had access to the son he hadn't spoken to in years; a man he kept close to his side in the only way he could; a stranger who had no intension of darkening his door.

Ed was going to die alone, with no one to hold onto, and it made me sad.

I still hadn't finished piecing together the full picture that was Mustang and Ed. I only had one side of the story, but it was enough to know Ed wasn't blameless. His medical history was further proof. Only, I wasn't sure if the remaining puzzle pieces would truly fill in all the gaps. I didn't know the version of Ed Mustang remembered. To me, Ed wasn't an abusive alcoholic. He was a sick, frail man with the saddest eyes I'd ever seen.

I remembered what Jenna told me back at the start of all of this. Maybe the best comfort I could offer him was the knowledge that his son had turned out okay. *Better* than okay. And maybe it was my job to tell him before it was too late.

My phone alerted me to my ten-minute timer, and I sighed as I silenced it.

I was late.

I needed to head inside.

After gathering my things, I made my way to the front door, using the spare key to let myself in. "Ed? It's Tess," I called out, as I always did.

"Yup," he grumbled from the next room.

He was propped up in bed, a sloppily made, half-eaten sandwich on a plate beside him. I set my bag down on the chair nearby and offered him a smile.

"How you feelin' today?"

"Like shit. Not much different than yesterday."

My smile stretched into a grin. It was the same answer he always gave me—not the least bit informative, aside from the fact that it was my clue he still had hold of his mind.

"Let's try that again," I suggested good-naturedly.

He let out a heavy breath and answered, "Tired."

I eyed his abandoned sandwich. "How's your appetite?"

I asked him a series of questions then proceeded with his physical exam. When he assured me he was finished with his sandwich, I went to the kitchen to discard it and took the liberty of making another one. When I was finished, I wrapped it and stowed it in the fridge for later. Upon my return, I sat in my usual chair with my tablet in order to work on his chart.

Like most of my visits, Ed didn't talk while I worked, so I hummed to help keep myself awake. I knew he liked it, and I peeked over at him every once in a while to find him sitting peacefully while he listened.

Today, even that brought me guilt, knowing I could give him more.

I blacked out the screen of my tablet and laid it flat across my lap.

"Ed? I have to confess something."

He looked at me, his brow dipped slightly. "Confess? What could you have to confess to me?"

I couldn't tell him the whole truth. Not merely because I'd broken my number one rule when it came to the family members of my patients. This was bigger than me. My relationship with Mustang was just that. A relationship—*his* as much as it was *mine*. I didn't think I had the right to give away pieces of Mustang that weren't mine to give.

But there *were* parts of him he'd given to me, little tidbits I figured I could share with whom I liked.

"I went to that bar," I told Ed, pointing at the picture frame. "I went looking for Mu—um, for Sully. I went looking for Sully."

It felt weird to call him by a name that was only his on paper, but the mention of it brought a sharpness to Ed's hazel-blue eyes I'd never seen before.

"You talk to him?"

"Yes. I—um..." I tried to choose my words carefully, wishing not to lie. "I've been back to the bar a few times. The article was right. Steel Mustang is very successful. Mu—uh, Sully brings in some really great musicians, and the bands draw crowds of people from as far south as Cheyenne or even places in South Dakota."

He considered what I said for a moment, then muttered, "You don't strike me as someone who fits in at a place like that."

I smiled and glanced down at myself to remind me what I was wearing before I told him, "Don't let my lavender scrubs fool you."

He didn't smile back at me. Not exactly. But his eyes brightened a little before he asked, "What's he like?"

"He's..." I started and then I stopped, unsure if I could shove Mustang into the confines of a description. Like anyone else, he was a lot of things—but unlike most, the dichotomy between the man he was on the inside and the man he was on the outside was vast.

The more I thought about it, the clearer it became that it wasn't so much who he was on the inside or the outside; it was the parts of him that were Sully versus the parts of him that were Mustang; the parts of him nurtured and loved by Mary-Kate the elder, and the parts of him he'd carved out and rebuilt in an effort to escape Ed.

I didn't know how to explain all that. Instead, I decided to describe the man in the photo.

"He's a Wild Stallion, obviously. He goes by Mustang now. He's actually one of the higher ranked members of the club. They're his brothers, and you can tell they all mean a lot to one another," I said, thinking of Bull—of Maverick and Rodeo, protecting him from himself. "They look out for one another." I paused, wanting Ed to know his son wasn't alone in the world, but also aware that in delivering that message, I was reminding him that *he* was. "And he's smart. He's business smart, and he works hard," I finished.

"He's been riding since he was just a teenager. I gave him his first bike, you know?"

His comment sent a pang through my belly. The way he said it—as if the act had been a kindness—robbed me of my words. For a brief moment, I thought I saw a shadow of the man Mustang once knew. A man who could take everything I'd said and somehow think he had anything to do with it.

Ed focused his gaze on the newspaper clipping and asked, "Is he happy?"

"Yeah," I answered softly. "Yeah, he seems that way."

He nodded but didn't say more. He didn't even ask about whether or not I could convince Mustang to come for a visit, as if he knew there was no chance of that.

When I felt certain we were done discussing his son, I finished charting and then left him with the promise that I'd be back in a couple of days.

All the way home I thought about our conversation, short lived as it had been. It was the first time I'd been given two sides of the same story. Only, Ed's recollection had been brief. I knew the complete history of that bike—how it brought Mustang to the Stallions. To Bull.

I shoved aside all thoughts of Ed when I pulled into my driveway, past the familiar, blue Harley parked along the curb. I'd finally made it to my favorite part of Wednesday, and I could hardly wait to get inside.

The smell of my early dinner greeted me as soon as I walked through the door. I dropped my purse in its usual spot and made a B-line for the kitchen. Mustang was at the stove, but I didn't hesitate to walk right up to him, pressing myself into his side as I curled my hand around the back of his neck and drew him to me for an open-mouthed kiss.

This time *I* was the greedy one, my lips turning down in a pout when he pulled away before I was ready.

He grinned, then reached to squeeze one of my butt cheeks as he said, "Dinner's 'bout done, Tess. You get me goin' now, I won't get to fuel you up before we get to your workout."

I smiled, conceding to his point.

"Do I have time for a quick shower?"

"Yup."

"'Kay. Be right back." I pressed a kiss against the corner of his mouth then hurried upstairs for that shower.

By the time I came back downstairs, dinner was served. While we ate, Ed kept forcing his way to the front of my mind. I knew I needed to tell Mustang what I had done—what I had shared—but I wasn't sure how he'd take it.

He told me once he didn't hate his dad, but indifference seemed worse. Moreover, I didn't think he'd be *indifferent* to the fact that I'd made him a topic of conversation at that afternoon's visit.

During a lull in our conversation, the truth grew so loud in my head, I couldn't focus on anything else. Without warning, I blurted, "I told Ed today that I met you. I told him I went to the bar looking for you, and that I'd been a few times since, and that I talked to you."

Mustang stared at me, saying nothing.

Feeling nervous, I kept going.

"I didn't tell him about us. I didn't mention Mary-Kate. I just told him you were a Stallion, that you go by Mustang now, and that the bar is really successful. He asked if you were happy, and I told him you were.

"I just felt so guilty every time I walked into that sad, empty house knowing that while he lay dying alone each night, I was going home to the son he only had in an article clipping framed by his bed. I get the real, full-color, vibrant version of you that is better than I ever could have imagined, and it seemed so unfair of me, as his hospice nurse, to keep you all to myself when I could offer him even a tiny little bit of you. So, I told him about you.

"And I'm really sorry if that was the wrong thing to do. I've never been in this type of situation before, so I'll admit, I'm not entirely sure how to handle it. Maybe I should have—"

"Baby, stop," he interjected.

I snapped my mouth shut, only then noticing I was a little out of breath.

He paused, as if wanting to make sure I wouldn't start up again.

"Would appreciate it if you didn't make that a habit, but I'm not mad. You think you're caught in the middle of somethin'. I get that. But, sugar, you're not," he said calmly.

I hesitated a moment before I murmured, "I know you said no before, but—"

"Tess, there's nothin' in that house but a dying old man I don't know. And I'm sure it hasn't escaped you that I live hardly more than five miles from that bastard—have for the last twenty fuckin' years—and not once did he ever come knockin' on my door."

I let out a slow breath as I sat back in my chair.

Mustang was wrong. I hadn't considered that. Not even once.

Every one of my patients had a life they lived before I entered it. In the best-case scenarios, that life had been long. But I was only ever a part of their last few months, sometimes weeks, or even days.

When I met Ed, all I got was a snapshot of his life *now*. It was a life filled with holes—holes punctured by sadness and regret. I understood there were significant moments, life changing mistakes that had been made shaping his *now;* but all the space between those decisions and moments were filled with other details and choices I'd never thought about, because I never did. Not with any of my patients.

Like he'd been doing since the night he'd thrown all those puzzle pieces at my feet, Mustang helped me fill a couple more spots in the picture I so wanted to see. He'd run away from home at sixteen years old, but he hadn't gone far.

The puzzle was almost complete, and I knew then, I wasn't going to ask him about Ed anymore. Ed was dying now, but their relationship had died a slow death long before me.

I couldn't help but wonder if the name *Sully* had died just as slowly, or if that tie had been severed quicker.

"Is that why you don't like to be called Sully?" I asked softly.

He sighed, reaching up to run a hand down his face. This was clearly not a conversation he anticipated; neither was it one he was enjoying, but he answered me anyway.

"First time you met me you called me Sullivan. It's what he used to call me. Didn't like it then. Still don't fuckin' like it."

I frowned, fairly certain it had been Ed who corrected me when I had used the name mentioned in the newspaper caption. "He didn't call you Sully?"

Mustang shook his head once. "Mom called me Sully."

I thought about this for a moment. Then I remembered how little Mary-Kate referred to all her uncles by their given names, not their road names. But Otto had called Mustang Uncle Stang, not Uncle Sully. Rodeo didn't even know Mustang's real name.

"I just assumed—I mean, everyone calls you—"

"Mustang suits me. Didn't choose it, but it fit. I liked it. So, it's the only way I introduce myself."

"You didn't choose it?"

This came as a surprise to me. I'd all but memorized the mustang tattoo he had inked on his chest. The name more than suited him, it identified him.

"No one chooses their own road name, sugar."

"Who decided you were Mustang? And why?"

"Winnie—but so far as the club knows, it was Bull's idea. As for why, mustangs are free-roaming, feral horses. She knew from the moment she found me in her office I'd escaped my own forced captivity. And when I had a bike that could ride, nothin' I wanted to do more than ride it. Didn't matter where."

Ride wild. Roam free.

That wasn't the club's motto—it was *Mustang's.*

Winnie had been right. She had my man pegged before he even had a chance to earn his first patch. Yet, she wasn't the first woman to name him or the first woman to love him. That honor had been reserved for Mary-Kate. She was responsible for the parts of him I was beginning to understand were Sully.

"You *are* Mustang," I said, searching the depths of his eyes. "Almost like you were born to be no one else. But there are parts of you—parts of you I think are Sully, too. The way you love, the way you take care of the people who mean something to you—I think that comes from your mom, which is the part of you that can't be identified as the man called Mustang. It can only live inside the protective shell that is that man. She never got the chance to know this complete version of you. She died loving her boy, Sully."

He stared at me for a long time, saying nothing and everything all at once.

"Babe?" I whispered after a while.

"Sittin' right next to you, Tess," he replied softly, as if the moment in which we found ourselves might have been broken if either of us spoke too loudly.

My gaze still locked with his, I asked what I'd been wanting to know for weeks.

"How did she die?"

He answered me without a second's hesitation.

"There was a spring storm blowin' through. We'd barely finished dinner, mom and me, and the phone rang. Ed was at the bar, gettin' shit-faced. They were shuttin' down early. Bar owner had the house number on fuckin' speed dial. Rang her up, told her she needed to come get her man. So, she went. Like always. Made it all the way there. Picked him up. Lost control on a patch of ice comin' home. Car flipped. Mom died. Drunk bastard didn't."

"Oh, Sully..." I breathed.

I didn't know why, but that name slipped out as my heart broke for him.

"Baby," he began, leaning towards me. He rested his hand on my thigh, bare since I'd changed into a pair of sleep shorts. His touch was as warm and rough as the man I knew him to be. "I'm all grown up now. Don't need anyone feeling sorry for me. Shit happens. People die. That's life, and there's no changin' it. You know that better than most.

"As far as I'm concerned, there's no sense dwellin' on the past, either—especially when the future involves you, naked, moanin' my name while you come hard for me after not comin' at all the last three days."

Just like that, he had me smiling.

That was my man—hard on the outside and sweet on the inside.

The Wild Stallion *Mustang* cocooned around Mary-Kate's *Sully*.

"Is that your way of telling me you're ready to go upstairs?"

"Fueled you up, sugar. Time for that workout."

He was right. It *had* been three days, and I'd missed him more with each one.

I stood, but he caught my hand before I could take a single step.

"One more thing," he said, tugging me until I was close enough for him to snake his arm around my waist.

"What's that?"

"Sturgis. It's in a couple weeks."

My eyes widened as a thrill raced up and then back down my spine.

I'd never been to Sturgis.

If the crooked smile pulling at Mustang's lips was any indication, I was not hiding my desire to experience the biggest motorcycle rally in the *world*.

"Pretty in pink and wild like the wind, my Tess," he muttered.

I smiled huge, leaning into him as I sank my fingers in his hair.

"The plan is to roll out the day before the rally starts, soon as I drop MK with Trix. Won't stay but a few days. Want to be back for MK Sunday, plus we'll get hit, too. Bein' in the path of the rally, the garage and the bar see plenty of business those two weeks. Be stupid to shut it all down.

"Want you there with me. Can you get the time off? Real time off. None of this on-call even when you're off bullshit."

I fought the urge to squeal as I nodded. "Yes. I haven't taken a vacation in forever. I can get the time off."

"Good. Do it."

"'Kay," I said, bending to bring my lips to his. Before I kissed him, I added, "Can't wait."

We soon abandoned our dishes and went to the bedroom.

A while later, when I came—I did it hard, and I did it moaning his name.

Mustang.

CHAPTER *Seventeen*

Mustang

Two Weeks Later

I T WAS FRIDAY NIGHT, and they were fifteen minutes from the heart of Sturgis at the Full Throttle Saloon. The place was packed, the country rock headliner of the night on the mainstage. Mustang was standing in the crowd with Bull, Twister, Maverick, Wrangler, and a few of his brothers from Wild Stallions' other chapters who'd been interested in the concert that night.

Winnie and Tess stood in front of their men. Twister had a topless chick covered in body paint hanging all over him, while Maverick had a woman under each arm, both of them in hardly more than pasties and fishnet stockings.

The night was young. The music was great. The company was even better.

There was no place else Mustang wanted to be.

Bull nudged him with his elbow, earning him Mustang's attention before he leaned toward him and yelled, "Looks like she's settlin' in just fine."

Mustang shifted his gaze back onto his woman, admiring the view.

She was in a pink Harley Davidson tank top, the iconic wings printed on the back. He'd purchased it after she'd spotted it the day before. She wore it tucked-in to her blue jean, high-waisted, cut-off shorts, exposing her sexy legs. Classic Tess, she made sure to pack the perfect pair of shoes that weekend—her feet buried in her cowgirl boots.

When they first arrived in Sturgis, he could tell Tess was overwhelmed. It wasn't just the crowds. That part, she'd expected. That part, she'd been looking forward to. It was the unfiltered, no boundaries, raw nature of the rally she hadn't expected.

His Tess was wild like the wind, but gentle as a breeze, too.

He didn't want her any other way.

But Bull was right. After two full days immersed in the biggest biker party of the year, she was cutting loose and having fun—something he loved to see.

Much like she'd settled in to the wild ruckus of the rally, she'd gotten comfortable in his world back home. He'd known for a while now he wasn't going to let her go; but every day, she did something to remind him he'd be a fool not to brand her as his.

She was good, clean, and pure. Yet, somehow, she'd accepted him for who he was without a fight. She'd swallowed the truth about the club, and she didn't shy away from him after he'd doled out justice with his fists. At the end of the day, she loved him, and she wasn't afraid to show it.

He had no intension of ever peeling the curtain all the way back. He wanted to preserve his sweet Tess as best he could, and it was his job to protect her and his baby girl with everything he had. Regardless of what he might keep from her, it was a comfort he never thought he'd know, having a good woman who would stand by his side no matter what.

He'd seen such a thing with Bull and Winnie, but it was rare amongst his brothers. Most of them were too wild to even consider settling down. Those who had tried had failed—the life of a Stallion not a simple one. The women who hung around the club were either there for a good time or lost, neither of which made for a decent partner.

Some days, Mustang still found it hard to believe his woman had walked right into his bar asking for him.

Now she was tipsy, having had a couple of beers, her third draft in her hand halfway gone. She was swaying her hips to the beat of the music, singing to the chorus with Winnie at the top of her lungs. As he watched her, Mustang felt compelled to give her something that made her feel as content as she made him.

He took a step closer, reaching his arm around her middle before pulling her back against his chest. She came without resistance, instantly melting into him as she continued to sway her hips from side to side.

A half-smile tugging at the side of his mouth, he brought his lips to her ear and muttered, "Fuck, I love you."

He felt her gasp as her body froze, and his half-smile stretched into a grin.

Then she whipped around, sloshing her beer as she wrapped her arms around his neck and sought out his eyes. Hers, golden-brown and gorgeous, were glassy with tears.

That was his Tess. Pretty in pink.

Leaning into him, she pressed up onto her tiptoes and sought out his mouth.

He gave it to her, reaching down to palm her ass as he kissed her long and hard.

She kissed him right back, deep and greedy, like no one was watching.

That was his Tess. Wild like the wind.

CHAPTER
Eighteen

Tess

One Week Later

I WOKE LATE FRIDAY morning in Mustang's bed, immediately rolling toward my phone. When I found I had no missed notifications, I flopped onto my back and yawned.

I'd just opened my eyes and already I knew I was going to need a nap before my shift that night.

Since we got back from Sturgis, I hadn't slept in my own bed.

Or, as I preferred to think about it, since Mustang told me he loved me, he'd been pretty insistent we were no longer to sleep in separate beds—even though our sleep schedules didn't always mesh.

Seeing as Mustang had a way of getting what he wanted, especially when it came to me, I'd made it work to be at his place before I fell into bed that whole week.

Sunday to Wednesday we had Mary-Kate. While I didn't get to see much of her Tuesday or Wednesday, she and I got to spend some quality time together Monday night. Steel Mustang was usually closed

Mondays and Tuesdays—but with the rally still going on, they were open for business, which meant Mustang was putting in some extra hours.

Fortunately, Mary-Kate was more than happy to have a girl's night with me.

It was debatable which one of us had the better time.

Spoiling her was too easy.

Her best friend might have been a boy, but she was a girly girl at heart.

By Wednesday, even though I would be asleep while Mustang worked, and he'd sleep the following morning after I left for my shift, I ended up in his bed because it was convenient. My toothbrush, shampoo and conditioner were already in his bathroom.

Thursday evening had been a long one, Mustang again working behind the bar on a busy night. I hung out, because we'd been two ships passing in the night for a couple of days. When we got home in the wee hours, Mustang promised me he'd take me on a real date as soon as the Sturgis rush had died down.

Seeing as we'd spent four unbelievable nights together at the rally, he heard no complaints from me about the crazy work week that followed.

It was my bladder that beckoned me out of bed. After I'd seen to my needs, I went looking for Mustang. I found him at the kitchen island, sipping coffee, his attention directed at his phone.

"Morning, sweetheart," I said, stopping at his side only long enough to press a kiss against his Wild Stallions tattoo before heading for the coffee pot.

"Hey, baby," he muttered distractedly.

I glanced back at him, curious what was on his mind, but I didn't ask. I'd doctored my coffee the way I liked and was standing opposite him at the island when he put his phone down and gave me his full attention.

"You okay with a sandwich for lunch, or do I need to get more creative?"

"I'm good with a sandwich—but you don't have to make them. Let me. I just need, like, five minutes with this coffee."

"Yeah. Okay. I'll get a quick shower. In about an hour, we've got to head to the clubhouse. A few of us need to have a chat."

I nodded, cupping my mug with both hands. "Is everything okay?" I asked cautiously.

"Just some shit gettin' stirred down south. We're handling it."

While his answer hadn't revealed much, it was more than he gave me the last time there was club business. I wasn't entirely clear on how tight they were with the other chapters, but Mustang didn't seem to be too concerned about it, so I decided to follow his lead.

He went to take a shower while I made us sandwiches for lunch. After we'd eaten, I took my turn under the water. I was running out of clothes, with only a clean pair of scrubs to change into. I made a mental note to ask Mustang if he wouldn't mind sleeping at my place the next couple of nights, so I could catch up on laundry and restock my non-work apparel.

If we were going to keep up the back and forth, it was possible we needed to consider doubling up on essentials while each of us spared a dresser drawer for the other. Living out of a suitcase was bound to get old fast.

My scrubs and sneakers were probably the most practical outfit I'd ever worn while riding on the back of Mustang's hog, and I enjoyed our comfortable—albeit *short*—ride to the compound. We walked hand-in-hand into the clubhouse only to find Bull, Twister, Maverick, Wrangler, and Slick—a guy I didn't know nearly as well as the others—were already there.

"Hey, Tess," greeted Bull with a jerk of his chin. "Winnie's in the office over at the garage if you want company."

"Alright. Thanks."

I looked up at Mustang and he squeezed my hand, sliding his sunglasses over his hair. "I'll come grab you when we're done."

"Sure."

He kissed me before he went to join the others, and I set out to find Winnie.

I'd been thrilled to learn she and Bull would be joining us at Sturgis. Given they still had three kids at home, I wasn't sure how they'd swing it. Apparently, Miles—their oldest—was left in charge. As Bull put it, *under threat of death,* he was to keep watch over his brothers while they were away.

I was merely relieved I wouldn't be the only woman riding in our pack. Not that there weren't plenty of women at the rally to keep the other boys company—there certainly was no shortage of half-naked enthusiasts in attendance—but it was nice to have a known female friend there. And after our long, adventure filled weekend, I definitely considered Winnie a friend.

I was halfway to the garage when my phone sounded with a text alert. I dug the device out of my purse and found a message from Jenna.

Pedicures Sunday? I want to hear all about Sturgis before the memory starts to fade.

I laughed quietly to myself, shaking my head as I typed out my reply. A part of me knew my memories from Sturgis *would* indeed fade, as all memories did—but I couldn't imagine forgetting any of it any time soon.

Yes! We're overdue. Would you mind if I

brought Mary-Kate? I'm sure she would love a little pampering.

Jenna's reply came just as I reached the open door of an empty garage bay.

Can't wait to meet her.

I caught the attention of one of the guys not busy under a hood and asked if he could point me in the direction of Winnie's office. I was surprised when he asked if I was Mustang's woman but didn't hesitate to answer in the affirmative. Armed with that knowledge, he didn't point me in the right direction, he escorted me right to the office door. When I thanked him, he gave me the universal badass chin jerk of acknowledgment, then I knocked twice and poked my head in to see Winnie.

"Hi! Get in here. Have a seat," she insisted.

"Am I interrupting?" I asked, moving to sit on the couch facing her desk on the opposite side of the small room.

"Not at all. I'm just putzing around. Miles is working his apprentice shift out there today, and he's off in another hour or so. Otto's at a summer day camp, and Jett is with some friends. I was caught up about an hour ago, so I'm killin' some time."

"Oh, I didn't know Miles was an apprentice."

Winnie raised and lowered her eyebrows, like she could hardly believe it herself. "Yeah. Before I know it, he'll be a Stallion probie."

I considered this and asked, "Do you think all your sons will want to follow in Bull's footsteps?"

Winnie propped her forearms atop her desk and casually leaned against them. "There were a few years when I thought I might catch a break with Jett, but the older he gets the more unsure I become. He could still surprise us all, but only time will tell."

She shrugged before she continued.

"Miles will be a senior this year, and I'm sure the *only* reason he'll graduate in good standing is because he knows his father will kick his ass if he doesn't. He'd live on the compound if he could. I knew a long time ago he was born and bred to be a Stallion.

"As for my baby, his daddy is his idol—but he's five, so I don't have to worry about him for a while," she said with a smile of relief.

I thought about why I was sitting in Winnie's office, and the meeting that was happening in the clubhouse. I wondered if Winnie was guaranteed to live a life of worry until her dying day, every one of the men in her family destined to wear the Stallions patch on their backs.

Except, she'd been part of the club life for a quarter of a century, nearly all her adult years. Maybe she'd built an immunity to all the ins and outs of their world.

"Do you get used to it?" I wondered aloud. "I mean, the worry about...*club business*?"

Her face softened in understanding before she told me, "Yes and no. You get comfortable once you learn the world they live in has its own set of rules, and that familiarity eases the worry. But I'd be lying if I said I didn't sleep a little less any time Roy goes out on a run."

"And what about what's going on right now? Mustang keeps telling me it's nothing—but is that true?"

She paused before answering, and I could tell by the look in her eye she was about to drop the kind of wisdom only a veteran ol' lady would know.

"Most valuable piece of advice I could ever give you: never doubt your man. Not ever. I know Mustang. He doesn't play games, and he shoots it straight all the time. It's why Roy trusts him so much. He'll tell you what you need to know. Nothing more, nothing less.

"I've lived through some dark times with the Stallions. I wasn't caught up in the thick of it, but my old man was at the heart of it, so

I felt it just the same. Your man won't lie to you. Mustang loves you, and it's plain as day you love him. When things are tough, he'll need you, and you'll feel the weight of that responsibility—but he won't burden you with the small stuff.

"They're handling it. Remember they're not alone. They have each other, and that means more than either you or I could ever truly understand."

I nodded, on the fence as to whether or not anything she'd said made me feel better. On the one hand, it seemed I didn't have anything to worry about at present. On the other, it sounded like worst things could and *would* happen, and I needed to be ready to take that on when they did.

Then I thought of Mustang. I remembered him pulling me back against his chest, holding me tight as he told me he loved me for the first time, and I knew I'd walk through fire for my man.

Before either of us could change the subject, Winnie's mobile began to ring on top of her desk.

"Hmm," she hummed, glancing at the screen. "It's Mustang."

She swiped her finger in order to answer the call and put it on speaker. "Hey Mu—"

He didn't even let her finish before he barked, "Need the keys to your cage. Give 'em to Tess and tell her to meet me outside. *Now.*"

I was on my feet in an instant, my heart rate picking up speed in response to the tone of his voice.

As Winnie began digging in her purse for her key fob, she asked, "Is everything—?"

"*Fuck*, no," Mustang interrupted again. "It's MK."

Neither of us even noticed when he disconnected, the two of us staring at each other, suspended in a moment of terror, the possibilities of what that could mean unending and unfathomable. The fact that he needed Winnie's car—that whatever was happening was so urgent we couldn't take five minutes to go get his truck—made my belly ache.

It was Winnie who broke free of our shared moment of shock first, continuing her dig before she produced the key.

"Here," she said, standing and thrusting it at me. "Go, go."

I practically lunged across the small office, snatched her offering, then sprinted for the door.

Mustang

"I need an ambulance," he spoke into his phone, relaying what little information he knew and the address of the emergency. Tess came running toward him as he yelled, "I don't fuckin' know! I'm on my way there. Just send an ambulance."

Dispatch let him know an ambulance would be on its way, and he didn't bother to listen to anything else as he disconnected the call.

"Babe?" asked Tess, holding out the key.

He grabbed it, shoving it into his pocket as he changed direction, headed for Winnie's SUV. He hadn't answered the inquiry found in that one word greeting, but Tess didn't miss a step as she hurried alongside of him. Less than ten seconds later, they were in the car. Mustang didn't bother with a seatbelt but started the engine and gunned it out of the parking lot.

Tess braced but didn't speak a word in protest.

"Fuckin' done," he muttered. He slammed his hand against the steering wheel and repeated, "Fuckin', fuckin' *done*."

And he meant it.

'Mustang, she's not waking up. She's not waking up!'

He replayed his brief, panicked exchange with Trix, then pressed his foot down harder on the gas.

It took five minutes to get to Trix's apartment.

The fastest he'd ever made it was three.

That afternoon, he was there in two.

He came to an abrupt halt as he parked, jumping out of the driver's seat with the vehicle still running. He made his journey to Trix's door at a jog.

His Tess kept pace, following after him, still not uttering a word.

When he reached the right unit, he tried the handle, but the door was locked.

He didn't bother knocking.

He kicked twice, and the old, wooden frame cracked around the barrier, allowing it to fly open.

His heart dropped when he saw MK, sprawled unconscious on the floor, her head in Trix's lap.

"Oh, my god," breathed Tess.

It was the only voice he registered before both of them raced toward his girl.

He was there first, lifting MK's small frame into his arms. She was light, even in her unconscious state, and Mustang felt her precious fragility as profoundly as he had the first time he ever held her in his arms.

"MK? Baby?" he called, his desperation heard even in his own ears.

"What happened?!" cried Tess.

It was then when Mustang heard Trix wailing on the floor and saw her man pacing frantically back and forth across the room, his fingers buried in his hair.

"How many?" he asked Trix.

She looked up at him, tears streaking her cheeks and snot dripping from her nose as she shook her head in reply.

"*How many?!*" he repeated at a yell.

"I don't know! I don't know!"

"Babe," Tess called, drawing his attention.

She had hold of one of MK's hands, but her pleading expression was aimed at him.

"She's calmy and her pulse is weak. What the hell happened?"

"She got into Trix's edibles," he spat, instantly irate at the fact that they'd been left in such an easily accessible place.

Tess's face paled. "Edibles?"

"They're just weed. They're just *weed!*" the man cried.

Tess shook her head, never breaking eye contact with Mustang. "They could be laced with anything, and we don't know how many she had or how long ago. We need to go. Right now."

As if on cue, the sound of sirens could be heard as an ambulance approached. Tess started for the door without a moment's hesitation. Mustang began to follow just as Trix stood to her feet.

His grip around his girl tightened as he turned to face the woman.

His voice low and menacing, he shot her a glare and warned, "You do *not* want to see my face again. If you do, and my girl is not in my arms, mine will be the last fuckin' face you see."

"Mustang, please," she begged.

He paid her no mind, turning toward the busted door.

"Mustang!"

He was gone, hurrying for the stairs even as he saw the paramedics headed his way with their gear and a stretcher. Tess reached them first, filling them in on everything she knew. When Mustang caught up, he reluctantly surrendered his daughter into their care.

"There's room for one in the back. Which one of you is coming?"

Before Mustang could answer, Tess was standing in front of him, her hands taking hold of his arms. "Babe? Babe, listen to me."

He looked down at her and, for the first time, noticed the calm he saw in her golden-brown eyes. She was steady. Unwavering. His anchor in the storm.

"Let me go," she continued. "I know you're scared, and I know you don't want her out of your sight, but I'm an extra pair of hands, sweetheart. I can help. Please, let me be the one to go."

It wasn't until he tried to speak that he noticed his fear had morphed into a knot in his throat and all he could manage was a curt nod—but it was enough.

Tess pressed a kiss on the underside of his chin, giving his arms a squeeze before she joined the paramedics in the ambulance, not even sparing him a second glance. When the doors shut behind her, he ran back to the still running SUV.

She had to be okay.

He needed to believe his MK would be okay.

If she wasn't, he'd come unhinged.

Even *he* feared that version of himself.

Mustang rode the ambulance's bumper the whole way to the hospital.

He paid little attention to where he parked, but he did manage to kill the engine before he got out from behind the wheel.

As soon as the doors to the ambulance opened, Tess was jumping out, and a team of nurses and a doctor were there to help escort his baby girl inside.

"Oh, shit. Tess?"

Mustang jerked his head in the direction of Jenna's voice. She was already gloved, her hair pulled back into a messy ponytail, obviously on duty that afternoon.

"She's still not waking up," said Tess. "Jenna, she's overdosing."

Mustang's blood turned cold at the word.

The paramedics started relaying more information, the doctor in the lab coat asking questions as they all rushed into the emergency room, but Mustang could make sense of none of it. There was only one word circling around his brain.

Overdosing.

His four-year-old was *overdosing.*

When Tess was no longer of use, the ER staff busy at work in the bay they'd taken MK, she came to his side and took hold of his hand. Reflexively, he squeezed hers in return.

"They're going to pump her stomach," she told him. "It could take twenty minutes or so. Tell me what you need."

He didn't take his focus off his daughter as he muttered, "Need my girl to open her eyes."

"I know. I know, babe, and they're working on that."

She hugged his arm, pressing her lips against his bicep comfortingly. His brow furrowed as it hit him *where* she'd kissed. In the center of his tattoo. The tattoo he'd gotten in an attempt to memorialize another Mary-Kate he'd lost way too soon.

"*Fuck,*" he spat through gritted teeth. "*Fuck!*"

"Hey. Hey, look at me," Tess demanded, cupping a hand around his cheek.

He found her golden-brown gaze and held on, desperate for the calm she still exuded.

"She's in good hands. All we can do now is wait, babe. While we do that, you need to keep it together. Mary-Kate needs you to be strong. And I have every confidence that you will do that for her, because I know—to the depths of my soul—you would do *anything* for that little girl.

"And if you need a little help, well, I'm right here, sweetheart. I'm not going anywhere. If you want me to call Bull or Winnie or anyone? Just tell me, and I'll do it. Whatever you need, Mustang. All you have to do is ask."

He forced in a deep breath and let it out slowly, all the while drawing strength from the hand he still gripped tightly in his. When he felt a little less like losing his shit, he touched his forehead to hers and nodded.

"Need Bull. Winnie'll be worried, too."

"Okay. I'll call them. I'll call them right now."

Before she could move away from him, he buried his fingers in her hair, gripping a fistful and keeping her close.

"I can't lose her," he whispered. "I'll kill her. With my bare hands, Tess. If anything happens to my baby—"

She cut him off, pressing her lips to his in a hard, close-mouthed kiss. She hardly pulled away when she mumbled against his mouth, "If she's anything like her daddy, and we both know she is, Mary-Kate isn't going down without a fight. And so far as I'm aware, her daddy always wins—so I'm willing to bet, she will, too."

Her words buoyed him, and he tightened his grip in her hair before delivering his own hard, close-mouthed kiss. Then he let her go.

"I'll be right back. My phone is in my purse. I left it in Winnie's car."

She hurried toward the entrance, and he looked back at the bed that seemed to be swallowing MK. He folded his arms tight across his chest, the sight of a tube shoved down her throat making him want to come out of his skin.

Tess had been right.

He needed to keep it together.

If he lost his shit, it wouldn't help his girl.

As far as he was concerned, she had only one parent left—and she needed him.

Twenty minutes later, the contents of MK's stomach emptied, and her bloodwork on its way to the lab, they were still waiting for her to wake up.

"We're going to get her admitted," said Jenna, hugging the tablet she'd been updating only a minute earlier. "We'll move her to the pediatrics clinic just as soon as we can sort out a bed." She hesitated, her attention drawn across the room before she said, "You and Tess can stay with her, but we'll have to ask your friends to stay in the waiting room."

They both followed the line of her gaze, watching as Bull, Winnie, Twister, Wrangler, and Maverick headed their way. Mustang felt bolstered by their sudden presence. He also knew, if Bull had brought Twister and Wrangler, he wasn't just there to check in on his brother and his daughter.

"Stay," he told Tess, pressing a kiss into her hair. "I'll talk to them."

"Are you sure? I can—"

"Stay, baby," he semi-repeated.

Before he left, he reached out, gently grazing his knuckles over one of MK's pale cheeks.

"Daddy'll be right back, princess."

He wasn't sure if she could hear him, but he wanted her to know it just the same.

When he reached Winnie and his brothers, no one spoke. Winnie grabbed his hand, giving it a squeeze before she continued toward Tess and MK. Bull nodded toward the exit, and Mustang jerked his chin in agreement before the five men stepped outside.

There was a warm afternoon breeze that blew past them as they stepped out of earshot of any passersby. Mustang raked his fingers through his hair, squeezing the back of his neck as he scowled down at his boots.

"What do we need to know, brother?" asked Twister.

Mustang told them about the gummies, his call from Trix, and the subsequent chain of events that brought them to the present moment.

"Shit, man," muttered Wrangler. He rested a hand on Mustang's shoulder and gave it a squeeze.

Bull, who stood with his hands at his hips, leveled Mustang with an unwavering stare.

"Know what I'd do if it was Otto in that hospital bed. But it's not. Regardless of the patch on the front of my kutte, this isn't my call. She's the mother of your child."

Retribution.

Mustang didn't need Bull to make it any clearer.

Neither did he need time to think about it.

He'd known since the moment he'd gotten that call.

He was done.

She'd been warned, time and time again.

His daughter fighting an *overdose* was beyond the pale of anything he could have imagined happening while she was in Trix's care.

He tolerated her because MK loved her—but he'd lost his mother because she loved a man who loved himself more. He wouldn't lose his MK to the same fate.

Trix wasn't an ignorant innocent.

She'd wanted to tie herself to a Stallion.

It hadn't turned out the way she hoped, but she sure as fuck was tied to him—and she knew what that meant.

She also knew there were consequences should she fuck up.

And she'd fucked up in record breaking fashion.

Anyone who could boast a braincell knew you didn't mess with a Stallion and his kin.

Meeting his piercing blue stare, Mustang simply replied, "She doesn't see my girl again."

Bull nodded. Then, without a word, he cut his eyes at Twister.

Twister clapped Mustang on the back. "Hang in there, brother," he said before starting for the parking lot. "Let's roll," he called.

Wrangler gave Mustang's shoulder another squeeze, following after their VP. Maverick, too, gave a silent show of affection before he was headed for his hog.

"That's handled," said Bull. "What else you need?"

Mustang thought back to when Tess asked him a similar question, and he found his answer hadn't changed.

"Need my girl to open her eyes."

He said nothing more before turning to head back inside.

CHAPTER *Nineteen*

Tess

I'D BEEN CALLING MUSTANG to check in between every patient visit throughout the night.

Mary-Kate's vitals were improving. She was stable, but she hadn't opened her eyes.

The adrenaline which had coursed through my veins and spurred me into action the previous afternoon had long since left my body. I felt dead on my feet.

Still, when I finished my shift at six A.M., I hadn't spared a single thought to going home and climbing into bed.

There was only one place I wanted to be.

One place I *needed* to be.

Mustang wasn't the only one I'd been communicating with through the night. When I arrived at the hospital, instead of heading to the pediatrics clinic, I went looking for Jenna at the nurses' station in the emergency room. I found her leaning against the outer lip of the desk, a paper cup of hospital coffee in her hand as she stared unseeingly into the distance.

She looked about how I felt.

"Tell me you get to go home soon," I said instead of hello.

Jenna shook her head clear as she looked my way. "Uh, yeah. I'm actually already off the clock. I knew you'd be in soon, and I wanted to see you before I left."

She set aside her coffee and came toward me with open arms. I accepted her embrace and returned it with more gratitude than I could ever put into words.

"Thanks," I breathed.

"I stopped by as often as I could throughout the night," she began as she pulled away. "I gotta say—when I told you I couldn't wait to meet Mary-Kate, this wasn't exactly what I had in mind."

"Yeah, no shit," I muttered, pulling my fingers through my hair.

"Tess, I've seen a lot of things come in and out of this hospital, but I've never seen so many bikers show up, and all for a little girl."

I gave her a tired smile. "That doesn't surprise me. They're badasses, but they're each other's family. In Mustang's case, his only family. I'm glad to know he wasn't alone after I left."

"So, the part about them being badasses?" She looked around then took me by the elbow, drawing me further away from the nurses' station before she continued in a hushed voice. "Obviously, when a child comes in overdosing on edible weed laced with LSD, the cops show up, as does CPS. And I don't know what kind of connections these guys have, but the officers were in and out of here in five minutes. It was almost like they showed up just so they could make a record of it. After what happened with Lance Jones, and how he didn't press charges following the public beating that broke more than a couple bones, I'm beginning to think the Stallions and the cops are more friendly than makes sense."

Staring into her hazel-green eyes, I tried to absorb all she'd said. Mustang and I had never discussed the Stallions' relationship with law enforcement, and I hadn't given it a ton of thought. What I knew was what I had always known from afar—the Wild Stallions didn't make headlines; and now that I was thinking about it, it made sense that in order to avoid making headlines, they couldn't get caught.

But no matter how careful they were, I knew things sometimes got messy. Lance being the perfect example. So, if they did get caught, there must have been some way for them to get out of it.

"I know we're both exhausted; but, honey, you don't look at all surprised by this," murmured Jenna with a concerned frown.

I didn't like keeping things from my best friend, but the Stallions' secrets weren't mine to share. Rather than lie to her, I came at the truth from a different angle.

"Look, I've met Mary-Kate's mom. Well, sort of. What I mean to say is, when Mary-Kate is with Mustang, she eats up his attention and his affection like she's starved for it. I don't have to be a social worker to see Trix isn't going to be nominated for mother of the year—and what happened yesterday was awful but not altogether shocking. If CPS is going to revoke her parenting rights, good. Whatever handshakes were exchanged were not in vain. The safest place Mary-Kate could ever be is with Mustang."

Jenna's frown still tugged at her eyebrows, but she nodded as she folded her arms across her chest. "That I believe. He hasn't left her side. I don't think he's slept, either. And in spite of our reassurances that she appears to just be sleeping it off, he's as worried now as he was when you first showed up."

"I should go check on him," I replied, now more anxious than ever to be with him.

"Hey," said Jenna, her brow finally relaxing. "He's a badass, and I wouldn't want any of my friends to go up against him in a fist fight, but I can see he's a good man underneath that leather vest."

"He is," I agreed on a whisper.

"Text me when she wakes up?"

I nodded, and she offered me a tired smile of her own.

"We'll reschedule that pedicure for when she's all better."

"Absolutely."

We parted with another hug—her finally heading home, and me headed to the pediatrics clinic. It wasn't that far of a walk, but it felt like it took me forever to get there. When I came upon Mary-Kate's room, Mustang sitting alone in a chair pulled up close to the bed, my heart swelled with love.

He looked my way as soon as he heard me open the closed door.

"Hi."

"Hey, sugar."

I didn't stop until I was standing next to him. He reached out and curled an arm around my hips. As I combed my fingers through his hair, he propped his forehead against my abdomen, and that was all the sign I needed. Using both hands, I repetitively made my way from the top of his head down to his neck, gently scraping his scalp with my fingernails.

"How you doin', babe?"

It was a question I asked so often with my patients, always willing and hoping I could help. Never before had I wanted so badly to be of use, all the while fearing I'd fall short.

"Tired of waitin', Tess. It's been sixteen hours."

In an effort to be encouraging, I reminded him, "In a non-drug in-duced sleep, she could easily be out for ten. She'll wake up, sweetheart. I know she will."

He didn't get a chance to respond before my stomach growled. On an exhale, he lifted his head in order to look up at me.

"You haven't been home," he muttered, as if he'd just noticed my scrubs.

"Not yet."

"You should go get some food in you. And you haven't slept."

I moved my hands until they framed either side of his face and replied, "Rumor has it, neither have you."

"I've been sittin' here all night. You've been workin'."

"Mustang? I'm not going anywhere. Not without you. *Both* of you."

For a long moment, he said nothing, his hazel-blue eyes—tired and worried, but vibrant as always—fixed steadily on me.

Finally, he said, "She'll be with me full-time now."

"I know, sweetheart."

He paused once more, his grip at my hips tightening before he told me, "Like my house just fine—but you want to change any of it, run it by me. I've got to say, baby, I've got better cookware than you. Better dishes, too. But I do like your couch."

I knit my eyebrows together in confusion, my hands slipping away from his face.

"What?"

"I know you barely had a chance to do anything with your place after we painted it, but fresh paint will make it more attractive when you put it on the market. You want to sell it, great. You want to rent it out, I'm good with that, too."

My exhaustion was temporarily assuaged as a tremor of shock raced up my spine. What he was implying was suddenly starting to make sense.

Except, even though I understood what he was getting at, I couldn't believe it.

"What?" I managed on a breath.

"Tess, I got MK full-time, my ol' lady can't reside at an address that's not mine. Especially with the schedules we got. Not sayin' that because I need you to be my backup. Not puttin' that on you. But I gotta mind my girl; and I can't mind my girl and take care of my ol' lady if they don't—"

I cut him off with a kiss.

I couldn't take anymore.

If he kept talking, I knew I'd burst.

Ol' Lady. He'd called me his ol' lady.

I felt my face scrunch as I fought back tears even while I parted my lips, inviting my man inside of my mouth.

He accepted. Generously.

As I kissed Mustang long and hard, I did so with the knowledge that I had more than met my match. I'd met a man who was ready to shift gears before I was.

I'd never find another like him.

Seeing as I'd already planned on never letting him go, that was perfectly fine by me.

I broke our kiss, pulling away only as far as I needed to touch my forehead to his as I promised, "I'll be your backup, babe. I'll be whatever you need. We'll work it out. I want all of you, Mustang—and all of you includes that little girl."

Tilting my head until my lips grazed his once more, I whispered, "The Wild Stallions, Steel Mustang, banana pancakes with Mary-Kate—the open road, with you and that blue Harley—that's all you, sweetheart. And I love every bit of you."

This time it was Mustang who crushed his lips against mine, punctuating the end of our conversation with a deep, greedy kiss.

It was everything.

Well, almost everything.

Twenty minutes later, Mary-Kate finally opened her eyes.

It was late Monday morning when I saw the news.

Elaine was a bit of a news junkie. I was used to conducting my visit with the local news playing softly in the background. Even though she was getting close to the end and was losing her cognitive ability to remember any of it after it was over, I understood the comfort of familiarity and why her daughter, Sarah, turned it on routinely.

Usually, I didn't pay much attention to it.

That morning, a casual glance at the television had me stopping in my tracks.

They flashed her photograph on the screen, identifying her as Beatrix De la Cruz.

She'd been killed in a tragic motor vehicle accident in the middle of the night.

With the volume turned down, I couldn't catch everything the news anchor said, but I did hear *brake failure*.

My stomach sank and I had to concentrate on my breathing as I wrapped my head around this news.

Mary-Kate's mother was dead.

They'd said her brakes had failed, and I believed that.

I also knew, I *knew* it wasn't an accident.

The Wild Stallions were in the business of protection.

They were also professional mechanics.

Mustang told me they weren't assassins. He also said in a kill or be killed situation, they did what they had to do. It didn't take much for me to figure out that wasn't a logic which applied exclusively to the men in the club.

Trix's negligence had threatened Mary-Kate's life. The Stallions did what they thought they had to do.

A month ago, this realization would likely have freaked me out majorly. In all honesty, it was a bit terrifying to think about it even then—but I knew these men. They were outlaws, but they weren't monsters. What I saw on the news was only half the story. The full story was a tale of vigilante justice.

I was well aware that any justification of their actions was an acceptance, on my part, of their criminal nature. But I was in love with a Stallion. I trusted him with my life. I trusted him with his daughter's life.

Winnie had told me the most valuable piece of advice she could ever give me was to never doubt my man. Not ever.

It might have made me a stupid woman, but I was too far gone.

I was going to heed that advice.

I loved him too much not to.

"Did you know her or something?" asked Sarah from where she sat in a nearby armchair, her gaze cast in my direction.

I inhaled deeply and let it out in a calm exhale as I nodded. "I did, actually. Well, I met her a couple times. We weren't friends or anything."

"It's too bad, what happened to her. Only thirty years old."

I nodded in agreement.

There was no denying it was too bad.

But as it always did after death, life would go on.

CHAPTER
Twenty

Mustang

Four Days Later

H E STOOD IN THE driveway, leaning against his Road King, arms folded across his chest as he thought back over the last few days. It had been a whirlwind, but at least most of the physical labor was behind them. Now, him, his ol' lady, and his girl could focus on settling.

It was early Monday morning when the cops knocked on his door to make the notification regarding Trix. Mustang waited until MK woke on her own before he broke the news.

It had been his call, but he wasn't heartless.

He knew what it was like to lose the only mother he'd ever known, and he knew—regardless of the circumstances—MK would feel a similar loss. She was still young. She couldn't fully wrap her head around the concept of death, but she had her moments of grief, moments he let her have. He didn't regret his decision. He was grateful his daughter was alive to feel anything at all, even if that was sadness for a woman he knew didn't deserve her tears.

Mustang was certain his MK would be alright—especially because now she had Tess, too.

His backup. His partner. His ol' lady.

In spite of everything they had going on, she planned on taking his princess to get her first pedicure in a couple of days.

Fuck, but he loved that woman.

He'd known since the moment he'd seen Tess take MK's hand in her own, she was exactly the kind of mother-figure his daughter deserved to have in her life.

Tuesday they started packing up her townhouse. Winnie helped.

When he decided they were taking too long, Mustang rallied a couple of his brothers to help finish the job while Tess was at work on Wednesday. By Thursday, all her shit was in his garage. This meant his truck and his hog were in the driveway.

His hog didn't belong in the driveway.

That morning, he'd told Tess she had a week to figure out what she wanted to keep and then the rest had to go.

It had been a hell of a few days, but it had all been worth the hassle.

They would settle. It would take some time, but they'd get there. Together.

That night, Winnie was at the house with Otto and MK. She planned on staying until he got home from the bar. Mustang would take Otto home the next morning, after Tess made her banana pancakes for the kids before she crashed.

Mustang had been at the bar until about fifteen minutes ago. Business was still kicking their asses, and he hated to leave, but he had something to do. It wouldn't take long.

As he waited for Tess to turn down Thornhill Road, he hoped she wasn't running behind.

He hadn't told her he was coming.

Five minutes later, he saw her headlights signaling her approach.

He didn't move as she pulled into the driveway next to him, killed the engine, and stepped out of her car, patiently waiting for his moment.

"Hi, babe," she said, surprise evident in her tone. "What are you doing here? Is everything okay?"

"Got somethin' to say," he muttered.

She took a step closer, eyeing him with curiosity. "Okay."

"Not to you, baby."

She gasped softly as he uncrossed his arms and stood upright, headed for the front door.

"Oh, my gosh. Uh—wait," she stammered, hurrying after him. "Wait, I have a key."

He stood out of her way, allowing her to free the locks.

"He might not be awake. It's hit or miss lately, especially at night," she warned him.

"I'm here now. If he's asleep, we'll wake his ass up."

She knit her eyebrows together as she looked up at him, and he could tell she wasn't thrilled by this idea. She nodded anyway before pushing open the door.

"Ed? Are you awake?" she called softly. "It's Tess."

"The pain is..."

Ed's familiar yet aging voice trailed off when he saw Mustang enter the room behind Tess. For a moment, all he could do was stare. Mustang took him in, the withering man on his deathbed, then glanced around the room. Tess always described the house as sad and empty. That's exactly what it was, but Mustang wasn't caught off guard by this. He knew the moment his mother died, the house was destined to be nothing *but* sad and empty.

"Sully?"

Mustang looked back at the man who'd given him his eyes and got on with saying what he came to say.

"Not here for you. Here for her," he said, nodding toward Tess. "The best thing you ever did for me was die. It brought Tess to you and then to me. Aside from my little girl, nothin' matters to me more than this woman.

"She didn't want you dyin' alone. She's good like that. Better than me. Can't give her what she wants—not when it comes to you. But I can give her this. You get to see me one more time. See how I turned out. Fuck of a lot better than you—*in spite* of you."

Ed's eyes grew laden with tears, but Mustang was not moved.

"I'm sorry, son," he whispered.

Mustang stared at him a minute longer, wondering if he believed him. Then he realized it didn't matter whether he did or didn't—Mustang had no intention of forgiving him.

Without another word, he turned toward Tess, pressed a kiss into her hair, then took his leave. It wasn't much, but he'd given all he had to spare to that man, and he'd done it just in time.

The next day, in a sad, empty house, Edmond Thomas died alone.

Epilogue

Tess

Ten Months Later

IT HAD BEEN ONE year—to the day—since we first met. It wasn't hard to convince Mustang the occasion warranted a date. It was even easier to get him to agree the only logical place for us to go on said date was the biker bar in which we'd met.

It didn't matter that he was there all the time, or that I still found myself at the bar, in a pair of kickass jeans and killer heels on a somewhat regular basis. Neither did it matter that he was thirty-seven years sober, and I was four months pregnant—which meant we'd be at the bar, surrounded by a bunch of patrons getting drunk, while we simply enjoyed the live music and each other's company.

Steel Mustang was, no doubt, the *only* logical place for us to go.

So, we were there, at the bar, with Winnie, Bull, and a couple of their brothers, enjoying the live music and each other's company.

As Mustang grazed his knuckles repetitively up and down my side, I admitted that for me—it was his company I was enjoying the most.

It was hard to believe it had already been a year.

So much had happened in such a short span of time.

In spite of our weird schedules, our little family had managed to find a rhythm. Winnie remained a godsend, but we'd also totally lucked out with a new neighbor who had a daughter who happened to be perfect babysitting age. Grace was amazing, and Mary-Kate loved her.

Then again, Mary-Kate was a sweetheart. She loved almost everyone.

Grace had one more year before she graduated high school and left us all in pursuit of her dreams. I tried not to think about when the time would come that we'd have to say goodbye—though, as my belly began to expand with our anticipated new arrival, I knew everything would look different in a year anyway.

Even though we had a fair bit of summer ahead of us, Mary-Kate was already excited for the fall. She'd attended part-time preschool the previous school year, and she could hardly wait to start kindergarten. She thought school was so fun, and—in classic Mary-Kate fashion—she'd made friends with just about all her classmates. She was always quick to remind anyone that Otto was still her *bestest* friend, but she looked forward to getting to return to a classroom filled with kids she wouldn't see over the break.

Even though she'd suffered a loss the previous summer, Mustang's little princess was resilient. She was also thriving with the consistency of living under one roof. Mustang never said it out loud, but I could see how proud he was to be able to give her the kind of life where she couldn't wait to go back to school. It was so much more than the childhood he'd been given.

School had never been his thing, seeing as he had other things to worry about. Other *grown-up* things no kid should have to shoulder.

But Mary-Kate didn't have to carry such burdens. Mustang didn't care if it was school or something else. Whatever dreams his daughter wanted to go after, he intended to make sure she was free to chase them.

It was one of the many reasons why I loved him.

While it had been fairly easy to find a rhythm at home, life as an ol' lady to a Wild Stallion had come with its own challenges.

The guys were great. They were family—mine as much as Mustang's—and I'd learned quickly how much respect came with my title.

It was actually kind of badass.

Yet, while club business wasn't always a big deal, or even something Mustang put on my radar, there had been a few nights over the last year when I didn't sleep so well—my man out on business with his brothers.

Winnie hadn't steered me wrong. I wasn't sure I was ever going to get used to the inherent dangers attached to some aspects of their MC lifestyle, but it came with the territory. If nothing else, I'd learned to accept it. I trusted Mustang. Even more, I'd learned to trust the other Stallions to have his back. Their loyalty to one another was a beautiful thing, and that's what I loved about being a part of the Wild Stallions family.

No matter how ugly or illegal or terrifying things got, it didn't change the hearts of those men.

Deep down, all they really wanted was to live free and protect their own.

Most of them, anyway.

I felt Mustang's lips graze my ear a second before he asked, "You ready to ride, sugar?"

As I turned my head, touching my nose to his, I didn't hide my smile.

No way we'd been at the bar for longer than an hour, which meant we hadn't even hit ten o'clock—but we both knew I was never going to make it to the last act that night.

I was a woman who thrived on cat naps and coffee.

But I'd temporarily given up coffee, and a cat nap whilst growing a human was a joke.

I wanted three things that night.

First, to sit at the bar at Steel Mustang.

Second, to feel the wind in my hair as we took to the open road on his hog.

Third, to stay awake for the best part.

I knew, if he was ready to go, he was hoping to make sure I got all three.

I answered with a nod, he took my hand, and we were out the door.

I waved to Winnie as we went. She smirked and winked in reply.

The jeans I had on that night wouldn't close anymore, but thanks to my new maternity belly band, I still rocked them and was able to get on and off the Harley with practiced ease.

Sadly, I hadn't been able to get my feet into my pink Jimmy Choos—but on the bright side, the alternative was seriously badass.

For my birthday, Mustang bought me a pair of Christian Louboutin calf leather, red sole, Chelsea ankle booties. They had a three-inch heel, a rubber sole, and an elastic collar that all but guaranteed I could fit my swollen ankles inside throughout my pregnancy.

I loved my man.

My boots were proof he loved me, too.

He revved his Harley's engine, and I held him tight. I wasn't sure how much longer I'd be able to ride, but I intended to enjoy the freedom as long as it lasted.

It was around mid-December when Mustang and I started talking about trying for a baby. It was Mary-Kate who brought it up first when she asked for a sibling for Christmas. Apparently, one of her classmates was expecting a baby brother at the time, which made it top of mind as she curated her list for Santa.

That night in bed, Mustang asked me if I was ready.

The next morning, I stopped taking my birth control.

We hardly thought about the fact that we'd only been together six months.

Like every move we made together, we were all in fast.

It took us three months before we finally got that double pink line.

While it was a bit of a spoiler, with an ETA a year later than she'd originally hoped, on Mary-Kate's fifth birthday, we told her she'd be a big sister come Christmas.

Mustang drove a half hour out and then turned around and brought me home.

It wasn't a long ride, but it sure did do the trick.

I once told him I didn't want to get used to the way the rumble of his hog turned me on. Thanks to my pregnancy hormones, there was no danger of that. If anything, it made me even more ravenous.

Before I moved to climb off the back, I squeezed my arms around him tighter, propping my chin on his shoulder as I murmured, "You're gonna have to handle Grace. I can't do small talk right now. All I can think about is how badly I want you inside me."

Mustang gave my thigh a squeeze then demanded, "Off, baby."

I obeyed.

When he dismounted, he turned towards me, grabbed a fistful of my hair, then kissed me deep. I moaned, leaning myself against him as I pressed my thighs together, the ache at my center distractingly huge.

He ripped his mouth away from mine, leaving me panting as he said, "Don't lose that feeling, Tess. I'll meet you in the bedroom. You fall asleep before I get there, I'll spank your ass."

I shivered at his threat and the promise held therein.

There was no way I was falling asleep.

Still, I breathed, "Don't take too long."

He let me go and we made our way inside. I managed to breeze by Grace with a wave, a thank you, and the excuse that I needed to check on Mary-Kate before I fell into bed.

She didn't seem to mind. Besides, Mustang was always the one who paid her before walking her two houses down.

I peeked in on our little princess to find her fast asleep, and I lingered for a moment in her doorway. I blamed it on the baby inside of me, my new longing to watch her while she slept. Just for a couple minutes. Her curly hair was already everywhere from tossing and turning, like the wild sleeper she was, and it made me smile.

When I'd had my fill, I carefully closed her door and crossed the hall to our bedroom.

Mustang had agreed to let me spruce it up a bit and paint the walls that spring.

They were a dark shade of *graphic charcoal*, creating a warm, masculine, yet sexy vibe in the room. To soften it up, there were pops of light, neutral colors here and there, making it the perfect combination of him and me.

I'd slipped out of my boots and socks and was working my way out of my shirt when I heard Mustang's footsteps down the hall. My top hit the floor as he passed over the threshold, and he wasted not a second before he shut and locked the door. He shrugged out of his kutte next, hanging it on its hook before he prowled toward me.

My excited giggle couldn't be helped.

As soon as he had me in his arms, his mouth closed around mine, my giggle soon dissolved into a satisfied sigh.

I slid my hands underneath the fabric of his shirt, skimming my way over his abs and up his chest before he broke our kiss in order to yank the shirt over his head. It hadn't hit the ground, and he was already unclasping my bra while I reached for the button at his jeans. I got his zipper down before he was kissing me again.

He had one hand at the back of my head, the other holding one side of my butt, my naked breasts and pebbled nipples pressed flush against his warm, hard chest.

It was sensational—but I wanted *more*.

"Babe," I whimpered, clinging to his neck. "I need you. *Now*."

At that, he took hold of my hips, spun me around, then hooked his thumbs into the top of my belly band and began to shove. With my own hands, I helped him work the rest of my clothing over my hips.

Trusting him to handle the rest, I bent over the side of the bed, propping myself up on my forearms before glancing back at him from over my shoulder.

My jeans around my ankles, his jeans around his, he placed a hand on the small of my back, positioned himself at my entrance, then slammed inside of me.

It was *heaven*.

"Oh, yes," I moaned unabashedly, throwing my head back.

Three thrusts, and I was coming.

He didn't stop but continued pounding into me hard and fast.

When he reached underneath my hip and down between my legs, he found my clit blindly and I was pretty sure my first orgasm was quickly trumped by my second.

Freaking *sublime*.

The pleasure was so, so good. I balled the comforter beneath my hands into fists as I dropped my head, muting my cries within the folds of our bed covers.

My center was still constricting and releasing, my legs trembling when he pulled out of me.

I was vaguely aware of the sound of his boots dropping on the floor as I tried to catch my breath. It wasn't until he tapped the side of my leg, signaling me to lift one foot and then the other, that I stepped out of my jeans.

"Middle of the bed, baby," he instructed.

I nodded as I crawled to the middle of the bed and rolled onto my back.

Then he was there, his weight between my legs, his hard length heavy against my lower abdomen—slightly swollen with our baby.

Our baby.

I could hardly wait to make him a daddy again.

Leaning on one forearm, he gazed down at me, resting his hand at my left hip before he grazed his thumb over my pelvis. We both knew, without either of us looking down, he'd nailed the spot exactly. He touched me there often, and it still sent a thrill up my spine even months later.

He'd labeled me his ol' lady in August.

I'd moved in shortly thereafter.

By September, I was branded.

The tattoo was simple and feminine—a black and gray depiction of a mustang leaping through the air, the design following the curve where my thigh met my hip.

It hurt like none other when I got it, but it was beautiful, and totally worth it.

Especially because Mustang loved it.

And I loved it every time he touched me there, almost reverently.

When he moved to slide inside of me, he did so slowly, easing all the way in until I was full. Then he kissed me, deep and wet.

I hitched my knees up to his hips, wrapping my arms around his shoulders as he pulled out patiently before he came back on a hard thrust.

As he made love to me, I luxuriated in the slow burn of passion he stoked at my center.

He took his time, and I knew what was building inside of me was going to be out of this world.

"*Mustang*," I breathed, tightening my limbs.

"Hold on, sugar," he demanded, his hips jerking harder.

"Oh, god," I moaned, feeling my way up the back of his neck as my fingers sought purchase in his hair.

He nipped at my bottom lip as he pulled out, a low growl crawling up his throat as he pounded in.

"Babe!" I whimpered, on the verge.

"Let go, baby—I'm right behind you."

I lifted my head, sealing my lips with his, forcing him to swallow my moan as I came long and hard.

After he swallowed my cry, I inhaled his groan as he found his release, riding me until we were both spent.

He lay on top of me for only a moment, then he rolled us both until he was on his back, me plastered down his front. When I lost him from inside of me, a soft mew spilled from my lips, still hypersensitive to his every touch.

My hair fell on either side of my face, but he gathered it into his hands, holding it back so he could see clearly into my eyes. I was on the cusp of telling him I should probably go clean myself up before I passed out—but he spoke first.

"You're mine, baby. Known it for a while now. MK, the club—they all know you belong to me."

"Of course, I do," I murmured, slightly confused. "Always, sweetheart."

"It's time everyone else knew."

I shook my head, still not understanding.

"Marry me, Tess."

A zing shot through my belly, and I shivered as a thrill raced up my spine.

I knew he felt the shiver when his lips curled into a crocked smile.

"That a yes?" he muttered when I didn't respond.

A soft laugh bubbled out of me even as my vision began to blur with tears.

We never talked about marriage, and I couldn't believe he'd asked. I was perfectly content being his ol' lady, knowing that was as good as a wife in the MC world. I was pregnant with his child and branded as his—there was no question we were already tied together forever.

But after a year, I should have known better.

My man was always one step ahead of me.

My perfect match.

"Yes," I whispered with a nod. "Yes, Sully *Mustang* Thomas. Yes!"

He grinned.

Then he kissed me.

Deep and greedy.

Just like always.

Jenna Hayes is holding out for the ideal guy—a man capable of checking all the right boxes. Her best friend thinks she's picky, but Jenna's just selective. Rather than carelessly throwing herself into relationships, she practices a more calculated approach.

Except, she never factored in an encounter with a biker who kisses better than anyone she's ever met.

Maverick is a Wild Stallion and far from Jenna's type. While she can't deny he's easy on the eyes, to even consider him an option seems outrageous. He's in a notorious motorcycle club—which, among many things, means he's an outlaw. But he's also got a way of challenging how she thinks, causing her to wonder if she hasn't found the one because she's more close-minded than she realizes.

There's no way their chemistry is sustainable, but a date with someone new might not be a bad idea. She can live one night on the wild side.

Or so she thinks.

Turn the page and dive into Jenna's POV in the prologue of book one in the Wild Stallions MC series – Ridin' Wild.

PROLOGUE

Jenna

I was there to meet Mustang, the man behind the name *Steel Mustang*.

It took me approximately seventy-two seconds to understand why my best friend was totally head over heels. While he wasn't my type, I could still appreciate the appeal.

He was everything she told me he was.

Mustang was tall and built, with overgrown hair, a full-grown beard, his arms and hands accented with tattoos. He was handsome, if not rough around the edges—but it was the way he held Tess, possessively yet tenderly, that made me smile.

Simply watching their hello was worth the trip.

A biker bar wasn't exactly my scene, but I couldn't deny this one was pretty cool.

The left half of the space had pool tables in the back corner, and high-top tables with barstools crowded with people. The right half was full of low-set tables and chairs, equally packed and situated in front of the stage that accommodated the live band.

The walls were covered in metal biker paraphernalia, neon lit signs, and framed photos of famous old bands or classic motorcycles. The ceiling was completely plastered with vinyl record sleeves, and it was quite apparent the vibe of Steel Mustang was attributed to the music just as much as the bikers themselves. It made the place a little more friendly to those who belonged to a different world.

People like me.

The bar, where Tess and I sat, was L-shaped and tucked into the back of the room—the wall along the front decked out in a bunch of motorcycle license plates from all over the country. On the other side of the counter, the brick facing was full of shelves stocked with booze, and there was a custom neon Steel Mustang sign mounted, too.

There wasn't a television in sight, another reminder I'd entered a place that was all about good music and great company, which I appreciated.

The latter I had in spades.

Tess McBride, the knockout in the little black dress whose man had claimed her with one hell of a kiss, was my best friend and had been since we met at the hospital nearly a decade before. That was back when she first started as an oncology nurse, and I was a year in as an ER nurse. She'd since left the hospital to pursue her career in hospice care, but we remained close.

In a lot of ways, we were each other's support systems. We kept each other sane and pulled each other from the brink of burnout time and time again.

Though, while we'd chosen similar career paths, we were quite different from one another. In some areas of life, we were complete opposites.

Our love lives were the perfect example.

Tess always fell hard and fast, while I was usually measured and cautious.

She liked her men rough and wild, and I—well, I had an ideal in my head I'd been chasing for nearly twelve years. I'd looked for him in all sorts of men, and most of them were quick to fall short.

I had *zero* anticipation that the man next to me would be anything more than the guy buying my drinks that night—but he had a smile which took me by surprise, eyes that were flirty and engaging, and hair I envied in a way I didn't know it was possible to envy when comparing my own thick mane with a man's.

Maverick was the epitome of a biker, and a Wild Stallion at that.

His gigantic feet were covered in boots, and his long legs wrapped in holey black jeans. He had on a plain, white tee with a deep V-neck, and a black leather vest, which was the symbol of his membership to the Wild Stallion Motorcycle Club.

Even sitting down, I knew he was a tall man. Likely taller than Mustang.

He was also well built in his own right. Not overly chiseled, but obviously strong.

His right arm was covered in tattoos. I couldn't make out all of them, given his clothing and the angle at which he sat, but I knew the one on his outer bicep matched Mustang's—as well as all the other guys in the club. It was their logo; a skeletal stallion head that appeared to be made of metal, the mane a wild lick of flames rather than hair.

Taking up his entire, inner right forearm was a detailed close up of a lion's face. On his outer forearm was a slithering snake, which coiled once at his wrist, its head depicted on his hand with its mouth open and its forked tongue darting out toward his thumb.

On his left arm, the only ink I could see from my vantage point was the rosary he had tattooed on his inner forearm. The beads were wrapped just below his elbow, with the crucifix hanging closer to his wrist.

All of his ink was in black and gray; each piece, while certainly bold and masculine, was really well done.

He didn't have knuckle tattoos, like Mustang, but he seemed to have an affinity for rings. He wore three on his right hand, and two on his left.

Like everyone else at the bar, Tess, Maverick and I were facing outward, so as to fully appreciate the show. I was a couple sips into my ranch water when Maverick leaned onto his right elbow—propped on the bar next to me—and asked, "What do you think of the band?"

I shrugged and nodded, the universal nonverbal response for *not bad* and said loud enough for him to hear, "I'm impressed."

"Eighties rock up your alley?"

He smiled at me mischievously, his dark brown eyes bright and playful, like he knew I routinely blasted the likes of Luke Combs, Morgan Wallen, and Kelsea Ballerini on my way to and from work.

I fought a grin and replied, "It's classic. I can't deny that."

He frowned at me teasingly. "Don't tell me you're a Swiftie."

I laughed unabashedly, not having expected that.

"What do *you* know about *Swifties*?"

His smile stretched into a grin. For a second, I wondered if my drink was already going to my head, or if it was that grin which caused a tightness in my chest.

Maverick didn't have a full-grown beard. He grew out a mustache and a goatee, which were both somehow blond, even though he wasn't. The rest of his face was clean shaven—like any more would compete for the attention of his head full of hair.

As if there was any risk of that.

His mane was long, his tight, bronzy-brunette curls draping halfway down his chest and back. He wore it parted down the middle, and it looked thick and soft.

"Got a brother with a daughter who is full-on Swiftie, poor bastard," he chuckled.

I shook my head, still combating my amusement as I told him, "I think I'm a little old to be a Swiftie. Some might argue I'm wrong, but I think I may be offended you didn't give me more credit than *Taylor*. I do *know* who Bon Jovi is," I teased.

We were flirting, and I knew it.

I didn't often spend my Saturday night out at a bar flirting with a stranger. In fact, it had been a really long time since I'd been on a date, or anything resembling one. My schedule was not always conducive to an active dating life.

At least, that was my easiest excuse.

But that night, I felt like being in the moment.

Besides, Tess *did* tell me how fun it was to walk on the wild side.

It was easy to flirt with Maverick, and I knew why.

There was no pressure. No expectations.

We weren't going to be anything.

I didn't need to worry about all the reasons why he wasn't my type or why we probably wouldn't work out, because we were just two strangers who made each other laugh.

Simple as that.

"And what about you? I'm guessing this is your sweet spot? You've even got the *glam rock* hair."

"Eighties are good," he said with a nod and a smirk. "Seventies are better."

"Mmm, an old soul."

"Somethin' like that."

I took another sip of my cocktail then glanced over at Tess.

She really was fit for a place like this, even in her Louboutin stiletto sandals.

Her wavy, dirty blonde hair was tousled just right, hanging above her shoulders. I always thought her hair was an uncanny reflection of who she was on the inside. She was beauty and flare; compassionate and rebellious; light and dark; blonde and brunette all rolled into one.

Her golden-brown eyes caught my hazel-green ones as she smiled, bumping her bare shoulder against mine. "Are you having a good time?"

"I am."

"And you're not just saying that to appease me?" she asked, squinting skeptically.

"You were right," I assured her, this time nudging her with my shoulder. "It's pretty chill for a biker bar."

"Well, I mean, it's still a little early," she laughed. "Expect the crowd to get a little riled up after a few more drinks."

For the next forty-five minutes I bounced back and forth between Tess and Maverick, enjoying the cover band and a bit of people watching. When I got to the bottom of my ranch water, Maverick noticed right away and offered to buy me another. I took him up on it, and he ordered another beer for himself.

He'd just handed me my second serving when I was distracted by the sight of a strange man entering the bar. In any other place I could imagine, *strange* wouldn't have been the adjective I would have used to describe him; but the attractive, blond man in a button-up shirt looked odd even amongst the non-bikers.

Leaning toward Tess, I voiced my observation.

"I—I know him," she stammered in reply.

I gave her my full attention. "What? You do?"

She knit her eyebrows together and shifted her gaze until it found mine.

"I had a patient. She died a couple weeks ago. *That* is her youngest son. I have no idea what he's doing here, but something tells me I have to go talk to him."

I cut my eyes back toward the blond, then sucked in a breath through my teeth as I raised my eyebrows at Tess. "Um, something tells me you're right, because he just clocked you and he's headed this way."

"Shit," Tess whispered.

She slid off her barstool and tugged at the hem of her dress.

There wasn't much to tug, so it didn't go far.

I could tell she looked uncomfortable, and I didn't like that one bit.

"Are you okay? Do you need me to go with you?"

"No. No, I got it," she assured me. "I'll be back in a minute."

I watched her cross the room, meeting the man in the middle. They exchanged a few words before she looked back at us, then she followed the man outside.

I couldn't wrap my head around why he would come to Steel Mustang to talk to Tess. She had pretty strict boundaries when it came to how she interacted with the family members of her patients. Given this man's mother was dead, it didn't make sense that a relationship with the son would continue—at least, not in any way other than a kind hello if they ran into one another around town.

The biker who stood at the door frowned for a moment before he made his way toward us. He wore a vest, identifying him as a Stallion, and he had a biker mustache he pulled off surprisingly well—but I was too preoccupied to fully appreciate the details of his face.

He stopped in front of Maverick and stated, "That guy didn't smell right."

That's all he had to say. Without another word, Maverick set aside his beer and headed for the door.

"Yo! Mustang," called the man with the mustache. He waited for

Mustang to stop what he was doing and acknowledge him. "Joker walked in lookin' for your woman. She followed him outside for a chat. Didn't like the looks of him."

It was my turn to set my drink aside as I twisted on my seat and told Mustang, "She said he's the son of a former patient. She died a couple weeks ago?"

Mustang jerked his chin in acknowledgment then looked toward the door. Following his lead, the guy with the mustache and I did the same. Maverick had the door cracked open with his shoulder as he peeked out. He only looked for a moment, then he let the door close as he shifted his focus our way and shrugged, as if to silently report everything was okay.

"I don't like her out there alone," said Mustang.

I then watched as he turned toward the swinging door behind the bar. Not five seconds later, he was walking toward *Mustache*. They were on their way to the front entrance when Maverick took another peek outside. Only this time—he didn't shrug at what he saw.

He took off running.

My stomach dropped, instant panic weighing it down like an anvil.

Mustang and the other guy were hot on Maverick's heels, and my legs carried me in the same direction before my brain could fully register what was happening.

Even though no one had said a word, a half dozen men in vests were quick to head to the exit, curious about all the commotion.

I was in heeled ankle booties, so I wasn't moving quite as fast as the others, but I spotted Tess just as her knees gave out, her body sinking to the ground along the far side of the building as she heaved for breath.

I hurried straight for her, my heart racing.

"Hey, hey—honey—are you okay?" I cried, kneeling down beside her.

She was shaking when I wrapped my arms around her shoulders.

She shook her head, but I couldn't tell if it was shock or an answer to my question.

Tess shifted in my arms, and then I heard it.

My head jerked in the direction of the parking lot.

I couldn't see much from my low vantage point, but I was certain a punch had been thrown—and it landed.

Tess shifted again. When I looked back at her, I understood she was trying to stand. I adjusted my hold on her and helped her to her feet. She was still trembling as she leaned into me, her breaths quick and shallow.

A second punch was thrown. And a third. And a fourth.

I looked back toward the fight.

If one could call it that.

Now that I was standing, I could see it was Mustang's fist that was repeatedly making contact with the man in the button-up shirt. The guy with the biker 'stache had hold of the man, both his arms pinned behind his back.

The crowd around them shifted, and I lost sight of what was happening, but I could still hear it. The fifth punch, and the sixth.

I hadn't seen it happen, but there was only one reason why the guys would have gone running at what they saw; only one reason why I'd come outside to find Tess gasping for breath on the ground; only one reason why her man would see fit to beat the hell out of the guy in the button-up shirt.

Yet, while I understood what was happening, it didn't make it any less terrifying.

The fact that my friend had likely been assaulted was horrifying. And while I thought it valiant that her man would go to battle for her—what I saw wasn't a battle. It was annihilation. Totally one sided.

Button-up hit the ground, and I thought it might have been over.

Then I heard a boot make contact with something solid followed by a groan of pain.

Mustang kicked him three times before Maverick and another Wild Stallion grabbed hold of Mustang and pulled him back. I watched as he tried to resist, then heard as he yelled, "You sick *motherfucker*—you put those hands on *any* woman who doesn't want your limp dick, I'll find out, and I'll cut your fuckin' hands off. You put those fuckin' hands on *my* woman again—I'll saw your dick off and feed it to you."

Earlier in the night, I'd seen the man with whom my friend was falling in love.

I saw the way he adored and respected her.

He was kind to me.

But as I stared at the man who stood over his victim, beaten bloody on the ground, I knew who I saw wasn't just Mustang the man.

He was Mustang *the Wild Stallion*.

I didn't know much about motorcycle clubs, but I wasn't so naïve as to think the Stallions were a club that got together just to ride for fun. They had a reputation around town. They were respected and feared in equal measure. Except, I never knew *why* they were feared. It wasn't like they made headlines for breaking federal laws or menacing the community. Not as a collective, anyway.

Now, I not only knew why they were feared—I sort of feared them, too.

I was an ER nurse. I'd seen my fair share of crazy things. I'd seen gunshot wounds, stab wounds, broken and bruised bones. I'd seen victims of violence, but never *before* they got to the hospital. Never *while* the violence was happening.

Justified as Mustang's actions might have been, it still didn't make it any less *terrifying*.

He shrugged off the men who were holding him back, his attention wholly focused on Tess. I heard her breath catch, her body still trembling against mine. Then Mustang was headed our way.

When Tess took a step toward him, I let her go.

Neither of them hesitated.

He opened his arms, and she fell right into them, burying her face under his chin as she burst into tears. With one arm wrapped around her waist, his other hand gently holding the back of her head, I stepped away and stared.

Whatever rage that coursed through him, causing him to lose his shit on Button-up, it was gone. Now, all that remained was his concern for his woman.

I couldn't make sense of the dichotomy between Mustang the Stallion and Mustang the lover—but I knew instinctively that Tess was safe now. I knew because I trusted Tess, wholeheartedly. She had a tendency to be a bit impulsive when it came to matters of the heart, but she was completely self-aware. She wasn't stupid.

If she saw what I saw, and the first place she wanted to be after she'd seen it was in the arms of her man—then that's where I wanted her to be.

And now that Tess was where she belonged, I couldn't ignore I was needed, too.

I looked toward the limp body in the parking lot, and the few remaining men who stood over him. One guy nudged him with a boot, spat at him, then headed back for the entrance of the bar. I could still hear the band playing as the door opened and closed behind the men who passed through it.

Inside, it was like nothing happened.

I wasn't paying attention to who was left as I made my way toward the man. In all the commotion, I'd managed to keep hold of my purse, strapped over my shoulder—except, I knew there wasn't going to be anything inside that would be of much help. He probably needed an ambulance. I wondered if he'd hit his head when he fell to the ground.

"What do you think you're doin'?"

I looked up as Maverick stood in front of me, blocking my path to my new patient.

For a fraction of a second, I noted that I'd been right. He was tall. Taller than Mustang. At least six-four.

"He needs help," I answered before I attempted to step around him.

"He'll be fine," Maverick replied, extending an arm to block my path.

The other two remaining guys snickered as they walked away, leaving just Maverick and me with the unconscious man.

I looked at my patient, then up at Maverick. "He *might* be fine, if I get him some help."

I tried again to get around him, but he shuffled and remained in my way.

"Leave him, babe. He ain't dead."

A scowl tugged at my brow as I replied, "I don't expect you to understand, but I am a healthcare professional. I have an obligation—"

"He put his hands on your girl," he interrupted. "Why the fuck do you even care what happens to him?"

I balled my hands into fists, the impact of his words knocking me square in the chest.

He'd been the first to see. Maverick had been the first to run out the door.

Tess had been assaulted by the scumbag now unconscious on the ground.

I glanced over at my friend and saw her staring back at me. She was still standing in Mustang's hold. I knew there was nothing I could do to help her—not like Mustang could. And she and I both knew I couldn't in good conscious leave a bloody, beaten man to succumb to his injuries. I had an ethical obligation.

She'd understand. I knew she would.

Looking up at Maverick, I explained, "I don't get a choice. I have to treat everyone—even sons-of-bitches like him. It doesn't excuse what he's done. Not even a little. But Tess is exactly where she needs to be right now, and if you would *move*, I could be where I need to be."

Maverick didn't respond, so I took that to mean he was going to let me have my way.

I was very wrong.

As soon as I began to step around him, he bent down and hooked an arm around my thighs. The next thing I knew, my feet were no longer on the ground.

I squealed, gravity pitching me forward, my torso folded over his shoulder as he began to carry me away.

"Maverick! Maverick—what are you doing? Put me down!"

He still said nothing.

My focus was glued to the ground, which passed beneath us quickly with his long, efficient strides. My hair hung all around my face, and my hands were pressed against his back.

Admittedly, I couldn't ignore the way my bare arm brushed against his curly hair.

It was as soft as I imagined it would be, which meant he took good care of it.

But I tried not to think about that.

Instead, I insisted, "Maverick! Seriously, put me down."

Two seconds later, I was on my feet.

Though, whether or not it was because I'd demanded it or he simply had me where he wanted me, I wasn't sure. A quick glance around let me know I was on the far, opposite side of the building.

And we were all alone.

"I hope you know, you can drag me back here over and over again, but I'm going to help that man. Out of sight does *not* mean out of mind. We can't just *leave* him there."

"Don't sass me, woman, or I'm gonna have to do somethin' about it."

I jerked my head back, adjusted my purse on my shoulder and replied, "I'm not *sassing* you. I'm doing my—"

I didn't get a chance to finish telling him what I was doing before I was suddenly doing something else entirely.

His fingers combed my hair away from my face, making way for his lips to find mine. He tilted my head back, I sucked in a startled breath, and before I could think of a response, he was teasing my mouth open with his tongue.

There was something about the way he did it—the sure, decisive sweep of the muscular organ between my lips that made me obey.

Given full access to my mouth, he cradled my head in his large hands and *devoured* me.

It took me approximately two seconds to get lost in the moment with him, my stomach full and buzzing with a million little butterflies.

The way he held me. The way he consumed me.

He was in control, but he wasn't aggressive.

He was tender, but he wasn't soft or timid.

He felt *incredible*. I couldn't remember the last time I'd been kissed so well.

I pressed up onto my tiptoes, my hands automatically lifting to take hold of his wrists as he beckoned my tongue to dance with his.

This close, he smelled like coconut, birchwood, and leather—earthy and manly and delicious.

My senses overwhelmed, I was so wrapped up in him, I almost forgot where I was.

Then I heard the rumble of a motorcycle, and I was immediately freed from my trance.

I reared my head back and yanked at Maverick's wrists.

He let me go, breaking our kiss, but remained close—close enough for me to feel his panting breaths as they mingled with mine.

Staring up at him, everything that had happened over the course of the last ten minutes flashed before my eyes.

I blinked, *hard*, and shook my head.

I was at a biker bar and totally out of my depth.

Maverick was a Wild Stallion.

I now understood why a Stallion should be feared.

He might not have been the one throwing punches, but he was not the kind of guy I should kiss.

Not to mention, there was an unconscious man still in the middle of the parking lot I'd claimed as my responsibility. I wasn't about to abandon him for a man who was hardly more than a stranger who had bought me a couple drinks—no matter how well he kissed.

"I can't do this right now. There's a man lying in the middle of the parking lot."

I let go of his wrists and moved to walk around him, *again*.

He extended his arm, pressed his palm against the building at my back, and stopped me, *again*.

"Babe, I can guarantee I'm a hell of a better time than that punk-ass bitch."

The dying butterflies in my stomach fluttered for the last time, reminding me of what it felt like to have Maverick's mouth on mine. I avoided his gaze as I ducked under his arm, murmuring, "No doubt," as I went.

Finally out of Maverick's reach, I hurried back to my patient. As I went, I dug my phone out of my purse.

"Sir? Can you hear me?" I asked as I knelt beside the man. He didn't respond, and I reached for his neck in search of a pulse. Sweeping my hair behind my ear, I also leaned over him in an effort to hear his breathing. I found his pulse, but I was only marginally relieved. There was still no telling what was happening on the inside of him.

I was on the verge of dialing 911 when my phone was plucked right out of my hands.

"I know you're smarter than that, foxy," Maverick muttered as he deleted the numbers.

"Hey!" I gasped, exasperated as I scowled up at him.

He didn't give me back my phone. Instead, he dialed a number and initiated a call.

"What are you doing?"

"Gettin' your number," he answered matter-of-factly.

I shot to my feet, my patience completely spent.

"What is wrong with you? This man needs help!"

I didn't wait for him to respond but reached for my phone and wrenched it out of his grasp, ending the call.

"No ambulances. No fuckin' cops. Not on the compound," he warned me.

My lips clamped shut, I tried not to lose my temper as I glared up at him.

I was so irritated it was hard to believe I'd had his tongue in my mouth not two minutes ago.

"Fine," I bit out as I turned on my heel.

I marched across the parking lot, skirting motorcycles and vehicles until I reached mine. I didn't exactly relish the idea of putting a bloody man in the backseat of my car, but a girl had to do what a girl had to do. I was not going to be bested by my circumstances.

Maverick was still standing by my patient when I screeched to a halt next to him.

Of course, he was.

After I stepped out from behind the wheel, I went straight to the back passenger door and pulled it open. Tess and I had ridden to the bar together, as I didn't want to show up by myself. The plan was always for her to leave with Mustang, which was why her overnight bag was in my backseat. I grabbed it and shoved it at Maverick.

"Make yourself useful, would you? Be sure Tess gets that."

Kneeling once more, I tried again to rouse the unconscious man.

"Sir? Can you hear me?"

I huffed in frustration, wondering just how I was going to get a man who was likely twice my weight while passed out into my car. I didn't want to jostle him too much, just in case, but that was likely not going to happen.

"You've gotta be fuckin' kiddin' me," grumbled Maverick as I positioned myself to make my first attempt.

I then watched as he walked around me, dropped Tess's bag on top of my car, then came to stand beside me.

"Move."

I looked up at him, wondering if I could trust him.

"Babe—doin' you a solid. Fuckin' move."

I dropped my chin and hid behind my hair as a smile played at my lips.

I couldn't help it.

When I thought I had my face under control, I watched as Maverick unceremoniously hauled the man off the ground and shoved him across my backseat. It was far from graceful, but it was all I needed. As soon as I got to the hospital, there would be more than enough hands to help.

Maverick slammed the door shut then grabbed Tess's bag, headed for the bar without a backwards glance.

"Thank you," I called after him.

I barely heard it when he muttered, "Pain in my ass."

As I got behind the wheel and started for the hospital, something told me Maverick *wouldn't* be calling the number he'd been sure to procure earlier.

I didn't even know why the thought crossed my mind.

I didn't want him to call.

Even if he was a great kisser, he wasn't my type.

Follow me on Instagram (@annie.winston_author) and stay upto date on what I've got coming next!

xoxo — Annie

ALSO BY

LOVE ME TENDER

Toughest Catch
Tattered Edges

WILD STALLIONS MOTORCYCLE CLUB

Ridin' Wild

Follow me on Amazon and never miss a release!